DEATH HAS DEEP ROOTS

by Michael Gilbert

"Gilbert's time-scheme is a very tricky one, arranged to woo every excitement from the situation. The consequence is a tale both wry and agitating which must have been designed to select the strengths from both of its predecessors—a thriller called 'He Didn't Mind Danger' and a pleasing legal fiction called 'Smallbone Deceased'—into something that is better than either and very good indeed."   —*New York Herald Tribune Book Review*

"Rapidly changing points of view don't minimize the interest of this case, nor mar its crisp and entertaining style."   —*San Francisco Chronicle*

Other titles by Michael Gilbert available in
Perennial Library:

The Danger Within
Blood and Judgment

DEATH

HAS

DEEP

ROOTS

by MICHAEL GILBERT

PERENNIAL LIBRARY
Harper & Row, Publishers
New York, Hagerstown, San Francisco, London

This story was published serially in England under the title of *The Trial of Victoria Lamartine*.

A hardcover edition of this book was originally published by Harper & Row, Publishers.

First PERENNIAL LIBRARY edition published 1978

ISBN: 0-06-080447-5

78 79 80 81 82 10 9 8 7 6 5 4 3 2 1

Part One

Chapter One

By nine o'clock the queue was long enough to engage the attention of two policemen. At ten it contained enough people to fill the Central Criminal Court three times over. Two more policemen arrived and latecomers, who had now no choice of a seat, were directed to the front of the building where they might have the pleasure of watching the legal celebrities as they arrived.

"There's something about a woman, I mean—a murderess," said Baby Masterton to Avis—they were standing about tenth in the queue. "You know what I mean. Just to see her standing all alone in the dock."

"I know what you mean," said Avis.

"It's such a long time since we've had a real woman— not awful old bags like Mrs. Wilbraham or that Carter creature who chopped up her grandson—but a girl. French too."

"I didn't think she was particularly pretty, dear."

"Not pretty, no. But smart. French girls know about clothes."

"Yes."

"Then, you know, if she did do it—I mean, pretty cold-blooded. Even if they don't hang her they'll sentence her to death. There's something about a girl being sentenced to death. You know what I mean."

"Yes," said Avis truthfully. "I know exactly what you mean."

Mr. Ruby, who was twentieth in the queue—he had attended so many of these functions that he was able to gauge to a nicety the moment of his arrival and had even managed to get a proper breakfast, which was more than most of the queue had done—turned to the untidy young man next to him and said, "Your first murder trial, I expect."

"Well, yes," said the young man. "As a matter of fact, it is. I don't get much opportunity for this sort of thing you know—live in Doncaster. But being up in London for a few days—I say, though, how did you know—?"

"Your camera," said Mr. Ruby with a dry smile. "If you try to take that inside the court you'll find yourself in the dock, not the public gallery."

"My goodness," said the young man, hurriedly slipping the camera strap off his shoulder. "How very lucky I happened to speak to you—what had I better do with it?"

"I should put it in your pocket, or hand it to the attendant at the door. He'll look after it for you."

"Well, thank you," said the young man. "It's really very kind of you."

"Don't mention it," said Mr. Ruby. "I go to a lot of these criminal trials. In fact, I should describe myself as rather a student of the forensic science. Now this one should be particularly interesting. There's no doubt, I think, that the girl's guilty—but with Claudian Summers prosecuting and Poynter for the defense—they're both Silks, of course—I think we shall see some great cut and thrust."

"Yes, yes, I suppose we shall," agreed the young man. Indeed his eyes were already alight, as one who waits to hear a *geste* or a tale of ancient chivalry. "Both K.C.'s you say?"

"Yes," said Mr. Ruby. "You'd hardly expect anything less than a leader in a capital case. But Poynter's a magician with a jury. If the prisoner *is* guilty—and as I say, from reading the proceedings at the police court I can hardly see how she can be anything else—then she couldn't have a better counsel than Poynter. I've seen every man and woman in the jury in tears—all twelve of 'em—before he'd finished with them."

"Well, I never."

"And with Claudian Summers for the Crown, she's going to need all the defending she can get— Oh, here comes a photographer." Mr. Ruby straightened his bow tie and smoothed his thinning hair.

The press, having time on their hands before the arrival of the principals, had turned their attention to the queue and were getting some human stuff for the center pages. The man and woman at the head of the queue had already revealed, for the benefit of the five and a half million registered readers of the *Daily Telephone*, that their names were Edna and Egbert Engleheart, that they came from East Finchley and that they had already been waiting five hours and forty-five minutes, when, on a signal that the judge was arriving, the pressmen vanished as suddenly as they had come.

"They're opening the door," said Mr. Ruby. "Come on, we shall get a good seat."

This was optimistic if taken as describing the seat itself which was as hard as teak and as narrow as a legal distinction; but they certainly had a good view of the court. The box-shaped room, looking oddly foreshortened as seen from above; the benches at the back for the legal hangers-on ("My God," said Baby. "Young Fanshawe pretending to be a law student or something." "If anyone takes him for a lawyer," said Avis, "they'll mistake me for the Queen of Sheba." "Well, I wouldn't go as far as that," said Baby)—in the middle the dock, enormous and, as yet, empty. Then the cross-benches, steadily filling with wigged and gowned counsel and dark-coated solicitors.

"Lord bless me," said Mr. Ruby, suddenly leaning forward and gripping his companion by the arm, "what's happening?"

The young man was pardonably startled. It crossed his mind that someone might be attempting a last-minute rescue of the prisoner. Mr. Ruby, after several shots, got his pince-nez from their case and focused them on the foremost cross-bench.

"Yes," he said. "Yes. It is! I thought I couldn't be mistaken."

"What is it? What's happening?"

"It's Macrea."

"My God, so it is," said a middle-aged man on the right. "There's no mistaking him, is there? I thought Summers was leading for the Crown."

"He is—he is," said Mr. Ruby impatiently. "He's just come in—that's him talking to the usher—" He indicated a thin, slight figure, standing by the door. "Macrea must have been brought in for the defense—or else—where's Poynter? He can't have refused the case at the last moment."

In the midst of this speculation the prisoner suddenly appeared in the dock. One moment it was empty, the next moment she was sitting there, with the wardresses on chairs behind her.

"I see what you mean," said Baby to Avis. "But you must admit she's got a certain sort of chic. Does she speak English?"

"Oh yes, quite well. They had an interpreter at the police court but they didn't have to use him. She's got a funny sort of accent."

"I expect it's a French accent."

At this point the clerk to the court got up from his desk in front of the judge's rostrum and was observed to go across and have a confabulation with Mr. Summers; who took off his wig, scratched his fine gray hair with a long forefinger, and then replaced his wig slightly askew.

"This really is extraordinary—quite inexplicable," said Mr. Ruby. He was sidling backward and forward along the limits of his narrow perch like an agitated parrot. "There's Mackling—he's a company counsel, you know—" he indicated a tubby little man in the tiewig of a junior, who was talking to Macrea, whilst Macrea was shaking his head backward and forward in an emphatic manner— "and what on earth—"

"Pray silence," said the clerk suddenly, in a very loud voice. "Everybody will stand."

Mr. Justice Arbuthnot appeared from the door in the rear of the rostrum, bowed slightly to the leaders, who bowed back, and took his seat. He was a healthy-looking, middle-aged person with kindly gray eyes and a very long protruding nose. In plain clothes he looked like a farmer or a sporting squire. He was a good lawyer for all that, and an excellent and impartial judge.

"I understand that there is an application," he said.

"If your lordship pleases—" said Mr. Macrea.

"Very well, Mr. Macrea."

"Your lordship has, I believe, been informed of the circumstances. The prisoner decided very recently—in fact at midday on Saturday—that is, the day before yesterday—for private reasons, to change her legal advisers."

The pressmen scribbled busily and wondered what was up.

"I myself," went on Macrea, "was only instructed yesterday morning. In the circumstances, therefore, we have taken the somewhat unusual course of asking that this case be postponed to the end of your lordship's list."

"The accused is, of course, perfectly entitled to change her legal advisers at any time," said the judge. "I ought, I think, to be enlightened on one point. Was her reason for requiring this change that she was dissatisfied with the way in which her case was being conducted?"

"In a general way, no. That is to say, neither she nor anyone else imputed anything in the nature of negligence or impropriety to the very eminent firm and persons concerned with her defense. It was simply that she disagreed with their view of the correct policy to be adopted."

"I quite understand, Mr. Macrea, I won't press you any further. Your application is granted."

"I am much obliged."

"You are certain that in the circumstances you would not rather ask for an adjournment to the next session. If I take this case at the end of the list—let me see—it is a short list—it may not give you more than eight days at the most to prepare your case."

"That should be quite sufficient, my lord," said Macrea. "I should have made it plain that we are not greatly at variance over matters of fact in this case—which has, indeed, been very carefully prepared by our eminent predecessors. It is just that a certain shift in emphasis—"

"I quite understand, Mr. Macrea."

"How excruciatingly polite they are," said Baby. "What does it all mean?"

"In that case—" suggested the judge.

There was an immediate general post in the front benches, and out of the turmoil Mr. Mackling rose to his feet. He cast a speculative eye over the packed gallery, inextricably wedged on their comfortless seats, and announced with barely concealed satisfaction that the matter before the court arose out of an application under Section one hundred and ninety-four Subsection two of the Companies Act 1948.

Chapter Two

The trouble, as Macrea had indicated, had started two days before, at eleven o'clock on the Saturday morning.

Noel Anthony Pontarlier Rumbold, the junior partner in his father's firm of Markby, Wragg and Rumbold, Solicitors, of Coleman Street, was at his desk in his office, conscientiously filling in a corrective affidavit for the Commissioners of Inland Revenue. Markby, Wragg and Rumbold was the sort of small firm in which all the partners could, and quite often did, fill in inland revenue affidavits all by themselves.

Since it was Saturday morning, the office was comparatively empty.

Mr. Rumbold, senior, was in Scotland. He was engaged, like some persistent middle-aged admirer, in courting a golf handicap whose figure increased remorselessly with the years. Mr. Wragg was at Golder's Green arranging, without enthusiasm, for the cremation of a client who had at long last died, leaving behind her a codicil in which she had thoughtfully revoked the charging clause in her will.

The telephone rang and Nap picked up the receiver.

"It's Chalibut and Spence, sir," said the desk sergeant. "They hadn't got any reference and they wouldn't say what it was about, so I thought I ought to put them through to you."

"All right, sergeant," said Nap. "It may be an agency job. Put them through, will you. Hello. Yes. Mr. Rumbold, junior, here."

"I'm afraid this is going to be rather difficult to explain, over the telephone," said a thin voice. "This is Mr. Spence

9

speaking. The matter's rather urgent. I wondered if I could possibly come round and have a word about it."

"By all means," said Nap. "Let me have a look at my book. I'm not doing anything much on Monday morning."

"I'm afraid it won't wait until Monday morning," said the thin voice.

"Oh, I see." Nap was uncomfortably conscious that he had arranged to catch the 12:15 from Waterloo.

"I could be with you in ten minutes. Our office is in Old Broad Street. I wouldn't have troubled you unless it had been urgent."

"That's all right," said Nap. "Will it take long?"

"Yes," said the thin voice. "Yes. I expect it will."

"Hell," said Nap. His wife, though the sweetest of women, had old-fashioned ideas about mealtimes.

Ten minutes later Mr. Spence arrived. He seated himself carefully, took a large number of papers out of his brief-case and started to talk. Once or twice Nap tried to interrupt the flow, rather in the spirit of an amateur plumber trying to deal with a burst main. He soon gave it up. Mr. Spence intended to get it all off his chest.

"Yes—but—I say," said Nap at the end. "You know we're not—we don't specialize in criminal work."

"Neither do we," said Mr. Spence wearily. "We took this matter up as a kindness to this client, and—between you and me—without any very great hopes of getting our costs back. Now it seems to have rebounded on our own heads."

"She wants to change—"

"She was very definite about it. She wishes to instruct new solicitors and to brief new counsel."

"But why pick on us?"

"I was coming to that," said Mr. Spence. He selected a fresh sheet of paper from the pile. "It would appear that

Major Thoseby was acquainted with you and often spoke of you and your firm."

"Eric Thoseby," said Nap. "Good heavens!"

How a name can unlock a door, thought Nap; a whole series of doors, so that the hearer looks, for a startled moment, backward down the corridor of the past. A tunneled and a distorted view but, at the end of the corridor, clear and sharp and unexpected.

A warm June afternoon on the cricket field. The smell of a motor-mower; the maddening, indescribable, never-forgotten sound of an old leather cricket ball on a well-oiled cricket bat. That was the first picture. Then a country house, near Basingstoke, in the autumn of 1942. Coming into the lounge and suddenly recognizing a back. "Good heavens, sir, fancy seeing you." "Young Rumbold, isn't it. What are you doing here?" "The same as you, sir, I expect." That was the sort of way people cropped up in wartime. That house near Basingstoke was one of the training schools for the Free French Forces and their helpers. Nap was a learner—he was due to spend some months near Besançon before D-Day. Major Eric Thoseby was already an old hand, installed and in charge of the Basse Loire, but now home for a short spell of Staff talks and a refresher course in the new daylight sensitive fuse. A café in Sedan, in August, 1944—

"I beg your pardon," he said, becoming aware that Mr. Spence was asking him a question. "I was thinking—by the way, how does Thoseby come into it?"

"He was found," said Mr. Spence patiently, "in March of this year, in a hotel in Pearlyman Street. He had been stabbed with a knife. That is the crime of which Mademoiselle Lamartine is accused."

"I see," said Nap.

The affair had come quite close to him, and he was thinking about it properly now.

"If she killed Eric Thoseby," he said, "I should be the last solicitor in London to undertake her defense."

"Certainly," said Mr. Spence. "The basis of her defense, of course, is that she did not kill him."

"Of course. That's the only line she could take."

"Not quite," said Mr. Spence. "Our case, if I might speak perfectly frankly, would have been that it was not proved that she had killed him—and even if she had been found guilty of killing him, that she had a certain measure of justification."

"I see," said Nap. He also saw why Miss Lamartine had wanted to change her professional advisers. "What is the next move?"

"She wants to see you."

"Now!"

"There is very little time to spare," said Mr. Spence. "As I was telling you, the trial opens at the Central Criminal Court on Monday—the day after tomorrow."

"There certainly isn't," said Nap. "Are you coming with me?"

"I have made all the necessary arrangements," said Mr. Spence. "But I am afraid I shall not be able to accompany you. It is her express desire that she should see you alone."

An hour later Nap was talking across a bare table to Victoria Lamartine.

It was an interview which, by all the rules, should have been dramatic, even passionate. It was, in fact, businesslike and quite short. Mademoiselle Lamartine did almost all the talking and the measure of her success was that Nap, who had come to the interview determined to say No went away twenty minutes later with a full promise of assistance.

Victoria Lamartine was no beauty. She was nearer to

thirty than twenty and her figure, in five years' time, would be unhesitatingly described as dumpy. The skill with which her hair was done did not conceal the fact that it was basically straight and mouse-colored. But all, to Nap's mind, was saved by the eyes. Not only were they kind eyes, but from them looked that intellectual honesty which would seem to be bred in the bones of a certain sort of French girl: a nation famed for looking on facts as they are.

"I appeal to you, Mr. Rimbault," she said, and Nap was absurdly charmed, at the outset of the interview, by hearing his name in its original French form, "for you alone in London are a lawyer I can trust."

"You are too kind."

Mademoiselle Lamartine brushed this aside.

"First you must understand," she said. "I did *not* kill Major Thoseby."

"I see."

"I did *not* have a child of him. I had a child, yes. A boy. He would now be five years old, but he died. He was *not* of Major Thoseby. He was of another man."

"Yes."

"I did *not* hate Major Thoseby. Why should I? The child was not of him. Why should I hate him?"

"Why indeed?"

"Now you understand."

"Mademoiselle," said Nap, "I understand nothing. If you would be so kind as to begin at the beginning, telling me, as concisely as possible, what has happened to bring you—" he waved a hand round with an infinitely delicate gesture— "to bring you here. Also, if it will assist you, pray speak in French."

"*Voyons: un exposé.*"

She spoke composedly, with an indifference bordering on disinterest: as if she was a spectator of the misadventures she described. Nap, who spent a great part of his professional life in ordering facts into logical sequences, found time to admire the performance even whilst he listened intently to the performer.

It was a strange enough story.

At the end of it the girl asked, with the first hint of concern that Nap had yet detected in her voice and in her eyes, "You will help me?"

"Yes," said Nap. He spoke absently. He had made the decision ten minutes before.

"Good. Then since I am now your client you may cease to call me Mademoiselle Lamartine. 'Mademoiselle' does not well become the mother of a child. And Lamartine is a name no Englishman can pronounce. Not even you, and your French is very good. I do not flatter you. But even you cannot place the stress evenly on the second syllable as it should go. Will you call me Vicky—or Victoria, if you wish to be more formal."

"Vicky will do," said Nap. "Now tell me one more thing. Why did you change your mind? About your lawyer, I mean."

"It was after the first court—I do not understand your judicial system—it wants for logic."

"I couldn't agree with you more," said Nap. "The police court, I expect you mean."

"Yes. The police court. It was that Mr. Poynter. When he spoke to the magistrate, I understood for the first time what he meant. To me he had always been most polite. 'Yes, mademoiselle'—'No, mademoiselle'—'I am quite sure that what you say is the truth, mademoiselle.' But to the judge—he said something quite else. He said—'This woman is guilty.' Not in those words, but I could hear it in his voice. He said, 'She is guilty. But because she is a woman, and because she is a stranger to this country, and because she has had a child and has been deceived by this man who is older than she, you must not be too severe.' "

"That's all right," said Nap. "I thought that was it. I just wanted to be sure."

He was not surprised. He had heard it all himself, an hour before, in the thin tones of Mr. Spence.

Chapter Three

A telephone call to Scotland brought the disgruntled Mr. Rumbold back to London on the night train, and on Sunday morning, after breakfast, father and son held council.

"Tell me the story first," said old Mr. Rumbold, "and then we'll decide—about the other things."

"Well," said Nap, "it's only her version—but, with that reservation, here it is. She's French—Parisian. Like a lot of other French girls she had a filthy time during the Occupation. She hasn't got much left in the way of family. Her father was dead before the war, and her mother, who stayed on in Paris, died some time in 1943—phthisis, hurried along by undernutrition, I gather. To start with, she herself didn't do so badly. She'd been evacuated, in 1940, to an old friend of the family, near Langeais. He was a farmer. A farm meant food. Vicky earned her keep, I don't doubt, by working in the house. The farmer—Père Chaise—was a thoroughly warmhearted, garrulous, unreliable supporter of the local Maquis. Vicky helped him in that too—just in the same way as she helped him about the house. Ran errands, kept watch, carried food to the 'active' Maquisards."

"Thousands of French girls did as much, I suppose."

"Thousands of French girls did as much," agreed Nap. "I don't think it makes it any less creditable. It certainly didn't make it any less unpleasant for them when they were caught—as Vicky was."

Nap paused for a moment and looked out of the break-fast-room window, over the sensible, sunlit, rose garden: and tried to re-create in his mind something of life as he had known it in France during those times: the hate and the fear, the hysterics and the exaggeration and the heroism.

"Here's where we've got to be careful," he said, "because things which happened at that time always seem, some-how, to get a bit twisted in the telling. From what I know of the way things were worked, I should imagine that Père Chaise's farm was really a sort of flytrap. The old man was much too noisy to be a conspirator. You can bet your bottom dollar the Gestapo knew all about him. But they let him alone, for the time being, until something really worth while should turn up. And in August of 1943 it did turn up, in the form of a British agent—a young and very inexperienced agent, I'm afraid, called Wells—a Lieutenant Julian Wells. I expect the planners in London had their eye on the Basse Loire. It lay in the flank of the turning movement in Normandy which must already have been on their map boards. Quite a lot of agents were flown in. Some were lucky; some weren't. Wells had been told that his first job was to contact the British officer who was running the district—a very tough and crafty character called Thoseby—Major Eric Thoseby."

"Good Lord above," said Mr. Rumbold, "not that school-master."

"That's the one. You remember him?"

"Yes. I do. Good heavens! So that was the chap Wells was sent to contact."

"Yes," said Nap. "But he didn't do it, that was just

the trouble. He must have been dropped a bit off-course. He had to do the best he could for himself, and he holed up at the Père Chaise farm; he was there for about three weeks, hidden under a haystack, whilst the local Maquisards went to look for Thoseby. Unfortunately, before they could contact him—he happened to be across the Swiss border—the Gestapo descended on the farm and roped everyone in. Père Chaise and two other men were shot. Vicky, as being somewhat less deeply involved, was locked up whilst they made their minds up about her."

"And Wells?"

"That's just it," said Nap. "We don't know. After a raid of that sort the German policy was to keep the different prisoners separate. They could work on them better that way. One would believe the other had said things—and so on. Of course they told Vicky that they'd got Wells. They had a very good reason to think that they could influence her through him."

"You mean?"

"I mean," said Nap slowly, "that it soon became apparent that Vicky was going to have a child. Once she knew it was coming, she made no bones about it. She said it was Wells's child. And to do her justice, she has stuck steadily to that story ever since."

"One of them must have been a fast worker," said Mr. Rumbold. "Two perfect strangers of barely three weeks' acquaintance—"

"Well, do you know, I can believe that part of it easily enough," said Nap. "They were both living under tension —a hothouse sort of life; these things were apt to happen much more quickly than they might in normal times."

"And the Germans," said Mr. Rumbold, "believing this, used threats about what they would do to Wells in order to get information out of this poor girl."

"Good Lord, no." Nap looked mildly at his father. "They could have got any blessed information they wanted out of her in five minutes, with a blowlamp. In any case, I don't suppose she knew anything useful. As I said, she wasn't deeply involved. The few actual Maquisard locations which she knew about would have been changed within half an hour of the news of her arrest. No, it was rather more than that. They wanted her to work *for* them. Then they would have released her and used her as a decoy. But if they were going to play that game they needed a good permanent hold over her. Hence Wells."

"She never actually saw him in prison?"

"No. On one occasion, when she was getting difficult, they produced one of his boots, covered with blood——"

"What do you think?"

"I don't know," said Nap. "I really don't know. . . . The gentle Gestapo I knew would have been more likely to have shown her one of his boots with the foot still in it. Even that wouldn't have proved anything. You could fake a boot just as easily as you could fake a foot. On balance I'm inclined to think they did have him, but he came to pieces in their hands, so they buried him quietly. Anyway, nothing's been seen of him since. Time went on, and in the end she had the child, actually in the Gestapo prison hospital, just before D-Day. I don't suppose it was exactly like a high-class London nursing home, but I think they were reasonably efficient. It was a boy, called Jules—an after-thought for 'Julian' perhaps. Then D-Day happened—and she was moved back with a lot of other prisoners, to a place near Strasbourg. They didn't take her into Germany. Might have been better if they had. You know what France was like during the last year of the war. The baby must have had a, hell of a time. He was never very strong. Vicky's one idea was to get hold of Major Thoseby. She had two reasons for this, she says. He knew about her work with the Resistance, and might have persuaded the British Army authorities to look after the baby. Also he might have known where Wells was. Anyway, that's her version of it, and it's got to be borne in mind, in view of what happened later. She never caught up with Thoseby. As soon as his part of France fell he was flown back to London and he got an immediate job on the War Crimes Commission and spent most of the next three years in Germany.

"After the war things didn't improve much in France, and Vicky often thought of coming to England. She speaks quite good English, and she still hoped to find Thoseby. Then, in that very lean and very bitter spring of 1947 something did happen—it was sad, but in a way it made things easier. The child died. Vicky took what money she had, wangled her permit and came over and began looking for a job. There she struck oil almost at once—a man called Sainte who came from the same Basse Loire province. She didn't know him—but he happened to have known Père Chaise. He was running a hotel on Pearlyman Street, near Euston. He knew something of what Vicky had been through—and gave her a job and looked after her. It wasn't entirely charity. She worked hard for her keep. The French take a pretty realistic view on what constitutes a good day's work for a woman."

"Not a bad thing, in the circumstances," said Mr. Rumbold.

"No. It didn't give her too much time to think about things. Any spare moments she did get were spent pestering the War Office for news of Thoseby—and Wells."

"Judging from the upshot," said Mr. Rumbold dryly "she anyway succeeded in contacting Major Thoseby."

"In fact," said Nap, "Thoseby found her. The French run an organization in London—the Société de Lorraine

—which keeps an eye on all the French who, for one reason or another, decided to stay on here after the liberation. It's a sort of offshoot of their Embassy, and it has an office in Charles Street. Thoseby called in at this office when he was on a visit from Germany. He saw the name of Victoria Lamartine and asked the clerk about her. The clerk then remembered that Vicky had been inquiring about a Major Thoseby, did an unusually lucid bit of putting two and two together for a bureaucrat and turned up her address, the upshot of which was that Thoseby wrote to Sainte and booked a room at his hotel for the night of March fourteenth. He wrote on March twelfth, but I gather there was some difficulty at first in fitting the time in, as Thoseby was due back in Germany on the sixteenth and he was busy all day at the War Office. However, that's the way he arranged it, and he wrote this letter to Sainte, who, of course, told Vicky. On the fourteenth Thoseby telephoned to say he would be at the hotel sometime that same evening."

Nap turned over the papers.

"Various versions of what happened on the evening of March fourteenth can be found in the depositions at the police court—"

"All right," said his father. "I'll read these now."

And read them he did, from beginning to end, without any comment, whilst Nap sat on the window seat and smoked his pipe and thought about a number of things.

"This case has been remarkably well cobbled," said his father at last. "That'll be Claudian Summers. He started life as a Chancery draftsman and he's got a most damnably logical mind."

Nap nodded his agreement.

"You know," went on his father, "there's only one person who could have done this."

"And that's—?"

"Your young lady—Miss Lamartine."

"That's rather what Spence and Company thought," said Nap, "and I rather gather that's why they've had the case taken away from them."

"When you say that," said Mr. Rumbold gently, "you display to my mind a misunderstanding of the role of a legal adviser. I am prepared to take on this case, because I think that I ought to help anyone who went through what Miss Lamartine did, particularly when it was the result of her efforts—even indirect efforts—to help this country. Also I happen to be old-fashioned enough to think that a woman in distress ought to be helped. Especially when she is a foreigner and about to be subjected to the savage and un-predictable caprices of the English judicial system"—Nap had noticed before, in one or two men of his father's age, a certain conditioning of their adjectives, the result, no doubt, of five years of Churchillian oratory—"but you must not imagine that we are playing the heroes of this melodrama to Spence's villain. The only real difference between Spence and me is that I happen to be prepared to do some work on this case, whilst he is not. He is quite plainly prepared—" Mr. Rumbold ruffled over the depositions—"to go to the jury on what amounts to an admission of guilt with a plea in extenuation. Now I—assisted by you, Nap—am going to contest every step of the way. We're going to fight a long, dirty blackguarding campaign in which we shall use every subterfuge that the law allows, and perhaps even a few that it doesn't—you can't be too particular when you're defending. If we can't get witnesses of our own we must shake up their witnesses. If we can't shake them, we must discredit them. We'll have to brief the counsel best suited to such tactics—"

"They've already got Poynter."

"That old windbag," said Mr. Rumbold. "If we mean

business it would be about as much good putting him up against Claudian Summers as it would be for you or me to bowl leg breaks to Bradman with a ping-pong ball. That's exactly what I meant when I said that they weren't prepared to do any real work. If you look at the paper you'll see Poynter's got two more cases in the same list. And no doubt he'll find time to do all three of them, the way he prepares them. No. If we mean business, there's only one man for our money and that's Macrea."

"Would he take it?"

"I've already had a word with his clerk on the telephone. Just on the chance. I think he'll take it. I hope he will. There's no one I'd rather have with me in a roughhouse. We'll get him to ask for a postponement. In the circumstances Arbuthnot can hardly refuse it."

"Wouldn't it be better still to get an adjournment?"

"I'd thought of that. But I don't think these adjournments do a case any good. Bound to create prejudice. Besides I can't honestly think of anyone I'd rather take the case in front of than Arbuthnot. He's strict, but very very fair. And he does decide cases on facts, which is a good deal more," Mr. Rumbold added libelously, "than you can say for all of 'em."

"We're going to have to work fast."

"Fast and hard," agreed Mr. Rumbold. "You and me and anyone else we can rope in. What we must have is facts. Good hard provable facts. There's nothing here but wind and water." He shook Mr. Spence's dossier angrily in the air. "Nothing solid at all."

"Where do we start?"

"We'll start with the girl herself. We'll both go and have a word with her tomorrow afternoon—I want to spend most of the morning with Macrea. We shall have to do something about guaranteeing his fee, too. What's the present arrangement?"

"I gather that Spence's costs were being paid by Vicky's employer, M. Sainte. I also gather that he wasn't a particularly rich man and funds were running a bit low."

"Which accounts, no doubt, for his lack of enthusiasm," suggested Mr. Rumbold uncharitably. "Well, we won't worry too much about our fees, but we shall have to fix Macrea."

"I've got an idea about that," said Nap. "If it comes off, it might solve the financial difficulties. There's a sort of M.I.5. fund—a very privy purse—for cases like this. I know the chap at the War Office who might be able to pull the strings."

"Splendid," said Mr. Rumbold.

He had no objection to pulling any number of strings provided they worked in his direction.

Chapter Four

Mr. Hargest Macrea had his chambers on the east side of King's Bench Walk. He was their real, though not their titular head. His name appeared no higher than fourth on the long list in the hallway; but Sir Ernest Puckeridge, the expert on Privy Council Appeals, now devoted most of his time to the cultivation of tomatoes under glass; Judge Trimble had long ago sunk into well-merited oblivion by way of the County Court Bench; whilst Mr. Barter-Shaw (who confined himself to written opinions on canon law) had been quite mad for years.

Macrea was not a specialist. If called upon to define his pursuits he would have said that he specialized in advocacy. For a quarter of a century he had been bickering profitably with judges of every type from the rare heights of the House of Lords down to the earthy depths of the Land Tribunals. Be the going firm and the hedges stiff he had never yet refused to join in the hunt. He was the possessor of a Scots accent, which was apt to become more marked as the hearing grew more acrimonious (for he had early discovered that there was nothing which annoyed the opposition more than to have the name of their client repeatedly and markedly mispronounced). But his greatest single weapon was his monocle. It was a monocle of peculiar distortion and its application had more than once unnerved a recalcitrant witness. In addition he possessed a truculent intellect and a remarkable memory. Mr. Rumbold had been sending him briefs for more than twenty years.

That Sunday afternoon, following a telephone call, both the Rumbolds had a word with him in his Surrey home. Macrea tore the heart from the pile of documents with trained rapidity and his conclusion was the same as Mr. Rumbold's had been.

"We want facts," he said. "I'll read the papers more carefully this evening, and I'll make your application for you tomorrow, but if we're going to achieve anything we shall want more facts. You can't go out shooting without ammunition."

"I rather thought," said Nap, "that I might get a line on both those military witnesses through Uncle Alfred. He knows General Rockingham-Hawse in Establishments."

"Cedarbrook? Yes, that's quite a good idea."

"What about the hotel people? The proprietor and waiter and—what's her name?—Mrs. Roper. We've got to shake her evidence or we might as well pack up."

"I had an idea about that, too," said Nap. "What about McCann?"

"Who's he?"

"Well. He keeps a pub in Shepherd Market—I met him first in the army, and we've done one or two jobs together since. He'd do anything for a bit of excitement."

"Sounds a broad-minded man," said Macrea. "See if he'll do it for you. Nothing official, mind. Just an inquiry to see what he can pick·up. That leaves the main field clear for you." He thought for a moment and then said gently, "You've got to find.Wells."

This blunt statement of the problem produced a pause.

"Wells," said Mr. Rumbold. "The idea about Wells seems to be that he's dead."

"It hasn't been proved," said Macrea. "And even if he is dead he may have left some things—some sort of message. I take it," he added with a shrewd glance at Mr. Rumbold, "that the line we are going on is that everything this girl says is true."

"Certainly," said Mr. Rumbold.

"All right," said Macrea. "I just wanted to be sure. Well, the way to break the prosecution case wide open would be to produce Wells in court, to swear the child was his. That would dispose of the motive, and half their case—the stronger half—would fall to the ground."

"If he's alive."

"Even if he isn't," said Macrea, "there's a chance that he may have written—I suppose it was possible to send messages from Occupied France."

"Oh, yes," said Nap. "It wasn't a twice-daily collection, but it was fairly reliable."

"Well, then, if he wrote to anybody during those three or four weeks, he'd have been bound to mention the girl. Or he may have left a diary. People did that sort of thing. You'll have to find out all you can about the French side of it."

"The real question is, where do we start?"

"Start with the girl," said Macrea.

Accordingly, on Monday afternoon, after Macrea, as has already been related, had made his successful application for a week's postponement, Nap again visited Holloway Prison, accompanied this time by his father.

They found Vicky in excellent spirits. She had, it appeared, been most favorably impressed by the judge.

"*Homme très sympathique,*" she observed.

Mr. Rumbold agreed with her. Six months before he had heard him pronouncing sentence of death in just that cultivated, articulate, considerate voice. He did not, of course, mention this, but brought the conversation quickly round to the subject of his visit.

"Julian? He is still alive."

"You haven't heard from him—?"

"No. But I feel it. It is a matter, you understand, that one is bound to feel. A man who has been one's lover."

"Quite so," said Mr. Rumbold. "It had occurred to me to wonder if, during that time, when he was—when he was staying with you, did Lieutenant Wells give you any information which would enable us to trace his past life."

"He was orphaned—poor boy."

"Yes. We knew that. The military authorities have given us such data as they had in his records, date and place of birth and education, and so on. But the detailed records only start when he joined up, in 1940. He left his public school in 1937. Those are the three years we are most interested in. He must have made some friends. What did he do? How did he earn his living?"

"He spoke of a School of Preparation."

"A School of Preparation." The Rumbolds looked at each other thoughtfully.

"The School of Preparation of Saint Augustine."

"Sounds Anglo-Catholic," said Mr. Rumbold. "I'll have to get hold of Father Pasteur."

"He was a *professeur* at this school."

"Good gracious me," said Mr. Rumbold. "I should hardly have thought—at that age—he had only just left school himself you say."

Light dawned.

"You mean he was a master—at a preparatory school."

"A preparatory school, yes."

"St. Augustine's Preparatory School for Boys. Boys prepared for all the leading public schools and the Royal Navy. A staff of graduates and a lady matron. Whilst every effort is made to develop a boy's natural abilities, 'cramming' is not encouraged."

"You know it, then?"

"I've heard of it," said Nap. "It's one of the better known prep schools. It's not far from Winchester, I believe."

"Well, that's one line," said Mr. Rumbold cheerfully. "It really sounds very promising. It covers just the time we want—after he left school, and before he joined the army. Now what about the other side—your side of the story, mademoiselle. France."

"Of that," said Vicky, "I will tell you all."

Chapter Five

"So you see," said Nap. "It's really a three-man job."

"It has the look of it," agreed Major McCann.

"I shall have to go across to Angers, as soon as I've arranged the necessary contacts. My father will be up to his eyebrows in the legal work. We wanted you to look up these people in England—down at Winchester."

"I haven't just all the time in the world to go stravaiging about England for you. However—"

He looked at his wife.

"It can't take more than a week. If we don't do it in a week, we shan't do it at all."

"Hmph."

"Go on," said his wife. "You're spoiling for it. There isn't all that work to do, now the summer's over and the Americans have gone home. I can manage for a week. I managed alone for five years before I married you."

"Well, then." McCann stirred his tea thoughtfully. "Give us the strength of it."

They were sitting in the landlord's parlor, on the first floor of the Leopard; which, as you know, is one of the Shepherd Market houses. It was a comfortable little room, designed equally for eating, working and sitting, and the first fire of autumn was alight in the grate.

"There's one thing we'll have to get clear," said McCann at the end of Nap's recital. "How do we stand with the police?"

"I should like notice of that question," said Nap. "I think that we stand where the defense in a capital charge always stands. The police are as equally bound to help us as they are to help the prosecution."

"I should have thought," said Kitty McCann, "that human nature being what it is—"

"Yes, I know. I know what you're going to say. The police have got the case up, and they don't want to see it flop. But honestly, I think that most police officers take the reasonable view that a miscarriage of justice does them more harm—in the end—than an acquittal. I'm fairly confident that would be Hazlerigg's view—"

"It isn't Hazlerigg's case, is it?"

"No. It's a chap called Partridge. Inspector Partridge. The D.D.I. of that division. I don't know him at all."

"And you wouldn't mind me seeing Hazlerigg—you'll remember he's a friend of mine."

"No," said Nap. "I'm sure we shouldn't. He mayn't be able to help, but it can't do any harm. They're bound to know that we shall work like beavers on such facts as we have got. Only—I shouldn't be too explicit about the exact line we're taking."

"I wouldn't mind knowing that myself," said McCann frankly. "On the facts you have given me there's only one person could have done the job—"

"That's what they all say," agreed Nap. "I guarantee, though, that you won't talk for ten minutes to this girl and go away thinking she's guilty."

"He's very sensitive to atmosphere," agreed Mrs. McCann. "He proposed to me the moment he saw my wine list."

"I can well believe it," said Nap. "I'd have done it for your clarets alone. Now this is the idea. If the girl is innocent—and we're presuming she is—then there are two obvious lines. First we must destroy the motive put forward by the prosecution."

"Produce Wells."

"Yes. Or someone who heard from him after he was parachuted into France—someone to whom he may have mentioned Vicky."

"I don't think that's awfully hopeful," said McCann. "Even the most casual person would hardly write that sort of thing in a letter home, would he? 'Last week I met a smashing girl called Vicky Lamartine and with any luck she should be having a child by me sometime next June—'"

"There's no need to be coarse, Angus."

"I imagine he'd wrap it up a bit," agreed Nap. "But I can't be expected to tell you what we'll find until we find it."

"And your second line?"

"Well, that's not quite so simple to explain. What I feel about it is this. You start from one indisputable fact, that Eric Thoseby was murdered. Now, in a general way, Eric was an easygoing sort of chap. People who met him rather liked him. I can't imagine him making any mortal enemies —except in connection with his Resistance work. So far as *that* side of him was concerned, it was business first, business last, business all the time. He was amiable but absolutely and completely ruthless. Because he happened to believe in the job he was doing. Therefore, I think it's a fair bet that if he made any mortal enemies we shall find the beginning of the trail on the Loire."

"That's fair enough," said McCann.

"And another thing—we still want to know a great deal more about what actually *did* happen in September, 1943. All we've got to go on at the moment is a certain amount of hearsay and an account—admittedly rather a biased account—given us by Vicky herself. There may be people in the Maine-et-Loire district who know what actually happened—no one's bothered to ask them yet. I don't think you can blame the police for that—it just doesn't happen to be part of their case."

Kitty McCann finished the sock she was darning, rolled it into a ball and laid it with a heap of others on top of the cellar book on the big old-fashioned gramophone beside her chair.

Both men were silent with their own thoughts, and she addressed the remark to them equally.

"What are you going to do," she said, "if all the facts you unearth show more and more clearly that Miss Lamartine did do the murder?"

"Oh, I don't know." Nap sounded uncomfortable. "I suppose we'd have to pick out the ones that were least unfavorable and spring them on the other side at the last moment. Unexpected facts are better than no facts at all."

"Blind 'em with science," suggested McCann.

"I see," said Mrs. McCann thoughtfully. "Yes—I suppose that's what you'd have to do."

Chapter Six

On Wednesday morning Major McCann called on Chief Inspector Hazlerigg at Scotland Yard.

It was the same room, the one he had been in a number of times before, with the waxed linoleum, the green filing cabinets, the neat, unused-looking desk. The only thing which was missing was the camp bed in the corner; the one which Hazlerigg used when times of stress forced him to eat and sleep and live with his work. It had been there during the days of the Fifth Column in 1938. McCann himself remembered it there when the Gilbert-Jacoby crowd was being liquidated. Its absence seemed, in a way, encouraging.

They shook hands, and McCann lowered himself into the easy chair facing the desk.

It was left to him to open the conversation.

"I wanted," he said, "to have a word with you about the case of Mademoiselle Lamartine."

"Yes," said Hazlerigg. "I understood you to say so on the telephone."

It was not unfriendly, but to McCann, who knew Hazlerigg well, the tone of voice conveyed a warning.

Nevertheless he persevered.

"You remember young Rumbold—the solicitor you met in the Stalagmite Insurance Case—well, it's his firm that has been instructed for the defense. They have to look through all the evidence as thoroughly as they can—on behalf of their client."

"I thought a firm called Chalibut and Spence was acting for Miss Lamartine."

"She changed her mind at the last moment," explained McCann patiently. He was pretty certain that Hazlerigg knew this already, but if the inspector, for reasons of his own, wanted to take everything the long way round, McCann was quite willing to oblige him.

"Have you any idea why she should do such a thing?"

"I gather," said McCann, "that she didn't fancy the line they were taking."

"Which was—?"

"Broadly speaking, guilty, under provocation, with a strong plea for the leniency of the court."

"And the new idea? That is, if you've no objection—"

"The new idea," said McCann slowly, "is that she didn't do it at all." It is possible that he surprised even himself. It certainly got through to Hazlerigg. The inspector deliberated for a moment, opened his mouth to answer and shut it again without saying a word, then climbed to his feet and went over to look out of the window, across the grimy buttresses of the Embankment, at the wind ruffling the waters of the Thames where a strong tide was making past Westminster Bridge.

When at last he turned round, he seemed to have come to some sort of decision.

"I think you must leave it alone," he said.

"If—"

"I know, I know. It's your duty as a citizen to assist justice. You said so. Every person is presumed innocent until they have been proved guilty. That's an argument I recognize so far as young what's-his-name is concerned. He's a lawyer. He's got to make out the best case he can for his client. That's what he's paid for. But you're not a lawyer, you're a publican and—" the irritation in his voice made Hazlerigg sound faintly human for the first time during the interview—"a damned pragmatical lowland Scot. Why, you're doing this for the fun of it."

"Perhaps if you'd let me finish what I was going to say—" suggested McCann mildly.

"Go on, then. It won't do any good. Say it by all means."

"It was just this. *If* you have made a mistake over this case—you can put away your gun, I'm only saying 'if'— then it must be in the best interests of the people you serve to have the truth brought to light. The truth, the whole truth, and nothing but the truth. I don't imagine that any police force enjoys its Oscar Slaters."

"Agreed," said Hazlerigg shortly. There was an unusual anger somewhere down behind his gray eyes.

"Well, then—on the other hand, if the girl *is* guilty— and that's possible too, probable if you like—surely, even then, it's to your advantage to have the thing properly contested. It's only when the defense put up a proper fight that you can be sure of getting to the truth. However good the prosecution's case is, unless it's fought out you must be left with an uncomfortable feeling that the prisoner *may* be doing it out of bravado or lunacy, or a kink of some sort, or to shield a third party, or to get their name in the headlines, or—"

"All right, all right," said Hazlerigg. "I admit it all. I still ask you, personally, to keep out of it."

"Why?" said McCann bluntly.

"That's not at all easy to explain. If it was a straight-forward case, I'd be the first to say go ahead and do your damnedest. But it isn't a straightforward case. And above all—" it was evident that the inspector was choosing his words with great care—"above all, it isn't my case."

"I see," said McCann. "Yes. The man who's doing the job—Inspector Partridge, I believe."

"That's the chap."

"You think I ought to have a word with him."

"You could do that, of course," said Hazlerigg. "I don't think you'd get much change out of him though."

"A rough character?"

"No. He's a man of very decided views."

"I see," said McCann again.

It was a surprising explanation, and surprisingly delicately put. It also made things extremely awkward. Before McCann could make up his mind as to exactly what he ought to say Hazlerigg went on:

"If the case is conducted on the lines you suggest, with Macrea at the wheel—" McCann was not so tactless as to inquire how Hazlerigg, if he had not heard of the change of solicitors, was yet fully informed of the change of counsel—"then one thing's certain. There's going to be a lot of mud thrown around. And since a good deal of the evidence in this case is police evidence—I'm not using the word in any derogatory sense—then it follows that a good deal of that mud will stick to the police witnesses—you follow me."

"Very clearly," said McCann.

"Well, then," said Hazlerigg bluntly, "in a case like this I fight for my own side. If you and your friends want to take this up as a—a sort of private crusade—then I warn you that on principle I'm against you."

"I'm sure," said McCann steadily, "that you'll do nothing but fight fair."

There was a short and rather uncomfortable silence.

"I hope I shan't disappoint you, then," said Hazlerigg with an attempt at lightness which sat awkwardly on him. He leaned forward and pressed the bell.

Sergeant Crabbe appeared.

"Sit down, Sergeant," said Hazlerigg. "This is Major McCann. I expect you remember him."

Sergeant Crabbe, a sorrowful man, nodded heavily. He bestowed upon McCann the look which a St. Bernard might have given if, after a long trek through the snow, he had found the traveler already frozen to death. He then sat down dutifully on the edge of the hardest chair.

"Major McCann is interested in the Lamartine case, and has some questions to put to us—questions which I shall do my best to answer. I thought it might be useful if you made a note of the interview."

"Very good, sir."

"When you get it typed you might have a second copy taken for Inspector Partridge."

"Very good, sir. Do you wish me to make a verbatim record?"

"Oh, no, Sergeant. Just the gist of what passes. Head-notes will do. Now then—"

He turned invitingly toward his visitor.

McCann was not to be intimidated. Moreover, the by-play had given him an opportunity to set his thoughts in order.

"There were one or two points," he said, "that weren't quite apparent on reading the papers. First of all, the hotel proprietor. I understood from our client that he was a compatriot—that he came from the same part of France."

"That is correct. I understand that he was from Maine-et-Loire—that is the district of Angers—where Miss Lamartine was staying during the Occupation."

"How does he come to be in England now?"

"I understand that he was granted an entry visa in 1946. He had had a good record during the war and put down the necessary security. The Foreign Office could tell you more about that, of course."

"When you say 'a good record,' " said McCann, "you mean that he was a member of the Resistance—?"

"I suppose that any Frenchman who did not co-operate with the Germans could more or less be so described."

"Quite so. Anyway, he might have had some previous contact with our client. He certainly knew about her, and sympathized with the ordeal she had been through."

"I believe that is so. You could ask her about that yourself, of course."

"Were there any other foreigners in the hotel?"

"The staff or the residents? None of the residents, I believe. The waiter is an Italian."

"I take it," said McCann, "that in the course of your ordinary investigations, everybody in the hotel would have been scrutinized."

"That is correct."

"And you had nothing on the proprietor or his staff."

"If I understand your question, you mean had they at any time done anything to render themselves liable to criminal prosecution? The answer is No."

"Could you take it a little further than that? Had you any reason at all—I wasn't referring only to actual criminal offenses—had you any reason to suspect that the proprietor or any of his staff might have had any hand in this murder?"

"On the contrary," said Hazlerigg. "All the evidence we have scrutinized to date would seem to exculpate them. I have only read the evidence, you understand, but that is my opinion."

"I see," said McCann. "And the guests."

"There were only seven guests at the hotel. A family

party of three—who were coming into the hotel actually at the moment the crime was discovered—and two others, a clergyman and his wife, who came in later. We have not paid a great deal of attention to them—beyond the usual routine checkup. The two guests actually in the hotel—I think you have read their evidence."

"Colonel Trevor Alwright and Mrs. Roper?"

"Yes. Well, if I may employ the expression you used a moment ago, we have certainly got nothing 'on' either of them."

McCann thought this out carefully.

"I might add," went on Hazlerigg, "that Colonel Alwright—now retired—has an extremely good record at the War Office, where he was in charge of interdepartmental postings for many years, and gained an O.B.E. for his valuable services during the war."

The look with which Hazlerigg accompanied this statement halted McCann as effectively as a blow under the heart.

It had really, he reflected, been very neatly done.

Sergeant Crabbe's report would be a beautifully innocuous document. It could be produced, at any time, in support of Hazlerigg's discretion.

A straight tip had been passed, nevertheless.

Chapter Seven

"I tell you," said Major McCann, "he practically shouted it in my ear. He wrote it in letters a yard high and pushed it right under my nose."

"I still don't see it," said his wife.

She dipped some more glasses into a tub of hot water, pulled them out in a bunch, held them under the cold tap and handed them to McCann, who started to polish them.

"Listen, sweetest," said McCann. "First of all I asked him if he had anything *on* any of the staff at the hotel. Before he would even answer that one, he carefully defined what he meant by 'on.' He made it mean 'Had they ever been the subject of criminal proceedings.' "

"I understand that," said Mrs. McCann. "Be careful with those port glasses, the price Mandelbaum charges for them, you'd think they were rare old crystal."

"All right. Then we came to the guests at the hotel. There were seven of them, but five were more or less out of it. That left two."

"Five from seven leaves two," agreed Mrs. McCann, to show that her mind was on the job.

"Those two are Colonel Alwright and Mrs. Roper. Now first Hazlerigg said he'd nothing 'on' them. That is they neither of them had actual police records. He then went on to say that Colonel Alwright had a very good name—a very good general reputation. From what he let go it didn't sound a terribly distinguished military career, but the gist of it was plain enough. He was a good type, an upright steady-going citizen, who might park his car on the wrong side of the road but wouldn't otherwise bother the police from year's end to year's end."

"We can't all be commandos," said Mrs. McCann. "I don't suppose they were invented when he was young."

"I don't suppose they were," said McCann, "but that isn't the point. What about Mrs. Roper?"

"Well, she could hardly have been in the comm—all right," she added hastily, seeing that McCann was showing signs of nervous instability. "I see what you're getting at, only please put down those glasses first. You mean that

Mrs. Roper, although she mayn't have a record, may be known to the police in some way."

"That was rather my idea," said McCann, "and I think that's why Hazlerigg had Sergeant Crabbe in attendance. He was giving me a hot tip—the hottest tip he could. If there's trouble about it, all he's got to do is to call for the record."

"What do you imagine she'd be up to?"

"I should say, just for guessing, that she's on their 'Further Inquiries' list. That means that she associates with people who have got records, but either she's managed, so far, to get away with it, or they just don't think it's politic to pull her in yet. Here she is—it was taken when she was leaving the police court."

"She looks quite respectable."

"So did Messalina. If she's a hanger-on in an organized crowd—which I think is the likeliest thing—then it must be in one of four or five lines. I ought to be able to pick it up."

"Are you going out tonight?"

"I thought I would." McCann polished off the last of the glasses and removed his apron. "There isn't much time to spare and there's a lot of ground to cover. I thought I'd start at Philippino's at King's Cross and work back."

He outlined his itinerary.

"I still think you may be imagining the whole thing," said Mrs. McCann.

"If you'd heard Hazlerigg," said McCann, "you wouldn't think so. It was as deliberate as a dig in the ribs. In my experience, Hazlerigg always thinks before he speaks."

"If he'd known you as well as I do," said Mrs. McCann, "he'd have kept his big mouth shut."

After her husband had gone she played with the idea of ringing up Inspector Roberts at the West End Central

Police Station and telling him where her husband was going. This would have been quite a reasonable thing to do, because he was an old friend of theirs and would have refrained from asking any awkward questions.

Her hand was actually on the telephone when the barman came in with a panic about the gin supply and the project got shelved.

It made no difference, because McCann didn't keep to his itinerary, anyway.

The Britannia Café stands in one of the uninspiring streets in the Goods Yard area which lies to the north of King's Cross station. There is a ground-floor room, which contains six marble-topped tables, a tea urn and a specimen case containing withered sandwiches, geological rock cakes and tins of diced potato. There is also a flight of stairs, and at the top of them a frosted glass door. Nothing invites you to go up the stairs. On the other hand nothing forbids you.

McCann climbed the stairs, opened the door at the top, and went in.

Except that it had two big coffee percolators and no tea urn it looked exactly like the ground floor. There were half a dozen men and two women in the room. When McCann opened the door they all stopped talking and started looking at him.

There was a positive quality of hostility in their silence. It was the sort of silence that asks a question. McCann looked quickly round and saw the man he wanted; a middle-sized, thick man wearing a raincoat over blue-dyed battledress trousers. As their eyes met the man got to his feet and came forward. "Hullo, Major, fancy seeing you again." His mouth was smiling but the rest of his face had a battered permanence that defied any change of expression.

"Evening, Gunner," said McCann.

Conversation had started up again but McCann noticed that he was not invited to join any of the groups. The thick man came and sat down beside him at one of the empty tables.

"Have some coffee," he said. "Coffee's one of the things Philippino knows about."

He knocked with a coin on the marble top of the table and a little brown man appeared. His face shone like a well-polished brogue shoe and he had very black hair and a very white smile.

"Two coffees, Pino. This is my friend, Major McCann."

"He's welcome," said the brown man. In less than a minute he had reappeared with two large cups of black coffee.

"He'll know you now," said Gunner. "If you happened to come here and—you know, if I wasn't here."

"Thanks," said McCann.

They drank some of their coffee. Gunner had spoken no more than the truth; it was very good coffee.

McCann unfolded his evening paper on to the table and pushed it across. The photograph was lying between the sheets.

"Do you know her?" he said.

"Never met her."

"Could you find out if she's known in your crowd?"

"What's in it?" said Gunner.

"There's a five in it," said McCann. "Not more. It's just a routine checkup."

"Is the five there whether it's Yes or No?"

"Just the same."

"All right," said Gunner. The paper was slid across the table. The photograph was still inside and five pound notes had added themselves to it.

"It'll take half an hour—maybe more," said Gunner. "Enjoy yourself. Why not have a nice game of brag with those boys in the corner?"

"My mother told me never to play cards with strangers."

Gunner showed his few teeth in a smile and was gone. It was nearly an hour before he returned.

He handed McCann back his folded paper.

"Not known," he said. "You might try Berty's."

"Thank you," said McCann.

A minute later he was out in the street.

It was seven o'clock and almost dark. There was a nip in the air, which was sharp and grateful after the overheated room. The first mist of autumn was making halos round the street lamps in the Islington Road, and outside the brewery two huge dray horses stood in a cloud of steam and dreamed of nosebags and stable. A trolley-bus swished past him in the mist, its wheels purring on the smooth asphalt.

McCann was a Scotsman but he had spent most of his life in London and he loved every bit of it. He loved the dirty bits and the twisted bits. The nastiness of London was part of its flavor.

He was making for a small public house near the Angel. Here he stopped long enough to spend a further five pounds. After which he returned to his own territory, and put in an inquiry at a theatrical club in Compton Street. It would have been more convenient if he could have made this call first, but the man he wanted was never there until nine. McCann ate some sandwiches whilst he was waiting for him and drank some beer. When his man arrived he handed out more money in return for which he got a glass of apricot brandy.

At half-past nine he set out once more, his objective being a pool room near Fleet Street. At half-past ten he was on his way home to bed.

He had spent twenty pounds of Messrs. Rumbold's money, but he was not entirely dissatisfied with his evening's work. He knew for certain now that Mrs. Roper was on the fringe of the law. He knew that her activities, whatever they might be, were not connected in any way with racing or betting, with the food and drink racket, with drugs, or with organized prostitution; which was quite a lot of negative evidence.

· He was crossing Kingsway when he saw someone he knew. A small man, who had been walking ahead of him, stopped for a moment under the street light, to let a car go past.

"Blow me down," said McCann to himself. "I've seen that nose before. It's Mousey."

Mousey Jones was a small character who made a living by picking up the crumbs which lie round the wainscoting, and in the dark corners, of that big living room of crime, the West End. His staple occupation was the insertion of lumps of putty into the return-coin slots of public telephones—lumps which he would later remove with a piece of wire bringing down sometimes as much as a shilling in coppers, a shilling which should by rights have gone to previous pressers of Button B. Between times he ran errands for almost anyone who would employ him.

McCann had not seen Mousey for a long time. He had no further business that night; all other lines having petered out he thought that Mousey might lead him somewhere. He followed him discreetly.

The little man was clearly up to no good. He sidled along, with his chin on his shoulder, a picture of felonious intent. The appearance of a policeman drove him to take a deep interest in a shop window—a window which contained, as McCann saw when he passed it himself, a large Bible open at the appropriate text of Jeremiah 18:11: "... Return

ye now every one from his evil way, and make your ways
and your doings good."

Halfway down Long Acre, Mousey disappeared.

McCann was puzzled for a moment, then he saw the dark
entrance to the side turning—it was no more than a passage-
way—and, halfway down it, throwing a fan of light into
the gloom, the open door of the King of Norway.

McCann followed circumspectly. He did not at once go
in. He first tried a glance through the window but was
baffled by the display of stained glass.

He hesitated for a moment. One or two of the Covent
Garden pubs, as he knew, had recently been getting a
borderline reputation. Also he was out of his own territory.

Finally he went in.

It was a small, quiet bar. Mousey had got his pint and
was sitting at one of the tables by the wall talking to a
youth with red hair and pimples. Four men were playing
nap at another table. Two old ladies, dressed in tight black
were perched like a brace of crows on the bench by the
door, nodding over their Guinnesses.

"Half pint of bitter," said McCann. "Quiet tonight."

"We're always quiet in here," said the landlord.

"It's nice to be quiet," said McCann.

"That's what I always say," said the landlord.

As he said this he smiled. It wasn't a particularly nice
smile.

McCann had picked up his glass when he realized that
two men had come in without making any noise. One of
them, a tall thin man with a bent nose was standing just
beside him. The other was at the door.

"Were you asking after Mrs. Roper?" said the thin man
softly.

Quite suddenly McCann realized that he had been every
sort of fool.

He realized that he had been led by the nose to the place where things happened. He knew this from the way the two women had already disappeared, and from the way the landlord kept his eye on the doorway through which he was preparing to disappear (and from a telephone behind which he would, no doubt, in due course, and when it was too late, summon the police). He knew it from the painstaking way in which the card players went on with their game without lifting their eyes.

Meanwhile there was a question to be answered.

"No," he said. "It wasn't me. Perhaps you were thinking of someone else."

Considering that this was a flat lie, he managed to work a good deal of conviction into it.

"Like hell I was thinking of someone else," said the thin man.

"I expect it was the other man," suggested McCann.

"What other man?"

"The one who went out just now," said McCann.

"Like hell someone went out just now," said the thin man.

It seemed to be a deadlock.

McCann saw what was coming—he saw the ugly bulk in the man's coat pocket. He decided to take the initiative. He shifted his weight on to his left foot and kicked the thin man hard, on the edge of his Achilles tendon.

The thin man gave a scream and lifted his right foot to clutch at the injured member. This was exactly as McCann had planned. The thin man was wearing a pair of those very wide-bottomed trousers. McCann seized firmly hold of the trouser leg with both hands, turned his back, and heaved sharply. Then he lifted and slung his opponent, as a coal heaver heaves a sack of coal.

The thin man flailed through the air, landed on the table,

where he considerably deranged the card game, slid across the table top, carrying off four full pints of beer, and came to rest with a satisfying thud against the barroom wall.

McCann did not waste any time in self-congratulation. The more dangerous opponent, he knew, was the big man at the street door.

Had this second man started a fraction sooner he would have caught McCann off balance and the fight, as a fight, would have ended then and there. He came across the floor in a powerful but controlled rush, but his delay gave McCann time to sweep a table into his way.

This added up to a bare two seconds' respite; and moving with surprising speed he propelled himself under the bar flap, and was round again facing his opponent with the width of the bar between them.

There, for a moment, they stood watching each other. The next move was far from plain. Clearly the big man could not himself come under the bar, since this would put his head at McCann's mercy; equally clearly he could not execute the plans he had in mind for McCann with a two-foot mahogany counter between them.

McCann cast a sideways glance at the thin man. He thought it possible, from the angle of his head, that the thin man's neck was broken.

Taking his eyes off his opponent was a mistake which nearly cost the game. He only just ducked in time, as the big man swung at him, left-handed.

The loaded stick glanced off his shoulder, but missed his head. There was a sharp detonation, and something warm started to run down the back of McCann's neck. For a wild moment he thought it was his own blood and wondered why he had felt nothing, then the true explanation occurred to him. It was gin. The stick had fractured the bottle which hung, reversed, from a bracket on the shelf.

At the moment the big man jumped.

It was quite an effort. He came clean over the bar, like an athlete diving over a vaulting horse, and he landed in McCann's arms.

A second later they were both on the ground rolling round in the gin and broken glass in the narrow space behind the counter.

It was only the narrowness of this space that saved McCann. The big man, as he speedily found, was every bit as strong as he was, and a much more experienced fighter.

McCann had caught the man's left wrist in his own right hand, but the man's other arm was free. He was unable to swing it. He confined himself, therefore, to an attempt to get his fingers into McCann's eyes. Unfortunately for him he misjudged the distance and succeeded only in wedging three of his fingers into McCann's mouth. McCann bit hard. The fingers were dragged out. They brought a couple of teeth with them.

At this point providence placed a weapon into the big man's hand. In his groping he found the bottom of the gin bottle. This had come off more or less in one piece and was adorned with half a dozen needle-sharp spikes of splintered glass.

McCann saw the red light; almost literally, in the glare of mingled rage and beastly satisfaction which came into the eyes so close above his own. He moved his left hand instinctively and encountered the big man's right wrist, as it slid up. He caught it and held it, though awkwardly, and was thus able to inspect at a range of six inches the horrible weapon which it held.

The big man pressed downward, twice, with all his force. McCann exerted himself in an upward direction. The big man reversed suddenly, tore his hand free, and jabbed.

McCann jerked his head aside and the glass cut the lobe off his left ear.

McCann rolled back and grabbed again.

This time he was holding his opponent's wrist downward and was able to get some of his weight on to it.

The only disadvantage of this change was that it brought their faces even closer together.

The big man started to eat McCann's left ear.

McCann stood this for some seconds, then raised his head sharply from the floor.

The click which followed suggested that he had broken the big man's nose.

At this point, and not before McCann was ready for it, a third party appeared.

The space at the top of the bar was blacked out, an arm in blue descended, and a voice said, "Now then, break that up."

The big man removed himself slowly, and McCann, following, got his head above the counter in time to see the last act. Standing in the middle of the bar was a young and conscientious-looking policeman. In front of him was the big man, who had just got out from under the bar counter.

McCann prepared himself for some rather difficult explanations. The big man thought otherwise. With a speed and power which showed what he could do in the open, he jumped forward, hit the policeman once in the stomach and once under the jaw, jumped his body and disappeared through the door into the street.

McCann got on to his feet shakily.

He found himself in sole and absolutely undisputed possession of the field of battle.

The landlord and the customers had disappeared. The constable lay where he had fallen. The thin man had rolled off the table on to a bench.

In the silence the ticking of the bar clock sounded loud.

McCann picked out a piece of glass which had got between his collar and his neck and straightened the remnants of his tie. He walked over to the thin man who seemed still to be breathing. He put his hand into the thin man's inside pocket and found a wallet. It was quite a heavy wallet. McCann pocketed it.

It struck him that it was high time to be off.

Twenty minutes later Mrs. McCann was gazing at her husband.

For once all comment seemed to have failed her. At last she said, faintly, "It must have been quite a party. I take it Mrs. Roper is a gin drinker. It looks as if she's got rather long nails, too."

"I wouldn't know," said McCann. "I never caught up with her. Just two of her friends. And as for the gin, I only wish I had rather more of it in me and rather less of it down my neck. Come up and talk to me in the bathroom and bring the first-aid kit with you."

Before he went to bed he turned out the wallet he had taken from the thin man.

He found seventeen pounds and ten shillings in notes, which he reckoned would go some way toward buying him a new suit. The only other thing of interest was a letter. A name in it caught his eye, and he showed it to his wife.

"There you are, Kitty," he said, "that's his racket all right. And if it's his racket, then it's probably Mrs. Roper's as well."

"Stimmy," said Mrs. McCann. "I know I've heard the name but I can't—"

"Gold," said McCann. "And I don't mean gold shares, I mean the article itself. He's the biggest illicit gold dealer in London."

Chapter Eight

"I shall have to catch the night boat," wrote Nap to his wife, "for I shall be busy all this afternoon in London, making the necessary contacts. Unless I can do some really good groundwork at this end I fear my trip will be largely wasted. However, the expenses are falling, in the long run, on public funds, so why worry?

"I ran into Angus McCann this morning in Shepherd Market. He had a beautiful black eye, someone had chewed the bottom off his left ear, and he could hardly speak for a plummy mouth. From what I could understand he's now got a line on Mrs. Roper. He has found out that she's connected, though distantly, with the gold smuggling and currency racket. I'm not at all sure how this ties up with our case, but it should make quite good ammunition for Macrea in cross-examination.

"I'm off now to the Société de Lorraine to try my charms on the French bureaucrats."

"H'm," said Mrs. Rumbold thoughtfully.

She read the letter again, turned it over to make sure there was no postscript, and then handed it down to Phylida Rumbold, who was lying on her stomach on the carpet. Phylida tore it in four pieces and started to eat the largest piece.

Meanwhile Nap had discovered the Bureau de Lorraine. The French, who have a genius for melancholia in their conduct of public affairs, had selected the most repulsive of the large houses which make up the south side of Charles Street, had decorated the front with a tricolor, and had already succeeded in imparting to the interior that particular odor of airlessness, frustration and a distant hint of the concierge's cooking arrangements which characterize the French administrative building.

Nap found a room marked RECEPTION and looked in.

Seated behind a desk, sole occupant of the room, was a girl. She looked up, saw Nap and smiled. It did not need the new copy of *Le Figaro* in her hand or the elaborately simple, beautifully conceived clothes. The face itself was sufficient to place her within ten square miles of the world's surface. Only one capital city could produce that deepest of dark brown hair, with highlights of black, that white neck solidly angled to the shoulders, yet too well-proportioned to seem thick: Siamese cat's eyes of very light blue, which were so rarely found with such black hair.

Nap realized that he was staring, but that the girl seemed unembarrassed by this circumstance.

Possibly she was used to people staring at her.

"Can I be of assistance?"

"Well, yes," said Nap. "I expect you can."

"What is it you want?"

"I want to see Monsieur le Directeur."

"If you would very kindly indicate your business." The girl drew a printed form from a rack and smiled at him. It was the sort of smile that sent the temperature of the room up ten degrees and turned all the lights on.

All right, thought Nap. If this a bureaucrat, *vive le bureaucratisme*.

"I am inquiring," he said, "about three persons, of all of whom I had hoped your organization might have something to tell me. First, Mademoiselle Victoria Lamartine—" Nap gave such details as he had and the girl made a number of businesslike little notes on her pad. "Then of a Monsieur Sainte—Monsieur Honorifique Sainte—of the same department. He is now the proprietor of an hotel in Pearlyman Street. I believe that you have had dealings with him."

"*Bien, monsieur.* And the third?"

"The third," said Nap slowly, "is an Englishman. A Lieutenant Wells, of the British Army. He was parachuted into the district of Maine-et-Loire in 1943 and afterward disappeared. Any news which you could let us have would be very much appreciated. It is possible, however, that he is dead—killed by the Gestapo."

"Very well," said the girl. "Will you follow me?"

She led the way out into the passage and pointed to a small room opposite. Nap went in. It looked like a waiting room. Half an hour later he had no doubts about it. It was certainly a waiting room. Almost an hour had gone by before the door opened and a small man in black came in and asked Nap to be good enough to follow.

The *directeur's* office was at the other end of the passage. It was a large and pleasant room and it overlooked the garden. Despite the warmth of the afternoon its windows were tightly shut, and the only air in the room appeared to come from a door in the opposite corner which was a few inches open.

"Please be seated," said the *directeur*. "I must apologize that you were kept waiting. Inquiries such as yours cannot be answered on the moment."

"Of course not," said Nap. "It's very good of you to see me at all."

"To business," said the *directeur* agreeably.

Nap said, "It is of two of your compatriots that I am inquiring—two persons I believe your organization has helped in the past, Mademoiselle Lamartine and Monsieur Sainte—"

The *directeur* pressed the tips of the fingers of his right hand against the tips of the fingers of his left hand in an exceedingly bureaucratical way.

"First," he said, "one should be excused for asking your credentials."

Nap was ready for this one.

"I suggest," he said, "that you ring up the Governor of Holloway Prison—he might allow you, in the circumstances, to speak to Miss Lamartine, and in any case he knows my name. Or you might ring up my office and ask for my father. He will confirm that we act for the lady."

"I accept your credentials," said the *directeur* calmly. Despite his pompous manner he did not look like a fool. Indeed, it seemed unlikely that the head of such an organization could be a fool.

"A minute with my files," he said, and turned to the shelf beside him.

"Mademoiselle Victoria Lamartine," he said, "formerly of Paris—you do not want her former Paris address, I take it. The house has, anyway, been destroyed. Evacuated in 1939 to Langeais near Angers, department of Maine-et-Loire. Engaged in Resistance work. Arrested the fifteenth of September, 1943. In the hands of the enemy until August, 1944 during which time she had a son born in prison. The son died in 1947. Mademoiselle Lamartine applied for permission to work in England. In view of her known history the references and deposit were waived and work was secured for her in London at the hotel in Pearlyman Street near Euston Station."

"Thank you," said Nap. "Much of that was known to us but the confirmation, you understand, may be useful."

"Honorifique Sainte, hotelier, 15 Rue du Pont Saumur, department Indre-et-Loire. Of good conduct during the war, though not, so far as is known, actively engaged in Resistance work. Application to open a hotel in London made in May, 1946. Deposit of 500,000 francs. References, Pierre and André Marquis, farmers of Avrillé-les-Ponceaux, and M. Gimelet, lawyer, of 20 Rue de Gazomètre, Angers. Aged fifty-five."

"Thank you," said Nap. He made a note of the names and dates. "Finally—I hardly think it likely—but—"

"Monsieur Le Lieutenant Wells," said the *directeur*, looking down at the form on the desk. "We should hardly be able to help you. We concern ourselves, you understand, with French citizens who have come over to England. We have no right, even, to ask them questions, but we are able to assist them, and so they keep us informed of their movements. Inquiries in France, however, are another matter. If we wish to make inquiries in France we have to obtain the assistance of the proper authorities."

"The Sûreté," suggested Nap.

"If the matter is criminal, certainly. Or of the Department of the Interior."

"I see," said Nap. "Well, thank you at all events for what you have given me."

On his way out he noticed that the door of the reception room was open. He looked in, but the room was empty.

After Nap had left the room the *directeur* sat for a few moments in silence. Then he walked over to the door in the corner and threw it open. In a small anteroom the black-haired girl was sitting, a shorthand notebook on her knee. She did not get up when the *directeur* came in and it was noticeable that they spoke as equals.

"It would still appear to me," said the *directeur*—he seemed to be taking up an argument where it had been left off—"to be a perfectly normal inquiry. I have read of the trial, of course. And these are the inquiries which Mademoiselle Lamartine's friends might be expected to make. My only criticism is that they should have been made earlier."

"I agree," said the girl. "But there are facts which you do not know." She shut her notebook. "This morning, for instance, that young man, Mr. Rimbault, met his friend, Major McCann. They had a very animated conversation. The subject matter of this conversation is only conjectural, but Major McCann was last night involved in an altercation —an exceedingly violent altercation—with two of the minor members of the English end of an organization in which we happen to be interested."

The *directeur* rasped the tip of his finger against the shaven side of his chin but said nothing.

"It seems fairly certain," went on the girl, "that when Mr. Rimbault reaches France he will run into trouble. The people whom I have mentioned are remarkable for their good intelligence organization. Nor do they conduct their affairs with gloved hands."

"You think then," said the *directeur*, "that when he leaves England, you should—it is, of course, entirely your decision."

"I think so," said the girl. "Yes, I most certainly think so."

Chapter Nine

Nap wedged his deck chair into a convenient space between the end of a wooden seat and a steel bulkhead, buttoned up his overcoat collar and settled down to do some thinking.

A night breeze was scuffling the water as the steamer cleared Newhaven harbor, and, winking in and out against the blackness of the sea, Nap saw the whitecaps as the wind bit off the top of the little waves. There didn't seem to be enough power behind it to move the sea, for which

Nap was duly thankful for he was not the world's best sailor.

He had plenty to think about.

First of all he was trying to work out a plan of campaign which might have a chance of unearthing in five or six days something which had lain hidden for as many years.

The only line of approach which he could see was to visit the two farms—the Père Chaise farm where Vicky had worked and Wells had hidden and on which the Gestapo had descended with such disastrous results in September, 1943, and the farm of the brothers Marquis which, he had ascertained, lay about five miles to the north of it. Was it a coincidence, he wondered, that the brothers Marquis, who had stood surety for Sainte, should have a farm such a short distance away. Probably only a coincidence. The second possible line would be to question the brothers Marquis and Monsieur Gimelet of Angers, and try to discover something to the discredit of Monsieur Sainte. This would not, perhaps, help to unravel the mystery, but it might provide more useful ammunition for Macrea.

Lanegais, Avrillé-les-Ponceaux, Saumur, Angers. They all lay within quite a small circle. Somewhere within that circumference was a key to their riddle, if he had the wit to find it.

He looked out across the blackness of the sea and the gloss and shine of the waves suddenly put him in mind of a head of hair belonging to a girl he had seen that morning.

Upon which he raised his eyes, and saw her, leaning against the rail.

First, in silhouette, against the pale night sky, but he knew at once, from the tilt of the chin and the set of the neck. Then the companionway door, swinging open and shut as the ship rolled, loosed a shaft of light, only for a second, but it was enough.

Nap got up and moved over to the rail as quickly as he could for the deck chairs and the clutter of baggage. When he got there the girl had gone.

"She can't get away unless she swims for it," he said.

It wasn't a big boat and in ten minutes he had been through the few public rooms. Then he went out and made a slow circuit of the two decks. The blue night lamps were lit and he did the job thoroughly, staring at recumbent forms and disturbing an indignant couple in a dark corner behind the deck-chair house.

He went back again into the lighted interior and had a word with the purser.

Yes, said the purser, there were private cabins—only six of them and all were taken. If Nap would tell him the name of the person he was looking for, he would examine the list.

Nap said it didn't matter.

He would have to wait until they docked at Dieppe. If he stationed himself by the gangplank he could hardly miss her. Meanwhile, he thought he would kill time by having a drink. He made his way through the saloon into the bar.

The bar was empty except for a bearded Frenchman in one corner who was sacrificing to his Channel crossing in libations of cognac, and the French girl, who was perched on one of the high stools.

As he came in she looked up with a smile of plainest welcome and it occurred to Nap that he had no idea at all what he wanted to say to her.

He was saved the trouble. The girl indicated the stool beside her and Nap sat down.

She inspected him slowly but not rudely, and then said, "So young."

"You leave my youth alone," said Nap, who was apt to be sensitive about his appearance. "I would remind you that I am a married man."

"And a lieutenant-colonel," said the girl.

"War Substantive," said Nap. "We keep a Pekingese, too, and have a female child called Phylida."

"Charming," said the girl. "So *gosse*. One would scarcely credit that you were pubic."

"Oh, but I am, I assure you," said Nap. "Hairs on the chest and everything. Will you join me in a drink? What's that you've got there?"

"Pernod. Thank you."

Nap looked with increased respect at the girl. He knew the cloudy devil that lived in the harmless, lemonade-colored liquid. He considered that his safest course would be to stick to business.

"You appear to know a good deal more about me," he said, "than I do about you. I regret that I do not even know your name."

"That is easily remedied," said the girl. She opened her bag, took out a tiny snake-skin case, and picked out an ivory-colored card. Nap took it up and read: "Josephine Delboise." The card was edged in black.

"My husband," explained Madame Delboise.

"Killed in the war?"

"In the war, but not in action. He was tortured to death by the Germans." She said this in the extremely matter-of-fact voice which the French reserve for announcements of this sort.

"I am sorry," said Nap.

"Not so sorry as the Germans—of those concerned all were killed by us. Some sooner, some later."

"I see," said Nap. He felt himself being sidetracked again. He ordered himself another gin and, seeing that she had finished hers, another Pernod for Madame Delboise, and dragged the conversation ruthlessly back.

"What do you do in the Société de Lorraine?"

"We help Frenchmen," said Madame Delboise. "Englishmen, too, sometimes," she added, "when they are themselves engaged in helping Frenchmen."

"I see," said Nap. "Principally you find them jobs and homes."

"Principally, but by no means solely. We are prepared to offer them any help in our power."

"And is this all part of the service?"

Madame Delboise contrived to look puzzled.

"Escorting me across the Channel."

"Escorting—but he flatters himself. I go to Paris, on a visit to my child who is at school. I take this route because —since we are being frank—it costs the least. And you?"

"I'm on my way—" Nap changed his mind at the last moment, and cobbled the sentence awkwardly—"I'm on my way to Paris, too."

"Not to Angers?"

"Not immediately. I have first to visit the Sûreté, to make myself known to your police."

"Indeed! You are acquainted with officials of the Sûreté?"

"I know one of them. A man called Bren. I met him two or three years ago—he was helping the English police in some trouble we were having. A friend of mine called McCann was in that, too."

"What sort of trouble? Or may you not say?"

"I don't think there's anything very hush-hush about it," said Nap. "It was a sort of two-way smuggling business, gold sovereigns one way and jewelry the other."

"I see." Madame Delboise sounded thoughtful. "And Major McCann was involved in that, too. Do you know Monsieur Bren well?"

"Well enough to call him a friend. I think he will help me if he can."

"Friends are always helpful," said Madame Delboise.

"Would it be an irregularity if I were to offer to buy you a drink?"

"Thank you no. I think I'll have a turn round the deck."

"I trust that the motion—"

"Nothing of the sort," said Nap indignantly. "The motion is of the calmest. I thought I would like a little fresh air."

He took up on deck with him one more little problem. He was wondering why Madame Delboise should have known enough to refer to McCann as "Major McCann." Some of his friends still called him that, but Angus himself had not used the title since the war.

The night was darker. The moon had gone. Behind the ship the wake was barely visible on the black sea. Ahead, the lights of Dieppe were already in sight.

Part Two

Chapter Ten

The Clerk: Victoria Lamartine, is that your name?

The Prisoner: Yes.

The Clerk: You stand charged upon this indictment with the murder of Eric Paulton Thoseby, a Major in His Majesty's Army, upon the fourteenth of March of this year. Are you guilty or not guilty?

The Prisoner: Not guilty, sir.

The Clerk: The Prisoner at the Bar, Victoria Lamartine, stands charged upon this indictment with the murder of Eric Paulton Thoseby. To this indictment she has pleaded not guilty and puts herself upon her country, which country you are. It is your duty to hearken to the evidence and to determine whether she is guilty or not.

"Members of the Jury," said Mr. Claudian Summers in his clear, uninflected, Oxford common-room voice, "I shall direct your attention first to the events which took place on the night of Wednesday the fourteenth of March of this year in a small residential hotel called the Family Hotel, comprising Numbers 41 and 43 Pearlyman Street, near Euston Station.

"Now, I do not mean to imply that this was the beginning of the story. It was not. A good deal must have happened in the past to bring about the events of that night. The roots of this tree are longer than its branches. Nevertheless, I think it is as well to emphasize at the outset of the case that, although we may often have to turn to the past to explain the motives of the actors and the reasons for their actions, yet it is with their actions on this one particular night, at this one particular place, that you and I are actually concerned, because on that night, at that place, Major Eric Thoseby was killed.

"He was killed, as you will hear, with a knife, by an upward left-handed blow above the top of the stomach, a blow which passed through the liver and the heart wall and caused almost instantaneous death. It will be your duty to say who struck that blow.

"There has never been any suggestion of accident or suicide and I will not, therefore, waste your time with fanciful speculations about such possibilities. This was a deliberate blow, delivered with intention and, I may add, with considerable skill. Who struck it?"

Mr. Claudian Summers paused. He did not look at the jury. Nor did he look at the prisoner. He scarcely seemed to be looking at anyone in the court. His eye was turned inward, down the long intricate perspective of his argument, a needle-etched landscape in black and white, comprehended in its entirety in his own capacious mind.

"First of all," he said, "I will try to give you an idea of the sort of place where these things happened. The Family Hotel is in Pearlyman Street, near Euston. You must not suppose from its position that it is what is often referred to as a Station Hotel—you will know the sort of hotel I mean—where passengers stay for one night or perhaps two when they arrive by train in London or are waiting to catch a train on their way home from London. On the contrary, the Family Hotel, as run by Monsieur Sainte, who came here from France in 1946, appears to have been a quiet, well-conducted residential hotel. All of the people who were there on the night of the fourteenth—except Major Thoseby himself—had been there for some weeks, and two of them were living there on what you might almost call a 'residential' basis—a Colonel Trevor Alwright and a Mrs. Roper. Both of them were present on that night and both will be giving evidence before you, here, in these proceedings. Apart from the guests there was the permanent staff of the hotel. This was not large. Monsieur Sainte himself ran the business and acted as manager. The prisoner, Mademoiselle Lamartine, was employed as receptionist and hotel assistant—that is to say she worked in and about the residential and sleeping part of the hotel, but was not called upon to do any waiting at table—that was done by a waitress who, like the cook, came daily and slept out. Neither the cook nor the waitress was in the hotel at the time of the murder, and we shall not be troubling you with their testimony. Finally, there was the night-waiter, porter and general factotum, Ercolo Camino, whom you will hear, since his evidence, though indirect, is of great corroborative importance at a number of points.

"That was the stage on which this drama was enacted. This was the cast. I will now run briefly through the course of events, reminding you first that the facts which I shall set out are not simply *my* version or *my* opinion of what happened. They will be supported in every material particular by the evidence of witnesses who will be called before you at a later stage in the proceedings. If I make any statement which is *not* so supported I feel confident that eminent counsel for the defense will be the first to draw your attention to my oversight."

Mr. Summers inclined his head graciously toward Mr. Macrea, who remained, however, unmoved.

"The events of the evening, so far as they are material, start with the arrival at the hotel of Major Thoseby at about half-past eight. He had reserved a room by telephone. He had explained that he was busy at the War Office, attending a conference, and that he did not know when he would reach the hotel. He might be in time for dinner, or he might not be there until ten, or even eleven o'clock. He did not know. In fact, he arrived in time for a late dinner. After dinner, he had, as you will hear, a few words with Monsieur Sainte, in his office, and then retired to his room saying that he had a lot of writing work to get through, notes on the conference he had been attending, and so on.

"His reason for coming to the hotel is known. It is not, in fact, in dispute. He had come to see the prisoner."

Mr. Summers, for the first time, allowed his eyes to rest for a second on the figure in the dock.

"He had come at the prisoner's own earnest solicitation. The prisoner—and again this is not disputed—had for more than three years been trying to arrange an occasion to meet Major Thoseby. Her long search had been success-ful a few weeks prior to these happenings. She had got into touch with him through the good offices of a French or-ganization known as the Society of Lorraine. She had re-newed her pressure on Major Thoseby to come and see her. He had at last consented to do so. It was his suggestion that he should stay for that one night at the hotel. He ex-plained, in conversation with Monsieur Sainte, that his time was limited. He was in London on a visit of five or six days from Germany and much of his time was necessarily taken up with official business. He suggested, therefore, that he should book a room for that one night and could then, conveniently, have his discussion with Mademoiselle Lamartine either that evening, when he arrived, or, if he should arrive too late, then on the following morning. That was the arrangement, duly explained by Monsieur Sainte to the prisoner.

"This brings us to the first question on which there is a conflict of evidence.

"Why was the prisoner not there to meet Major Thoseby when he arrived? She was eagerly anxious for the meeting.

She had made long, persistent and, at last, successful attempts to bring it about. Yet, when Major Thoseby did arrive she was out.

"I draw your attention to the point because you may think it significant. On the other hand, you may just think that it is one of those occasions on which real life is not quite so tidy as fiction. Anyway, the prisoner says that Monsieur Sainte did not make it clear that Major Thoseby could be arriving before 'between ten and eleven.' Wednesday was, by custom, her weekly night out. She was in the habit of having a meal at one of the restaurants in the Soho area where cooking in the French style is a specialty, and then of going to one or other of the cinemas near Oxford Circus which show French or other foreign films. This was her program and, in her account of the matter, she says that since she was not expecting Major Thoseby until ten-thirty, she saw no reason to depart from it. In any event, it is not disputed that she did arrive back at the hotel at almost exactly half-past ten.

"However, I have allowed myself to go ahead of the strict chronology of this account. Major Thoseby, as I said, arrived at the hotel at half-past eight. He had his evening meal, spoke to Monsieur Sainte for a few minutes, and then retired upstairs to his room. His room was on the first floor, and was one of four rooms, two on either side of a short passage, which made up the annex at the back of the hotel. Perhaps I might be allowed to put in one exhibit at this unusually early stage—I will have the draftsman sworn in due course—I have had a large-scale plan prepared and it might assist us all if it was in front of us."

"If the defense has no objection," said Mr. Justice Arbuthnot.

"Anything," said Mr. Macrea with ferocious good humor,

"which can in any way assist in disentangling the prosecution's story must have my wholehearted support."

A large-scale plan, ready set up on a blackboard, was wheeled forward into the well of the court and Mr. Summers, after some maneuvering, arranged it so that the jury and the judge could both see it.

He then armed himself with a short pointer and took his stand beside the board, whilst Mr. Macrea said something to his learned junior, Mr. Lovibond, in which the word "mortarboard" was audible, at which Mr. Lovibond laughed unrestrainedly.

"When you consider the events of the next two hours," said Mr. Summers, "the time, that is to say, between about half-past nine and half-past eleven, some of you may perhaps be reminded of a certain type of detective novel. I have no doubt that a number of you read this very popular form of literature—as I do myself—and will be well acquainted with what used to be known as a 'sealed box' mystery. I mean that type of mystery where a body is found in a locked room with no windows, or in a strong room or in some other inaccessible place, and the question which has to be answered is not only who was the murderer, but how did the murderer get at his victim and how did he get away again. I do not suppose that such types of crime are as familiar in everyday life as they are between the covers of books, but if you look at this plan you will see that there is here an element of what you might call control. And that control is exercised—as might be expected in an hotel—by the reception desk. A person in this desk is in a position to note at once who goes up and who comes down those stairs. And those stairs are the only means of access to Major Thoseby's room.

"When I say the only means of access I do not mean, of course, the only physical means of access. It would be

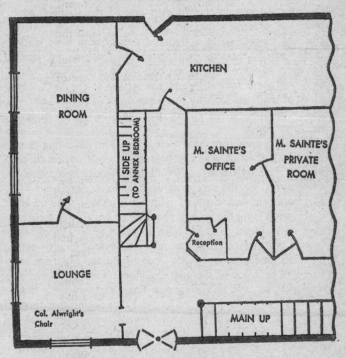

PART OF THE PLAN EXHIBITED IN COURT: GROUND FLOOR ONLY

possible to climb up by ladder from the street below or to descend by rope from the roof above. It is always within the bounds of possibility that there may have been a concealed trap door in the floor of one of the rooms." Mr. Summers presented the jury with a wintry smile. "All I can say on that score is that the police, who have made their usual painstaking examination of the building, have failed to discover any hidden trap doors, nor has any witness yet come forward—and the streets at the back and front of the hotel were by no means deserted at that hour—to say that they observed any persons climbing up ladders or down ropes.

"I think, therefore, that you are safe in assuming that this flight of stairs was the only method of approach to Major Thoseby's room. This flight of stairs was closely commanded by the reception desk, and the desk itself—" Mr. Summers demonstrated with his pointer—"was under observation from the lounge, the door of which was usually kept open. In this way we have a cross check. The closed box to which I referred just now really *was* closed—not by locks, and bars, and bolts—but by human observation. You will hear one of the guests, Colonel Trevor Alwright, state that he was in the lounge from eight o'clock that evening until about half-past ten, and that during that time, as he was able to observe, the waiter, Camino, was at the reception desk. The only times, in fact, when Camino left the desk were when Colonel Alwright asked him to fetch a drink for him. Mrs. Roper, another guest, was in the lounge until ten o'clock. She then went up to her room—duly observed by Camino in the reception desk. She herself left the lounge only once, to have a word with Monsieur Sainte in his office and will confirm Colonel Alwright's observations that Camino did not leave the reception desk during this period. This was the situation, then, between half-past nine and half-past ten. At half-past ten, the prisoner returned from her evening out. It was in accordance with normal arrangements that she would be back by half-past ten to take over Camino's duty at the reception desk. This was to release the waiter, who had other things to see to. He had to prepare the breakfast trays, bank the fires and do a number of other jobs in and around the kitchen—jobs which usually took him the best part of an hour—before he could go to bed himself.

"At about twenty to eleven, therefore, if I may again recapitulate briefly, the position was as follows. The lounge was by this time empty. Colonel Alwright had retired to his room—he slept in the main part of the building—Mrs. Roper was in her room, and the other guests had not yet returned. Camino was in the kitchen, the manager, Monsieur Sainte, was in his office, the prisoner was on duty at the reception desk. There is no dispute about all that. You will hear each of those persons testifying to it. There are, however, two radically different versions as to what happened next. It will be your duty to choose which one you will believe. I will come back to that in a moment.

"The next fact about which all parties are agreed is that at about a quarter to eleven, there was a very loud scream. The scream came from Major Thoseby's room. Mrs. Roper, who occupies, as you will see, the next room, ran into the passage. She saw that the door of Major Thoseby's room was ajar. Further screams came from inside the room. She says that they were so loud and so panic-stricken that she had no shadow of doubt that some awful tragedy had taken place. She pushed the door open and looked in. The prisoner was standing in the middle of the room looking down at the floor. On the floor was Major Thoseby's body."

"It really is quite astounding," said Macrea suddenly to

Mr. Rumbold, "how Summers does it—have you noticed? —without a single note. It impresses the jury, no doubt about it. I never could get the trick of it. I tried a scheme once of writing out the headings of what I wanted to say —a sort of mnemonic. Tried it out in a seduction case I was doing. I intended to start off by saying 'On the night of the sixth my client, the plaintiff, then a mere girl of nineteen, was induced to visit the defendant's room.' What I actually said was 'On the night of the nineteenth my client, a mere girl of six'—ruined the whole effect."

"The screams," said Mr. Summers, "had by now attracted others. Monsieur Sainte had heard them in his office and was running up the side stairs. Camino, coming from the kitchen, was a few steps behind him. At the same time three more of the guests, returning to the hotel, entered the foyer.

"As soon as Monsieur Sainte reached the room he realized that Major Thoseby was dead. He immediately sent for the police. You will hear their evidence, and the evidence of a number of experts, which I will not anticipate now, beyond mentioning one thing. The weapon with which Major Thoseby had been murdered was discovered at the preliminary search. It had been thrust down in the space between the back and the seat of the sofa. It was an ordinary black-handled kitchen knife. Under microscopic examination the handle gave the appearance of having been hastily wiped, but in spite of this attempted obliteration, prints were reconstructed. They were the thumb prints and fingerprints of the prisoner. The prints of her left hand. It is right to tell you that she does not deny them. She says that the knife was one which she often used in the course of her duties in the kitchen. It is right also to mention at this point her explanation of how she came to be in Major Thoseby's room. It is a very simple explanation.

She says that whilst she was in the office the bell indicator for Room 34 came up. She did not know that Room 34 was Major Thoseby's room. She did not even know that he had arrived. It was part of her duty to answer bedroom bells, and she therefore went up. When she got there she went in and found the body."

Mr. Summers paused again. He had presented the facts, together with the prisoner's explanation of them, quite flatly, neither agreeing nor disagreeing. This was his habit. It was one of the things which made him a very dangerous prosecuting counsel. Now, however, he was approaching more debatable ground and his style changed imperceptibly.

"I have reserved to the last," he said, "the question of motive. This is a matter which is apt to be misunderstood. It is the well-settled law of England—and his lordship will guide you on this, I am sure—that the onus is not on the prosecution to prove motive. Put in another way, we have not to undertake the task of explaining *why* a murder was done. Our duty is discharged if we show that a murder *was* done, and that, beyond a reasonable doubt, it was done by the hand of the prisoner. Why then is motive so often in discussion? The answer to that is, of course, that normal beings—sane human beings—do not commit murders. If, therefore, the prosecution can adduce an adequate motive it must have an immense additional compulsive force. I should explain, however, that by 'adequate' I do not mean what *you* might think adequate, or what *I* might think adequate. You may hold the act of murder in such horror—I trust you do—that *no* motive would seem adequate for it. That is what is meant when it is sometimes said that the motive must be measured against the actor. You have here a young woman trained, for many years, in violence. I shall deal with that training in evidence. Again, she is a woman who suffered treatment at the hands of the German police which might have turned the mind of the sanest. Finally, she is a woman—at the time of which I am going to speak, the middle years of the war, a young and inexperienced woman—who was seduced, and who gave birth to a child. In prison. In a Gestapo prison. A woman who was released by the happy turn of the war and who set out in search of the father of her child. Who in the course of that search saw her child die of malnutrition. Who came to England to further the search for this man. Who found him in Room 34 of this hotel."

"No," said the prisoner softly. "No, no, no, no, no."

"Well, that is all that I have to say at this juncture," said Mr. Summers. If he had heard the interruption he gave no sign of it. "We shall show you, in order, by the evidence of the witnesses that we shall bring before you that only one person had the opportunity. That the means were to the hand of one person. That the motive was the motive of one person. When that is established, whatever may be your feelings, and whatever may or may not happen to the prisoner afterward, your duty is quite clear. You must find the prisoner guilty of murder. Such a verdict may quite easily be distasteful to you. That does not absolve you from the obligation of giving it."

"My lord," said Mr. Macrea. He was on his feet so swiftly that both counsel were standing together. "May I make one matter plain. My learned friend has very freely offered my client his sympathy. I do not doubt for a moment that he is sincere. But on her behalf I must refuse the offer. It is not needed. Our case is not, odd though it may seem, that she committed this murder and is very upset about it. Our case is quite the opposite. It is that she did *not* commit this murder. I am sorry, but there it is." He sat down as swiftly as he had got up.

Mr. Summers resumed his seat more slowly.

All the crime reporters on the press bench looked up together and then looked down again and started scribbling away at twice the speed, like a bunch of second violins who have suddenly received a flick from the conductor's baton. It was clear to them, for the first time, that there was going to be a fight.

The judge said, "I think we have just time for your formal evidence, Mr. Summers. I shall then adjourn the court until two o'clock."

A thin young man with an ambitious mustache stepped into the box, told the court that his name was Edward Webb, that he was a qualified architect's draftsman, and that he had drawn the plan of the hotel which the jury had seen. Somewhat to his disappointment he was not cross-examined.

The court adjourned for lunch.

Chapter Eleven

Mr. Rumbold was one of the first to get clear of the building. He was not attracted by criminal work. He himself was a company lawyer and an expert on the leisurely intricacies of patent rights. So far as he was concerned a murder trial at the Old Bailey meant hurrying to and fro in taxicabs with suitcases full of papers, endless conferences and last-minute telephoning; it meant sandwiches for lunch and lateness for evening meals and working into the small hours of every morning. Unless he was very careful it was going to mean a thundering attack of dyspepsia.

He trotted into the A.B.C. opposite the court for a cup

of coffee, swallowed his drink before it had had time to cool, and hurried out to look for a taxi to take him back to the office. As usual he was unable to find one, and decided, as usual, that it would be just as quick by bus. As usual, as soon as he had got on to the bus four empty taxis went by.

At the office he found the boy standing by, and sent him out for sandwiches, shouted for his secretary and made his way to the sanctuary of his own room.

"Any messages," he said. "Anything from France yet?"

"Nothing from Mr. Anthony yet," said Miss Hardiman. She was a plump, cheerful girl, fortified in her not infrequent differences with Mr. Rumbold by the knowledge that she could never be dismissed since she was the only living person who understood his filing systems.

"What about McCann?"

"He rang from Winchester just before you came in. He didn't say much. He might be going on to Salisbury. There was one rather—"

"What on earth are all those?"

"Oh, that's the newspapers." Miss Hardiman tried not to sound impressed. "They've been ringing you up all the morning. I was saying there was—"

"Carrion," said Mr. Rumbold. He slit open half a dozen envelopes and consigned their contents to the "out" basket. "What were you saying?"

"I was telling you," said Miss Hardiman patiently, "Mrs. McCann has been on the phone."

"Mrs. McCann?"

"Major McCann's wife. She wants you to go and see her."

"Go down to Shepherd Market? Now?"

"She said it was important. She's got a witness. She wouldn't tell me any more over the telephone."

"Got a witness? For God's sake. A witness to what?"

"She wouldn't say."

"Have you got her number? All right, ring her up and I'll talk to her. What are those?"

"Egg sandwiches, sir. Real egg."

"Good boy. Oh—yes—yes—it's Mr. Rumbold. Mrs. McCann. You've got what? Oh, yes. Of course, certainly. No trouble at all. I'll come right away. See if you can get a taxi, Sam. Yes, I'll be there in about ten minutes. Don't let her go. Good-by."

He crammed one of the sandwiches into his mouth, gave the other three to Miss Hardiman, and made for the street at a trot.

At the Leopard he found Mrs. McCann waiting for him and was conducted through the lunch-hour crowd at the bar, up the stairs and into her sitting room.

"It's a girl," said Mrs. McCann without preamble. "Her name is Irene, and she sings—"

"Sings for her supper?"

"Yes, when she can get an engagement."

"Is she—?"

"No," said Mrs. McCann. "She isn't. I don't say that if times got hard she mightn't be, but at the moment, in my opinion, she's just an honest little trouper without much stuffing."

"Is she here?" said Mr. Rumbold, with a sideways look at his watch, "Because—"

"I've sent for her. I don't keep her on the premises. Whilst you're waiting why not have some lunch? You look about all in. I could have it sent in here."

"Well, really—"

"Steak pie. Some Dutch cheese and a small Guinness."

"All right," said Mr. Rumbold. "Only I shall have to hurry."

"What time does the curtain go up?"

"The court reassembles at two o'clock."

"You've plenty of time, then. It's not more than fifteen minutes by taxi."

"I can never seem to get a taxi," said Mr. Rumbold.

"Leave it to me," said Mrs. McCann. "I can *always* get a taxi."

Irene arrived with the cheese. Her coat and her hair were russet red and her skin had the yellowish oily look that stage faces often have by daylight. She was round and plump and the combination of colors made her look not unlike a little Dutch cheese herself. She was desperately genteel and she moved in a cloud of unidentifiable perfume. Despite all this, Mr. Rumbold found himself liking her. He agreed with Mrs. McCann. She was patently honest and could have had no conceivable motive for coming forward but the goodness of her own heart.

"I was in the Benbow Café," she said, "with a lot of the boys and girls. It's a little place we use when we're resting. Ellie Pinkerton who runs it was in Panto herself for years till one night when she was flying on to give the lovers her blessing—she was the good fairy—the wire broke and dropped her in the orchestra and that was the end of what you might call her active career—it's a little place in Gower Street—I said good night at just before half-past ten—"

"Wait a minute," said Mr. Rumbold, "what night was this?"

"I'm telling you—the fourteenth of March. The night that officer got done in at the hotel in Euston."

"How do you remember the date? Not that I disbelieve you but it's as well to be quite clear about it."

"I was telling you. It was my birthday. Between you and me, I'd hate to get up in public and say which number, but definitely my birthday. We'd been having a sort of do at Ellie's, to celebrate."

"Good enough," said Mr. Rumbold. "Please go on."

"Well, I live in Dunbar Street—that's this side of Mornington Crescent, so I thought I'd walk home. It was a nice night—warm for spring, and I'd been having one or two, just to celebrate—you know."

"I know," said Mr. Rumbold.

"I was about halfway home—just at the turning into Pearlyman Street—I thought I'd sit down for a minute and take my weight off my feet. You know the hotel—there's a little street runs behind it—Pearlyman Mews or Pearlyman Court or something like that—it's nice and quiet and quite dark."

"Pearlyman Passage."

"That's it. Well, I parked on a low wall and got my back against a buttress and started to think about life."

"How long would this have been after you'd left the café?"

"If you said a quarter of an hour you wouldn't be far off it. Well, I was sitting there, quite quietly, minding my own business, when I heard a window go up and someone called out, softly, but plain enough to hear."

She paused and Mr. Rumbold, aware of a slight dryness in the throat, asked, "Could you make out what was said?"

"Oh, yes," said the girl. "It was clear enough. It was a name—'Benny'—just like that, in a whisper, 'Benny.' I couldn't say I'd recognize the voice, not even to say whether it was a man or a woman, because when a person's whispering it's not easy to tell. But I heard the name of the person they were calling all right. There was no mistaking that—Benny."

Chapter Twelve

"Your name is Robert Chaunter Ammon, you are a major in the Royal Engineers."

"That is correct."

"Your work during the war brought you in touch with Major Thoseby."

"Well, as a matter of fact, I knew him before the war. I also worked with him during almost the whole of the war —1940 to 1944 to be precise."

"That was in his French Resistance work."

"Yes, I was in L.F.O.5."

"That was the official title of the Office of Liaison with the French forces."

"That is so. We used to run all the co-operation with the Resistance in France, supply arms and materials, drop agents in—and get them out again—sometimes."

"Major Thoseby was one of your agents."

"Yes. He was one of the first who went in. One of the best, too. He was in charge of the Basse Loire district from the beginning of 1941 to March, 1942. Early in 1942 he was picked up."

"Picked up?"

"By the Germans, yes. Luckily his cover story was so solid by that time that he got away with it. He produced two cousins, an aunt and his prewar employer to vouch for him. All quite genuine, by the way. It wasn't a nice thing to happen, though. We got him out soon after that for a rest and a bit of a technical refresher course in explosives. He went back in at the end of 1942 and was there for the whole of 1943 and down to D-Day in 1944."

"He was in France for the whole of that time?"

"Well, he went over to Switzerland once or twice. He never came back to England."

"During that eighteen months—I refer to Major Thoseby's second spell in Occupied France—French Resistance work was on the increase?"

"Yes. Toward the end, in the months before D-Day very much so."

"How was it organized in Major Thoseby's area?"

"Well, the actual command was French all the way up, from the leader of the individual Maquis up to the area commandants and then up to General Koenig himself. Our English agents were technically only advisers. They often attained a position of considerable influence. Particularly if they were lucky enough to last for some time."

"I take it that a man in Major Thoseby's position would move round as freely as conditions permitted, amongst the various French Maquisards. He would be personally known to most of them?"

"Yes."

"Did you in England have any record of the French members of the organization?"

"Oh, yes. That was one of the chief jobs of the liaison branch I was in. We kept records of everyone who was taking an active part."

"Was the prisoner's name in your records?"

"Yes, we knew about Miss Lamartine."

"Miss Lamartine was a member of the French Resistance and worked in Major Thoseby's district?"

"Yes."

"From your knowledge of the work would you have said that they would have met frequently?"

"Oh, yes. Major Thoseby often spoke about—"

"I am afraid," said Mr. Summers, timing his interruption to a nicety, "that you must not answer the question in that way. You must speak only of your own personal knowledge, not of what was said to you. However, the next witness will be dealing with the point, so I will not press it. Will you now pass on to the events of September twenty-sixth, 1943. I take it that you were kept informed of what happened?"

"Yes. An official report from Major Thoseby reached me within three or four days."

[*Some argument is omitted as to whether the report was admissible. The judge ruled that it was admissible.*]

"Will you give us the gist of it?"

"Yes. It told us that Père Chaise's farm near Langeais had been raided on the evening of September twenty-sixth. That Père Chaise and two other men had been taken and had been shot. That it was feared that Lieutenant Wells had been taken. That Mademoiselle Lamartine, arriving later at the farm, had also been picked up and was being held. That all necessary countermeasures were being put in hand, known localities changed, codes altered, and so on."

"When did you next hear from the prisoner?"

"Some months after D-Day. It would have been the end of March or the beginning of April, 1945."

"Were you surprised to hear from her?"

"Yes—very."

"Why was that?"

"I was always surprised to hear again from anyone who had been in the hands of the Gestapo."

"I see," said Mr. Summers. It was not the answer he had expected but he was too old a hand to look put out. "As a result of the message you received did you try to get in touch with Major Thoseby?"

"Yes. I did what I could. It wasn't easy because he was already in Germany."

"However, you did your best to put the prisoner in touch with Major Thoseby?"

"Yes."

"How many times did you hear from the prisoner?"

"I didn't keep a record. Half a dozen times at least between March, 1945 and 1946."

"Did this surprise you? I mean the persistence with which the prisoner communicated with you?"

"Well—certainly I—it's a very difficult question to answer yes or no."

"Nor," said the judge suddenly, "is there any reason you should do so. The idea that you must answer a question by yes or no is a relic of a system of advocacy now happily outdated. There are a number of questions which it is clearly impossible to answer by yes or no. You are quite entitled to give your answer, provided it is an honest answer, in any way you like."

"Thank you," said Major Ammon, looking a trifle overcome by this judicial broadside. "Well, first, I wasn't at all surprised that Miss Lamartine got hold of me. Anybody who knew anything about the system knew that I was Major Thoseby's official 'contact' in England. If you mean was I surprised that she wanted to get hold of Major Thoseby, the answer is that the first time or two it seemed quite natural. He had been her superior officer, her boss—in fact if not in name—and he would be the person to whom she would naturally turn for help—particularly as in 1945 the British Army were in a position to do a great deal to help their friends in France—they controlled a lot of transport and a lot of supplies. I don't imply anything improper. It was right that they should help their friends. Later it did seem a little odd. Major Thoseby was in Germany during the whole of 1946. He was on the War Crimes Commission. I gave Miss Lamartine several addresses at which she could write to him. It began to strike me that if he didn't answer her letters—or didn't do what Miss Lamartine wanted him to do—then he must have his own reasons."

"You use the words 'do what Miss Lamartine wanted him to do.' Had you any idea what this was?"

"No idea at all."

"You were acting simply as an intermediary?"

"That is correct."

"Very well, Major Ammon. One last thing. From your own knowledge of the Resistance organization can you say whether agents in your employment were always trained in certain personal methods of defense and attack?"

"Yes. Whenever possible they were so trained."

"I will be more specific. The nature of the blow which killed Major Thoseby has been described to you." Mr. Summer repeated the description which he had given in his opening address. "Would it be your opinion that such a blow had been given by a person trained in Resistance work?"

"There's no certainty about it. It might very well have been."

"Why do you say that?"

"Resistance workers were trained to use any weapon that came to hand—or even to manufacture them out of ordinary household implements—a sharpened knitting needle run through a thick cigarette holder, or a bicycle spoke held in a rubber bicycle pedal or household ammonia in a scent squirt—that sort of thing. It wasn't safe to carry weapons recognizable as weapons. Then again the blow, being left-handed and upward, is certainly significant. Amateurs were always taught to use a knife in this way."

"Perhaps you could explain very shortly why."

"Yes. The blow delivered in this way, from in front, goes in under the ribs, and the swing of the arm naturally takes it up into the region of the heart. If you hold a knife point downward—" Major Ammon demonstrated—"and strike at a person in front of you the blade usually turns on the ribs."

"Your agents were all instructed in these regrettable but necessary arts in case they had to kill Germans?"

"Yes," said Major Ammon. "Or themselves."

He said this casually, but many people in court suddenly found themselves looking back at an unknown and rather frightening landscape. A place where it might be necessary —where it might be most necessary and desirable—to be able to kill yourself quickly.

Mr. Summers resumed his seat well aware that this last answer might have done more for him than the whole of the rest of the examination.

"Major Ammon," said Macrea. "You knew the deceased very well?"

"Yes. I think I did."

"If I have your answer correctly, this was not only a wartime acquaintance. It started before the war?"

"As a matter of fact, I was at school with him."

"And kept up with him afterward?"

"In the way that two busy men do."

"Quite so. And afterward you worked very closely together over the French Resistance work. You spoke of yourself as his 'official contact'?"

"That is correct."

"Might I suggest that you knew him about as well as one man ever does know another?"

"Yes. I suppose that is so."

"Major Ammon, was Major Thoseby the type of man likely to indulge in an illicit union with a woman, to have —and later to refuse to acknowledge—an illegitimate child?"

"I—"

"Really, your lordship," said Mr. Summers. "I must object to the witness being asked to express what is purely a matter of opinion."

"Why not?" said Macrea. "It's a thing all men *do* have opinions about—where their men friends are concerned."

"I think," said the Judge, "in view of the motive which you have yourself suggested, Mr. Summers, it is a question which the witness can properly be asked. I think, however, he would equally be within his rights if he refused to answer it."

"As your lordship pleases," said Mr. Summers.

"Well, Major Ammon?"

"I don't mind answering the question," said Major Ammon. "The answer is, No. Major Thoseby was not, to my mind, that sort of man."

"You agree that men usually do know about other men, whether or not they are the type who is likely to—to have an affair of the sort suggested."

"In nine cases out of ten, yes."

"And Major Thoseby was not that type?"

"No."

"Now in connection with the numerous attempts—half a dozen I think you said—that the prisoner made to get in touch with Major Thoseby through you. You do not know if she was successful or not? You gave her his latest address and that was all?"

"That is so."

"Suppose then—I just put it to you—that the prisoner was not actually interested in contacting Major Thoseby himself, but was trying to contact someone else through him. And suppose that on each occasion Major Thoseby made suggestions to the prisoner as to how she could best do this—a line she might follow, a contact who might be useful to her—you can see what I mean?"

"Yes."

"Then when each suggested line petered out, she would naturally write to you again to put her in touch with Major Thoseby again."

"It is possible."

"There was nothing in her communications with you which was inconsistent with such an explanation?"

"I agree."

Mr. Summers did not re-examine.

Chapter Thirteen

"Your name is Marcel Lode? You have the rank of Commissaire de Ville?"

"Yes."

"During the war you were patron of the Maquis in the district of Angers? You were acquainted with the deceased and worked with him?"

"Yes."

"Were you acquainted also with the prisoner?"

"Yes, but to a lesser degree. She was not one of the workers with whom I had much contact. She came to me once or twice with messages."

"But you knew the deceased well."

"Major Thoseby? Yes. Very well indeed. I worked at hand-to-hand with him for many months in all the affairs of the Maquis."

"He was attached to your section?"

"To mine and to many others. He was chief adviser to all of us in the districts of Maine-et-Loire, of Indre-et-Loire and of Loir-et-Cher. The whole of the Basse Loire area."

"The farm which we have heard of—Père Chaise's farm —was in this area?"

"Certainly. It was near Langeais, in the Bois de Langeais —a few kilometres north of the river."

"That would not be in your own particular district?"

"No. It was in that of Tours. You must not imagine, though, that we were strictly—what is the word I want? —sectionalized. I would often visit Langeais, and Chinon —for the exchange of ideas—also, sometimes, for a change of air when that became necessary."

"So you can tell us, from first-hand knowledge, of the conditions at Langeais, and at this farm."

"Yes, I can. I think perhaps we were not very clever about Père Chaise's farm. I say so in retrospect. There were in every district certain households that were known to be safe. Certain householders in whom we had reliance. I think that in Père Chaise we had too much reliance. I do not mean that he betrayed us consciously. He would certainly never have done that. But he was a jovial, talkative man. A boaster. He had what we call the 'Gascon' temperament. Very soon I think the Germans knew that he harbored Resistance workers in his house in the woods."

"But they did nothing about it?"

"For a time, no. To catch one or two less important members of the Resistance—that was not their object. Soon, however, their patience was rewarded. A bigger prize offered. A British agent, Lieutenant Wells, arrived in the district. Even then they waited. It was no doubt in their minds that Major Thoseby or one of the other leaders might contact Lieutenant Wells at this farm."

"But they did not do so."

"Fortunately—fortunately for him, I mean—Major Thoseby was at that time in Switzerland. By the time he got back the Germans had tired of waiting and had raided the farm."

"When was that?"

"On September twenty-sixth, 1943."

"Were you in Langeais at the time?"

"No. When the raid took place I was at Amboise, that is the other side of Tours. I came quickly to Langeais to see if I could be of assistance. After such a raid there was always a lot of clearing up to do—of countermeasures to be taken."

"I quite understand. Was it your impression that Lieutenant Wells had been taken by the Gestapo, or that he had been killed in the raid?"

"It would have been very unlike the Gestapo to have killed him at once. They would require him for questioning."

"Was there any first-hand evidence that Lieutenant Wells was taken?"

"None. Such raids were almost always carried out at dusk or just before dawn. They were very quickly and efficiently conducted. Any prisoners were taken away separately, in closed cars. It was part of the German policy that no one should know who had been taken."

"It was known, though, that the prisoner, Miss Lamartine, was taken on this occasion?"

"Yes. The Germans had left a guard hidden in and around the farm. The people who were sent to warn Mademoiselle Lamartine—she was away on an errand—missed her and she walked into the trap. Our people, however, actually saw her taken, though they were just too late to stop her."

"How soon did Major Thoseby learn of this?"

"Two days afterward. In fact, I spoke to him of it myself."

"What were his reactions?"

For, the first time in his evidence Commissaire Lode paused before answering. "Major Thoseby was not a man who showed his emotions easily. Indeed, from a man in his position you would not expect it."

"You did not notice any reaction?"

"I did not say that. I said that he did not show his feelings easily. I, who knew him well, realized that he was shaken."

"Thank you," said Mr. Summers. "May we turn now to the time following the Liberation and the expulsion of the Germans from France. Did you see the prisoner again?"

"Not at once. The Germans, when they left, had taken a number of their special prisoners with them. I believe that the prisoner was taken."

"Yes. Well, no doubt she will tell us about that herself. I am afraid you must confine yourself to your own observation. When did you see the prisoner again?"

"In November or December of that year. I remembered her, of course. I was, I think, a little surprised to see her alive. I did what I could to help her, but I had at that time no official position. It was a very hard winter."

"Had she her child with her at this time?"

"Yes."

"You saw him?"

"I did. A tiny, thin child, of about six months. Very serious—but complaining little. I should say a child of natural fortitude."

"Why do you say that?"

"Monsieur, if you had been in France that winter you would not ask. The Germans did more damage in their departure than they had done in four years of occupation. There was no electricity for lighting or heating, little fuel, a great scarcity of food."

"I understand. Can you describe the child?"

"Most children of six months look alike, I think. He had what we call '*tête d'anglais*.'"

"You mean he had an English look."

"Anglo-Saxon, yes. Light hair and very light blue eyes. At that age most French children would have dark eyes and dark hair."

"I see. You mentioned just now that you did what you could to help the prisoner. What particular help did she ask for?"

"She wanted somewhere to live, some money. We were able to supply her with the necessities of life. All knew what she had suffered, and many were generous."

"Did she ask you for anything else?"

"Yes. She asked me to see if I could put her in touch with Major Thoseby."

"Were you surprised at this request?"

"No, I don't think I was."

"Why did you imagine she had made it?"

"I imagined, at that time, that she had thought that he would be in a position to help her."

Monsieur Lode gave this answer clearly and quietly and for a moment everyone in the court considered it, turning the words over to see what they could make of them. Macrea had his head cocked like a man who has sipped a fine brandy and is about to pronounce judgment on it. The prisoner was leaning forward with strained attention for counsel's next question.

"Thank you," said Mr. Summers, "that is all."

"Monsieur Lode," said Macrea, "I want to ask you a question which I put as one of my first questions to another witness. You knew Major Thoseby well. In your opinion was he the type of man to indulge in an illicit union with a young unmarried woman?"

"I do not think I can answer that question."

"Why not?"

"I do not think that any man could answer that question about another man."

"The last witness agreed that it was a matter about which one's friends could form an opinion."

"In England, perhaps so. In France I can assure you a man would never discuss such things with another man. With his mother, perhaps. Not with anyone else."

"With his mother?"

"Certainly. A Frenchman conceals nothing from his mother."

"I will put the question in another way. Was there anything in Major Thoseby's conduct to suggest to you that he was a man who would act in such a way?"

"That I can answer. No."

"Or that he, in fact, acted in such a way toward the prisoner?"

"No."

"Did he see the prisoner much?"

"Yes, from time to time—in the course of his duty."

"Would his duty ever be likely to lead him to spend the night with her?"

"On one occasion, at least. Yes."

"I see." Macrea had for the moment the look of a pedestrian who steps into a deep and unsuspected hole. "When was this?"

"It would have been in May of 1943. It was when the Gestapo were very active in the Langeais area and almost everyone concerned with Resistance work had to take to the woods. Major Thoseby was on his way through and had to spend the night in a barn—it was on the outskirts of the Forêt de Rochecotte. The prisoner also was sleeping in the barn."

"And was anyone else present?"

"Oh, yes—about fifteen other persons were sleeping in the barn as well."

"Yes—I see—not what one might call an intimate occasion."

"No."

"Monsieur Lode, after the war, in 1946, did you work for a time at Arolsen in North Hesse?"

"Yes."

"You were one of the French team on the UNRRA Tracing Staff."

"That is correct."

"You dealt, I believe, particularly with lists of persons who had been in concentration camps and in Gestapo prisons?"

"Among other matters, yes."

"Do you remember personally dealing with an inquiry for a Lieutenant Julian Wells?"

"Yes, I do. I recollected him, of course, since I had been so nearly connected with his original capture by the Germans."

"Would it surprise you to know that this inquiry was put on foot by the prisoner herself?"

"Yes. I certainly did not know that."

"Does it surprise you?"

"Yes. I think it does."

"Why?"

"I have explained why, in my opinion, Mademoiselle Lamartine tried to get in touch with Major Thoseby. He had been the senior British officer in the district and it was natural she should turn to him for help. The same reasons hardly applied in the case of Lieutenant Wells."

"I am obliged," said Macrea. "You would agree then that if the prisoner afterward sought news of Lieutenant Wells her reasons were probably personal ones?"

"My lord—" began Mr. Summers.

"I will put it to you in another way. It is within your knowledge that Lieutenant Wells spent three weeks at the Père Chaise farmhouse?"

"Yes."

"He was hidden there from the time of his arrival until the Gestapo raid. He would probably not have been able to go outside the farm?"

"That is so."

"And the prisoner was living at the farm all that time?"

"Yes."

"In fact, they were living together for three weeks?"

"I must protest—" said Mr. Summers.

"I anticipate my learned friend's protest," said Macrea smoothly, "by hastening to add that I was using the words in their primary sense only."

Chapter Fourteen

As Nap stepped off the boat, under the single unshaded electric light, on to the battered quay at Dieppe one thought was uppermost in his mind. That whatever steps he might have to take would be better taken out of the company of Josephine Delboise. Nor did he come to this conclusion from any motives of distaste for Madame Delboise as a person. Nevertheless, he felt it would be in all things safer, better and wiser did they part company.

Being a direct young man he therefore sought her out in the Customs shed, took possession of her two cases, led the way out on to the platform and found two seats in a first-class carriage in the Paris train which was waiting alongside the quay.

He placed his hat on the seat opposite, asked Madame Delboise to preserve the seat for him should any rival claimant appear—an unnecessary precaution really since the train was three-quarters empty—and went back to the Customs shed. A few minutes later he reappeared with a large and expensive-looking suitcase, which he placed on the rack. It was labeled for Paris and he imagined that the real owner would be able to identify it without difficulty at the other end. He then announced that there was just time to buy some newspapers before the train started, and went forth once more into the corridor. Madame Delboise appeared to be dozing, but gave him a sleepy smile of approval as he went.

Two minutes later Nap was stepping quietly off the darkened side of the train. He retrieved his own humble grip from behind a pile of lobster baskets and set out at a round pace along the quay.

There appeared to be no barrier to mark the end of the Gare Maritime and in a few minutes he was rounding the landward end of the jetty. The railway sheds were deserted and the arched colonnade where by day the fish sellers and the greengrocers hold their market, was black and silent.

As his footsteps rang out on the cobbles the stone arches threw back the echo. It was almost as if someone was walking behind him, in the shadows. He stopped abruptly. The echo stopped also. But did it stop quite quickly enough?

Imagination, thought Nap. Anyway, there was no time to lose for his train for Rouen left the Gare de Ville, at the other side of the town, in less than ten minutes.

He hurried on.

Dawn was coming up cold and gray as Nap's train crossed the watershed of the Alpes Normandes and plodded down toward the valley of the Seine. It was not a fast train. By the time it got to Rouen it was past six. Nap stood in the *place* outside the station and looked round him with unashamed nostalgia.

Despite the early hour most of the cafés were open and an old white-coated waiter was moving round outside one of them uptilting chairs and polishing the glass table-tops. A many-caped gendarme paced by on the sidewalk, lost in official thought. There were bicycles everywhere. Men bicycling to work; housewives bicycling to be early at market; women bicycling in from the country; elderly people bicycling with serious attention; children bicycling for fun.

Nap felt furiously hungry. He also felt grubby. The solution seemed to be a quiet hotel where he could wash and have breakfast, and possibly make up on some of the sleep he had lost the night before.

He looked round for a guide. The only stationary figure in the whole *place* was a young man who had dismounted from his bicycle and was now standing in the roadway looking up through steel-rimmed glasses at the train indicator board. He was wearing khaki slacks and sandals and his torso appeared to be covered by a curious tight-fitting brown garment. As Nap came nearer he saw his mistake. It was not a garment at all. He was naked to the waist.

"Hardy type," thought Nap. He was about to phrase his request when the young man rose suddenly on to his toes, placed his hands on his hips and started to rotate his body rapidly and flexibly, finishing with a backward bend which brought the top of his close-shaven head almost on to the pavement behind him. Then he rose slowly into an upright position, at the same time drawing in his breath until his s omach was perfectly concave. Finally he let his breath out with a rush and smiled. His eyes glinted behind his glasses.

"I was wondering," said Nap, "if you could possibly—"

"On the contrary," said the young man, "you were wondering what I was doing."

"I cannot deny it," said Nap.

"It is the new *gymnastique médicale*," said the young man. "It combats anemia and obesity. It is composed of two elements, the *gymnastique respiratoire*, which combats asthma and assists natural breathing and the *gymnastique orthopédique* which combats bad attitudes. In addition I practice a private system of deviations of the vertebral column, from which I have great hopes. How can I assist you?"

"I was wondering," said Nap, "if you knew of a quiet hotel which would be likely to have a room vacant."

"Certainly," said the young man. "Follow me."

Wheeling his bicycle with one hand he led the way at a pace which had Nap gasping. They forked left at the main crossroads, turned left again, and crossed the old market square whose ugly stone tower commemorates one of the ugliest deeds in Anglo-French history.

When the young man stopped Nap waited for the inevitable lecture on Joan of Arc, but it appeared that the young man's mind was on more recent history.

"Gestapo headquarters," he said briefly.

Nap could see nothing in the direction in which the young man was pointing except three large holes in the ground. Looking closer he saw, from the remnants of brickwork, that he was looking down into what had once been the basement of a fair-sized house.

"Not very habitable now," said the young man, showing his side teeth for a moment in a grin.

"Who—"

"The British Air Force, in March, 1944. An attack at rooftop level."

Nothing more was said, and in a minute they were outside the Hotel Apollinaire. Before Nap could thank him the young man had vaulted on to his bicycle and disappeared.

It was late afternoon when Nap came lazily up again to the uplands of consciousness. He lay staring at the ceiling. He had been dreaming that he was back in Occupied France. It was a dream he had once had quite often, but very rarely of late. He wondered what had brought it back: the talk with Madame Delboise on the boat, the young man he had met in the street, or the acorn coffee which he had had for his breakfast, many hours before, and the taste of which still lingered on his palate.

He looked down at his watch. The time was five past four. He had slept for eight hours, and he was beginning to feel abominably hungry. Lunch would now be over, and he was unlikely to be able to get dinner before seven. He lay for a few minutes thinking about that dinner. He would have plenty of time for it. The night train for Le Mans which he was planning to catch did not leave before ten. Nap had just decided that *tournedos Henri Quatre* would follow nicely on *rilettes de maison* when his attention was attracted by a slight scraping sound.

Sitting up abruptly he realized that he was not alone. From the arm chair, level with the head of his bed, a pair of muddy gray eyes looked at him. Their owner, as Nap saw when he had got over his first surprise, was an undistinguished little man with a crop of long well-greased black hair framing a young unhealthily white face. Nap thought he had rarely seen a man he disliked more at sight. One of his least pleasing characteristics was a sort of downy unshavenness, the result apparently not of Bohemian leanings but of the desire to avoid beheading a formidable crop of pimples in the jawbone area.

"What the devil," said Nap, "are you doing in my

room?" In his surprise he spoke in English, and seeing that this appeared to have gone over his visitor's head he repeated it in colloquial French with embellishments.

"I thought it would be a convenient place for a talk," said the man.

"If you don't get out at once—" Nap looked round for the bell— "I shall shout for the manager and have you put out."

"You can shout for a long time in this hotel," said the stranger. "People will only imagine that you are happy. There is always plenty of noise in this hotel."

Here Nap was forced to agree. He had eaten his breakfast to the accompaniment of one of the loudest wireless sets he had ever encountered. Even now he could hear it booming faintly in the distance.

"All right," said Nap, "then supposing I throw you out myself?"

"You could, of course, try that." The stranger made no appreciable move but his hand seemed to be resting under his coat.

There was a moment's silence. An air of unreality pervaded the whole scene. Nap fought with the idea that it was a continuation of his dream.

"What I have to say will not take long," said the man. Nap said nothing.

"You should return to England."

"Why the hell should I?" said Nap. "I haven't spent my fifty pounds yet."

"It is stupid to suggest that you are here as a tourist. We know why you are here. We know what you have come here to do."

"I only wish I did," said Nap. He was still trying to work out whether it would be worth starting a fight. The last thing he wanted was to make trouble or draw attention to himself. Also he disliked the prospect of fighting a fully dressed man when he himself was in pajamas and had bare feet. One would present too many vulnerable points.

"That is all," said the man. "I do not threaten. I just state the truth. What you are embarked on is not your business. It does not concern you. You should go back to England, now."

"I—" said Nap.

The man got to his feet, with no apparent haste. One moment he was standing there, looking down at Nap. The next moment he was gone. The door closed softly. Footsteps pattered away down the passage.

Nap put aside any thought of following him, and started slowly to get dressed.

Downstairs, in the lobby of the hotel, the white-faced man paused for a moment before he stepped out into the street. He looked quickly to left and to right, almost an automatic gesture.

He did not look behind him. If he had done so he might have seen a young man glance up from one of the tables in the coffee room and stare thoughtfully after him. A young man in steel-rimmed glasses.

Upstairs in his room Nap finished his dressing and started to write a letter. He sat on the bed, balancing the pad on his knee. It was quite a long letter, and it was in French.

When he had finished he read it over, placed it in an envelope and addressed it to Monsieur Bren, at the Sûreté, Paris.

Chapter Fifteen

"Your name is Honorifique Sainte?"

"Yes."

Monsieur Sainte, as he stood in the witness box, was a thick-set white-faced man. It would have been difficult to have guessed his age more closely than that he was over forty and under sixty. The fairest description of him could have been that he looked a complete hotelier—a calling which only the French, perhaps, recognize as one of the learned professions. He spoke in good English; as, indeed, he also spoke excellent Italian and fair Spanish.

"You were formerly the proprietor of an hotel at Saumur on the Loire?"

"That is so."

"Perhaps you would tell the court shortly how you came to England."

"Certainly. My hotel—it was on the river front at Saumur, near to the main road bridge, unfortunately—was completely destroyed by allied bombing in June of 1944. It did not seem at that time likely that I should be able to start again—or not in that part of France which I knew. Licenses to rebuild were almost impossible to obtain. Since I had to move, I decided to make a complete change. After some negotiation I got the necessary permission to come to England in 1946."

"I hope you have not regretted it," said Mr. Justice Arbuthnot courteously.

"On the contrary."

"I am glad to hear it."

"Now, Monsieur Sainte, can you tell us how you met the prisoner?"

"Certainly. Whilst in England I maintained a close contact with an organization called the Bureau de Lorraine, which exists to help Frenchmen in England. It was from them that I heard that Mademoiselle Lamartine was in England and was in need of work."

"You knew her name?"

"Yes. All in the Basse Loire district had heard of Mademoiselle Lamartine's misfortune."

"You had not met her before?"

"No. I had met her previous employer, Père Chaise, at Langeais. I had been once or twice to his farm during the Occupation but on each occasion, Mademoiselle Lamartine was absent, on errands, I think, for the Maquis."

"Were you yourself visiting Père Chaise's farm on Resistance work?"

The witness paused for a moment before answering. Then he said, "It would be easy and creditable at this distance to say Yes but in fact it would not be true. I went to see Père Chaise on business. He was one of the persons who supplied me with food for my hotel. During the Occupation it was patriotic, you understand, to work on the black market."

"You were not yourself a member of the Resistance."

"That is a very difficult question to answer. Many, I have no doubt, who did as much or as little as I did would now claim to have been the most active members of the Resistance. I gave what help I could and I did anything I was asked to. I did not go out of my way, however, to incur danger. I certainly took no active part in sabotage or resistance."

"I quite understand," said Mr. Summers. The frankness of the answer seemed to please him a good deal more than it did Macrea, who was observed to be savaging several pages of his brief.

"Will you now direct your attention to the period between the time when the prisoner came to work in your hotel and the events of March fourteenth of this year. During that time—a space of between two and three years—did the prisoner make any effort to get in touch with Major Thoseby?"

"Yes, she did."

"How often?"

"I cannot say. The occasions that naturally came to my attention were when she asked for a time off in order to visit the British War Office, as she did on several occasions. The Foreign Office, once, I think, and latterly the Société de Lorraine."

"It would be correct then to say that during that period she made consistent and repeated efforts to see the deceased?"

"I cannot say that she wished to see him. I know only that she was anxious to discover his whereabouts."

"Quite, quite. And it is very right to be accurate about it," said Mr. Summers sounding nevertheless rather annoyed. "Now let us deal with the events of March fourteenth. Perhaps you had better tell us in your own words what happened."

"Certainly. I was in my office at about half-past six when Major Thoseby telephoned."

"How did the witness know it was Major Thoseby?" said Macrea.

"Well—I—"

"My learned friend means that you had at that time no means of knowing who was speaking," said Mr. Summers smoothly. "No doubt it will satisfy him if you say 'a person announcing himself as Major Thoseby' telephoned to you."

"Of course I knew it was Major Thoseby," said Monsieur Sainte. "He himself said so. However, as you wish."

"Did you gather when he would be arriving?"

"I understood that he might be there as early as half-past eight or as late as half-past ten, or even eleven. I said that the hotel remained open until eleven. He said he would certainly be there by that time."

"What did you do next?"

"I sent for the prisoner and told her."

"Yes. What were her reactions?"

"She was excited—naturally. She already knew he was coming. We had had a message a day or two before. I asked if she would be staying in to meet him when he arrived. I knew it was the night on which she usually went out."

"And then—?"

"She said No. She would see him when she got back."

"Were you surprised?"

"I think I was—a little."

"And then?"

"The next thing was the arrival of Major Thoseby. I was in my office when he arrived. Camino showed him straight in."

"You had a talk? By the way, what time was this?"

"Just before half-past eight. Yes—we had about ten minutes' talk."

"What were your impressions of Major Thoseby?"

"I was very glad to see him—we had a very friendly talk."

"I didn't quite mean that. I meant, did he strike you as nervous or excited about his visit—or just casual?"

"Major Thoseby was a very reserved man."

"So we have been told. I will put this to you then. When you told him that the prisoner was not in to meet him did he seem surprised?"

"Yes. I thought he was surprised. Also, I thought, a little relieved."

"Can you explain that in any way?"

"Well, yes. The explanation that I offered to myself was that he anticipated a difficult interview—perhaps a stormy one—perhaps even an emotional one—and considered that such would better be postponed."

"Why did you think that a postponement would make it any better?"

"Well, it is difficult, for example, to be emotional after breakfast."

"I see—you thought—"

"Is this witness being presented as an expert witness on psychology?" said Mr. Macrea.

"Certainly not."

"Then are not all these answers rather in the nature of supposition—"

"I think I agree with Mr. Macrea," said the judge. "I don't think you should take these questions any further. The jury can draw their own deductions from the evidence without this witness's interpretation of it."

"If your lordship pleases. We will go on then to the later events of that evening. What was the next thing that happened?"

"Well—the next thing would be when I heard—No, I forgot. At about a quarter to ten Mrs. Roper came to see me."

"You were in your office?"

"Yes—I spent the whole evening in my office. Mrs. Roper was only with me for about five minutes. She wished to discuss her account. About an hour later I heard, from upstairs, one very loud shout or scream. I listened for a moment. There might have been an innocent explanation for it. Then there were more screams, loud and repeated. I jumped up and ran out."

"One moment, please," said Mr. Summers. "I am anxious

to fix this particular moment as accurately as possible." He walked over to the plan which still stood in the well of the court. "Did you leave your room by the door into the passage?"

"No, I went straight out through the reception desk. It is a few seconds quicker that way."

"Was there anyone in the reception desk?"

"No. Mademoiselle Lamartine was—"

"If you please, we will come to that in a moment. The reception desk was empty. What next?"

"I ran up the stairs."

"Did you observe anyone else whilst you were doing this?"

"Yes. I saw the door to the kitchen open and Camino came running through. I also heard the swinging doors which lead to the street begin to turn. I remember thinking, 'What a moment to have a visitor!' "

"Yes, and then?"

"I ran along the annex passage. The screams had stopped, but I had had the impression that they were coming from the end room. As I got there Mrs. Roper came out. She said something—I forget what it was. I pushed past her and saw Mademoiselle Lamartine. She was standing looking down at the floor. Major Thoseby was lying on the floor. He was half hidden by the door. His coat was open and the shirt and the top of his trousers were covered in blood. It did not seem to be flowing quickly. I put a hand on his heart, but I think that before I did this I knew he was dead." Most of the people in court—barristers, solicitors, law students, journalists—were by training accustomed to using their imaginations. As the witness finished speaking they could see a clear picture of the little, bare, upstairs bedroom at the back of the family hotel. The plain furniture, the yellow electric light, the worn carpet. Sprawled across the carpet the body of Major Thoseby, his shirt and trousers dark with blood—"the blood did not seem to be flowing quickly." But a lot of blood would run out if the stomach and the liver and the heart bag were punctured. The shirt, where it hung out from the top of his trousers, would be sodden with blood. The top of the shirt very white in contrast. "I put a hand on his heart." But it was too late. The heart had already ceased to beat. Major Thoseby, who had survived so many such imminent and urgent perils in Occupied France had come to his end in a residential hotel near Euston.

"Now, Monsieur Sainte," said Macrea.

[*The first part of his cross-examination is omitted. It was directed, skillfully enough, to showing in a sympathetic light the actions and sufferings of the prisoner in France. It did not succeed in shedding any new light on her relationship with Major Thoseby.*]

"Now. Monsieur Sainte. On the night of the murder Major Thoseby telephoned you at half-past six."

"That is correct."

"When did he tell you to expect him?"

"As I have said, it was not stated when he would arrive. It might be half-past seven—it might be eleven o'clock. He was at a conference at—"

"Yes. We have heard that. What time is the evening meal at your hotel?"

"At seven. Most people eat early nowadays."

"Yes. When does it finish?"

"It is finished by eight."

"Major Thoseby did not arrive until eight-thirty. Had you kept dinner for him?"

This very simple question appeared to confuse the witness. For the first time there was a perceptible pause before he replied.

"No, I did not keep dinner."

"But you said he had dinner when he arrived—" Macrea turned back some pages of his notes.

"A hotelier usually has something in reserve for an unexpected guest. Something in the kitchen."

"I see," said Macrea easily. "I was just trying to find out exactly how unexpected he really was."

"I do not understand that."

"I will make myself plain," said Macrea. "Will you tell us, once more—I haven't yet quite got it straight—when did you first hear from Major Thoseby?"

"Two days before. On the twelfth, that would be, his letter arrived. By the evening post."

"Have you still got that letter?"

"No. I think it has been destroyed."

"Why?"

"I am not a lawyer. I do not keep copies of all the letters that are sent to me."

"Would you not, as an hotelkeeper, preserve a letter of that sort?"

"If I had a secretary, no doubt all letters would be beautifully filed. I do my own work in the office. I have not time for such things. Letters get lost."

"Very well. When did you hear from Major Thoseby next?"

"As he had promised in his letter, he telephoned me at about half-past six in the evening of the fourteenth."

"I see. You have told us what he said. Then you sent for the prisoner."

"Yes."

"What did you say to her?"

"I cannot remember the exact words. She knew of the letter, of course. There was no need to say much. I may have said: 'He is coming this evening,' or something like that."

"Did you mention any time?"

"I think I repeated what Major Thoseby had said to me. He might be there at any time between eight and eleven."

"You are sure you said that?"

"To that effect."

"You did not say, 'He cannot be here before eleven.'"

"Certainly not."

"I want you to be very careful over this."

"I am quite certain that I did not say that he could not be here before eleven. It would not have been true. Why should I have said it?"

"Monsieur Sainte, you received a letter. That has been destroyed. You received a telephone message. Only you know what was said. The jury, if they are to judge the matter at all, have to judge by results."

"Yes."

"As a result of what you told her, Miss Lamartine left the hotel and did not come back until half-past ten."

"That is so."

"Is it not reasonable to suppose then—we know how anxious she was to meet Major Thoseby—I put it to you that it is a more reasonable explanation that you said something to her like: 'He cannot be here before eleven.'"

"I am certain that I did not say that."

"You agree that it would explain her actions in a logical way?"

"I do not think that you can ever explain the actions of a woman in a logical way."

Chapter Sixteen

Le Mans is not on the Loire, but it is the junction for all traffic coming south to the Basse Loire district. Nap got out of the train there at six o'clock on a gray morning. As he stood on the platform, looking like a ruff-necked starling, his overcoat turned up round his ears and his hair on end, he considered future moves.

It was Saturday. Such results as he might achieve, to be of any use to Mademoiselle Lamartine, must be obtained in three—at the most four—days.

The difficulty was to know where to start.

He would have to visit Père Chaise's farm near Langeais and get what information he could from the neighbors. Whilst he was there he thought he might have a word with one of Monsieur Sainte's "references" who lived at the Ferme du Grand Puits, not far from Langeais. His contacts after that were mainly in and around Angers.

An examination of the *indicateur* showed that he could either go straight to Angers and make his way up river or take the branch line to Tours and work back.

The deciding factor was the time of the trains.

If he went straight to Angers he would have no time for breakfast, and breakfast, after his second consecutive night in a French railway carriage, was beginning to assume a considerable measure of importance.

"Breakfast it is, then," said Nap.

On such small decisions do great issues hang.

He selected the Café du Colombier, a small cheerful eating house in the main street of Le Mans and ordered, with less difficulty than he would have experienced in England, an English breakfast of ham and eggs. Over a cup of indifferent coffee he started to read an early edition of the *Courier de L'Ouest* which he had found in the wicker rack beside the table.

It was more than two years since he had last set foot in France, and there were many things in the paper to surprise him. He read of a Gaulliste meeting at Saugny which had been broken up by Communists and had ended in a pitched battle. Allowing for a certain journalistic coloring in the report there was no escaping the ultimate, ugly fact that one man had been killed and fifteen seriously wounded. He read on the next page of the gang of currency smugglers who, apparently with the connivance of venial officials, had been running what amounted to a private airport for the cross-Channel carriage of dollar notes. The leader of the gang, who seemed to have boasted to the police after his capture, had stated that the profits of his group in one year's operations had exceeded a billion of francs.

It was not these events in themselves which Nap found so surprising. It was a coincidence of names. In charge of the investigations into the currency smuggling, he noticed, was Monsieur Bren of the Paris Sûreté. One of the wounded in the Saugny meeting—reading between the lines Nap imagined he must have been a Gaulliste organizer who had been roughly handled by the police—was a Pierre Roccambo. Now he had known both men. Both had worked with him in the affairs of the Franche-Comté Maquis.

For the first time he had a glimmering of an idea of the forces at work in France, forces which, did he know it, had already reached out and touched him at the extremities of their huge, opposed organizations.

Nap slept again in the train and woke at Tours. Here he found a branch-line train of toylike wooden carriages which brought him, in due course, to Langeais.

After lunch a bus, terrifyingly driven, took him out to Pont Boutard. From there, as he saw from his map, he had a walk of two or three kilometres, southward again, into the Bois de Langeais.

When, at about three o'clock in the afternoon, he came in sight of the Père Chaise farm, Nap knew that the first part of his journey had been in vain. The farm was now unlived in. A house which boasts four walls and a roof rarely goes out of occupation in the overfarmed country-side of France but this was an exception. The fields had gone back to fallow. They were being grazed, and Nap followed the track past the farm until he could see the roof of the next building, another kilometre further on. Here he found the farmer—it was his cattle that he had seen on Père Chaise's derelict fields—and a few words with him confirmed his first impression.

The Père Chaise farm had never been a lucky farm. The farmer produced a garbled account of the misfortunes of Père Chaise and his family during the war. The farmhouse had not been occupied since. Nap asked a few questions but it was evident that the farmer knew little more about it than Nap did himself. He knew the story of the English lieutenant. All the countryside knew it. He had been taken by the Germans and tortured to death. That was certain. All knew it.

Nap thanked him.

By the time he got back to Pont Boutard, the day was gone, and since there was no bus to take him to Langeais he spent the night, by invitation, at the corn chandler's house. The corn chandler, who was also the district money-lender, was an agreeable scoundrel and talked far into the night of the German Occupation, of the Gestapo, of the Resistance and of the present state of France. He put at Nap's disposal the marriage bed of his eldest daughter, a knobbed engine of brass and iron. Nap slept dreamlessly.

Early next morning he hired a bicycle from his host and set off for the Ferme du Grand Puits. It seemed, from the map, to be about eight kilometres away.

His way took him along the main road as far as Les Essards. Here he turned into a small, twisting, side road which climbed and dipped toward Avrillé-les-Ponceaux through the northern fringes of the Forêt de Rochecotte. It was a wild district of sandy uplands alternating with un-cleared wood. After half an hour of industrious pedaling Nap saw the signpost he had been warned to look for and turned again. He found an unmetaled track, deeply rutted by cartwheels in the mud of winter, but now dried into an infernal tramway along which he skidded and bumped. The track was still climbing, and suddenly he came out from the trees and saw the farmstead in front of him. It lay cupped in the side of the hill, hull down to the crest, hidden from the world by the woods which surrounded it, but watchful and dominant in its own upland clearing.

The buildings were massive. Fifty yards downhill from the farm Nap saw the mansard roof and the winding handle of the well which no doubt served to give the farm its name. "Grand" must mean "deep," he thought. You would have to go at least a hundred feet down into the chalk to get a water supply at a height like that.

He dismounted from his bicycle and stood for a moment surveying the steading. There was plenty of life about this farm. Chickens picking over the chaff at the barn door, a cat dozing beside the manure heap and keeping an eye on a gang of young turkeys braggarting up and down the yard.

A woman at one of the windows called something in a shrill voice and a moment later a fat man came out and stood in the doorway.

"Monsieur Marquis?" said Nap.

The fat man did not answer him directly.

"You are a stranger here," he said. "It is evident from your speech. You are from Paris?"

"Monsieur has a discriminating ear," said Nap.

"It is a facility," said the man. "You were asking after Monsieur Pierre Marquis. He is no longer here. I purchased the farm from him and his brother, André. It belonged to them jointly, you understand."

"That would be his younger brother?"

"On the contrary. Older. Much older. Seeing them together you would scarcely have said that they were brothers. I believe, however, that it was so. I see no reason to doubt it."

"Oh, quite," said Nap.

"As so often in these partnerships it was the younger who had the brain and the initiative. Or so it seemed to me."

"I suppose," said Nap, "you have no idea where they moved to. I have come a long way to find them—"

"I regret," said the man. "It was three—nearly four years ago. Just after the war."

"I see."

"Wait, though, an instant. Jeanne! Jeanne!" He had a thin piping voice for so large a man. The woman whom Nap had already seen came to the door. "What was the name of the advocate? You recollect. The one who negotiated the sale."

"Gimelet," said the woman. "Of Rue de Gazomètre at Angers."

"Why," said Nap. "But that—yes. Thank you."

"If Monsieur finds himself at Angers he might inquire. An advocate usually has the address of his client."

"If only to pester him with bills," said the woman, who seemed to be a realist.

"Thank you," said Nap. "Should I be in Angers I will certainly visit Monsieur Gimelet, and pursue my inquiries."

At the edge of the wood he paused and looked back. He found it difficult to account to himself for the powerful impression that the place had made on him. It was not the people. The fat self-satisfied man and his small dark wife: they were commonplace enough. It was not even the buildings, which were solid and well made, yet in no way remarkable. Was it, perhaps, the setting? The air of enclave; the suggestion of being the center of a maze; the heart, as it were, of its own private mystery?

As he was about to get on to his bicycle Nap noticed something else. But for his personal experience of such things he might very easily have missed it. At the point where the shoulder of the wood overlooked the approach to the farm someone had, at some time, constructed a camouflaged shelter. Nap could still see the trench and the step, overgrown but unmistakable. When he looked more closely he could see where small trees had been cut down to give a clear field of vision, and looking backward in the direction of the farm he could still make out the crawl trench which would have served a sentry for inconspicuous access and sudden retreat.

So the Ferme du Grand Puits had been a Maquis post too, in its time.

As Nap bicycled slowly back toward Pont Boutard and a late lunch, as he bounced in the bus which whirled back to Langeais, as he sat in the train which trundled him down the Loire Valley toward the town of Angers, the first very faint beginning of an idea was sown and planted its long roots in his mind.

Chapter Seventeen

On Tuesday morning before the proceedings opened Macrea found time for a word with Mr. Rumbold.

"Any word yet from that son of yours?" he asked.

"Not a thing," said Mr. Rumbold.

"Have we any means of letting him know what's happening at this end?"

"I've got a hotel address in Angers," said Mr. Rumbold. "He ought to be there by now. If he isn't I've wasted a lot of money."

Macrea cocked a tufted eyebrow at him.

"I sat up half last night," explained Mr. Rumbold, "cabling him a summary of all the evidence we've had so far—particularly Monsieur Sainte. It was a very compressed version but it seemed to add up to an awful lot of words when I came to paying for it."

"I hope we get something from him," said Macrea. "What about Major McCann?"

"He was in Winchester yesterday. He's in Salisbury today. He says he may be on to something."

Macrea looked thoughtful.

"I don't want to hurry your lieutenants unduly," he said, "but at the present rate this trial won't run much beyond Thursday midday."

"Your name is Adrian Arthur Crispin Trevor Alwright. You were a colonel on the general list in His Majesty's Army, now retired."

"Quite so."

"You have been resident since September of last year at the Family Hotel in Pearlyman Street and were resident there on March fourteenth of this year?"

"Just so."

"Now, Colonel Alwright, I would like you to direct your attention to the evening of March fourteenth."

"The night that poor fellow got killed."

"Yes."

"Shocking thing. Shocking. Well now, let me think. I had dinner at seven o'clock. I think we were only five at table that night—Mrs. Roper, the three Radletts and myself. The Radletts went out as soon as dinner was over."

"That would have been—when?"

"Oh. Just about eight—perhaps a little before."

"Thank you. What did you do next?"

"I went up to my room to see to one or two things. Came back to the lounge and settled down for the evening."

"Can you remember where you sat?" Mr. Summers moved over to the plan.

"Yes. My usual chair, between the window and the fire-place."

"About here?"

"That's about it."

"The point I had in mind is that you could see out through the door into the hall. Could you see the reception desk?"

"Yes."

"And the person in it."

"I could keep an eye on old Camino most of the time, if that's what you're getting at," said the colonel with soldierly directness.

"Well—yes. Most of the time, you say."

"If he moved to the back of the reception office, he went out of view. But he was there all right, I'm fairly sure of that."

"What reason have you got for saying that?"

"Well, he cantered up whenever I whistled for him—to fetch a drink, you know. That sort of thing."

"I see. Well, now, apart from Camino who did you see, in or near the lounge, that evening?"

"Are you talking about poor old Thoseby?"

"Yes. If you saw him. Just tell us who you saw."

"Of course I saw him. He had to come through the lounge to get to the dining room. I expect I said good evening. It seemed the friendly thing to do."

"What time would this have been?"

"I didn't keep looking at my watch. About half an hour after I'd settled down."

"The approximate time is all that we want. Now can you give us any idea of what Major Thoseby's demeanor was at this time. Did he look quite normal, or did he seem to you upset or nervous?"

"What had he got to be nervous about?" said the colonel reasonably. "He didn't know then that he was going to be murdered."

"Then he seemed perfectly normal."

"Quite normal."

"When did you see him next?"

"About half an hour later, when he'd finished his meal."

"He came back into the lounge."

"Yes."

"Did he say anything?"

"We exchanged a few sentences. I think I asked him whether he was stopping long in the hotel. He said no, just for the one night as far as he knew."

"As far as he knew—you're sure that's what he said."

"No. I'm not sure. How can anyone be sure about a conversation with a complete stranger in a hotel lounge six months ago?"

"But you remember that it was quite a short conversation?"

"Yes. Quite a short conversation. He then settled down

to read the papers and shortly after that he went out. I understood him to say he was going upstairs to his room."

"Can you give us any idea what time this would be?"

"Let me see—between a quarter- and half-past nine."

"Was there anyone else with you in the lounge?"

"Yes. Mrs. Roper was in the lounge with me all this time. She was there from after dinner until she went up to her room at ten o'clock."

"I see. Then what happened?"

"I must have been alone then, until I went to bed. I left the lounge at half-past ten. I ran into Mademoiselle—I mean—" The gallant colonel plainly boggled at the idea of saying "the prisoner" and concluded with a vague gesture in the direction of the dock.

"You encountered the prisoner?"

"Yes. I gathered that she had just returned from her evening out. I may have said good night. I really forget. I then went up to my room."

"What happened next?"

"Nothing happened next. I undressed, went to bed, and woke up the next morning."

"Your room, of course, is not in the annex with Major Thoseby's. Your room is in the main corridor?"

"Yes."

"Thank you, Colonel Alwright."

"Colonel Trevor Alwright," said Macrea. "Are you an accurate observer?"

"Am I—yes. I think I may say so. The Army teaches accurate observation."

"Then you will not object if I test your memory."

"Certainly not."

"Particularly as at one point in my learned friend's examination you indicated that you were not quite sure, after this lapse of time, exactly what did take place."

"I said that I couldn't remember exactly what was *said*."

"But your recollection of who was there that night, and at approximately what time they came and went—you are quite clear on that?"

"Oh, quite. Not to a minute, you know. I didn't have my watch in my hand."

"So you told us. Might I direct your attention to a statement you made in examination. You say 'Mrs. Roper was in the lounge with me all this time'—the time actually referred to was half-past nine, when Major Thoseby left to go up to his room—you go on to say: 'She was there from after dinner until she went up to her room at ten o'clock.' "

"Quite so."

"I do not particularly refer to the early part of the evening but that is a definite statement that Mrs. Roper was in the room with you from, let us say, nine-thirty until ten o'clock?"

"Yes."

"Is that true?"

"Really, sir. I hardly know how to answer you."

"Then try answering the question."

"It is my recollection of what happened."

"Your clear recollection?"

"I suppose so."

"You said, a moment ago, that your recollection of comings and goings was clear."

"Yes. I am sure that is correct."

"I see. I just mention it, because Monsieur Sainte, in his evidence, states that Mrs. Roper went in to see him in his office for a few minutes at a quarter to ten."

"In that case—yes. Well, she may have slipped out of the room for a few moments."

"I trust that you are bearing in mind," said Macrea screwing his glass into his eye and giving the colonel a stare of concentrated loathing, "that you are giving evidence upon oath?"

"Quite so."

"Evidence upon the accuracy of which the life of the prisoner may depend."

"Oh, quite," said the colonel unhappily.

"Later in your evidence you state that you went to bed, undressed and went to sleep. Can you give the court some idea of how long those—er—operations would normally take—approximately?"

"Well, about half an hour, possibly a little more."

"And you reached your room just after ten o'clock?"

"Yes."

"So that by a quarter to eleven you would not have been in bed for more than five, or at the most, ten minutes?"

"Yes."

"Your room is in the main corridor directly over Monsieur Sainte's office." Macrea demonstrated on the plan. "And being on the first floor is actually closer to Major Thoseby's room than Monsieur Sainte's office?"

"Certainly not. To get from my room to Major Thoseby's room would mean going back down the stairs—".

"If you would listen to my questions we should save the court's time. I did not ask if you could reach Major Thoseby's room more quickly than Monsieur Sainte could. I stated, as a mathematical fact, that your room is *nearer* to Major Thoseby's room."

"Yes. I expect that is so."

"Do you sleep with your window shut or open?"

"Open, of course."

"Then is it not odd that shouts—screams, I should say —that were loud enough to fetch Monsieur Sainte instantly to his feet, in a more distant room, with the window shut, made no impression on you, although you had only been in bed approximately five minutes?"

"I was asleep."

"Deeply asleep?"

"Yes, I sleep very soundly."

"You went to sleep at once?"

"I usually fall asleep as soon as my head touches the pillow."

"A very soldierly trait," commented Macrea. "May I revert for a moment to an earlier part of the evening? When my learned friend was pressing you to state definitely that the waiter, Camino, was in the reception desk, you said—I am paraphrasing your answer—that when he was at the front of the desk you could actually see him, and when he was occupied at the back of the desk, you were confident he was there, because he always responded to your summons. Is that right?"

"Yes. That is correct. The fellow always appeared immediately I called for him."

"And how many times did you call for him?"

"Well—perhaps half a dozen times."

"That would be six times in the period of about two hours. You are sure it was six times."

"I couldn't swear to the precise number. It might have been six or eight."

"I see. And what did he do for you on these six or eight occasions?"

"Well—it might have been an evening paper—or a drink."

"He will be giving evidence himself and will no doubt be able to assist us. Would you say that you sent six times for a drink?"

"Perhaps."

"And what were you drinking—no doubt you will remember that?"

"Whisky."

"Six orders of whisky. Single or doubles?"

"Really, I—singles. The first may have been a double."

"Well, I expect we shall be able to ask the next witness about that, too. You did say that you were an accurate observer, Colonel?"

"I did."

Macrea appeared to refer to a note in his brief.

"Is it correct that at the Kirkee Hospital in 1933, you called the attention of one of the medical officers to a cobra in a bathing suit and a fez which was tobogganing down the wall beside your bed?"

"I do not remember."

"I will not press the question. It would be true, however, to say that after six or seven glasses of whisky your observations might tend to be a little less reliable than they normally are."

The witness made no reply to this.

Mr. Summers, in re-examination asked, "When you were in Kirkee Hospital on the occasion to which my learned friend refers, were you suffering from malaria?"

"Yes."

"And that is a disease in which hallucinations are sometimes observed by the patient?"

"Certainly, why once in East Africa I saw—"

"Thank you," said Mr. Summers hastily.

Camino's evidence was given to the court through an interpreter and for this reason, and also because it tended chiefly to substantiate Colonel Alwright's, it is not offered verbatim.

The following is a short summary of the points elicited.

Camino was on duty at the reception desk from eight o'clock until ten-thirty. During this time he took four telephone calls and fetched Colonel Trevor Alwright seven

single whiskies, one double whisky and a copy of the
Evening Standard. He was quite certain that the colonel
was at no time intoxicated. Had the colonel been intoxicated
he would not have served him with further drinks. Cheerful, yes. At the end, possibly sleepy. But not intoxicated.
He had been relieved at the desk by the prisoner on her
return to the hotel at half-past ten. This was the normal
arrangement. He had many duties to perform before going
to bed—such as setting the breakfast, preparing early
morning tea-trays. He went straight into the kitchen and
was working between the kitchen and the dining room for
the next forty-five minutes. He was in the kitchen at a
quarter to eleven when he heard the screams. He ran
through the service door and up the stairs. Monsieur Sainte
was running just ahead of him. After the discovery of the
body Monsieur Sainte had instructed him to telephone for
the police and a doctor. In the excitement he had misunderstood and had telephoned only for the police. Afterward he
had summoned the doctor as well. He had been working
with Monsieur Sainte in the hotel ever since the hotel
opened.

Macrea leaned over and said something to Mr. Lovibond
who was taking this cross-examination.

"One last question. I understand that you are by birth
an Italian?"

"Yes."

"Did you come to England direct from Italy?"

"No, I was in France during the whole of the war."

"In what part of France?"

"Near Angers."

"I only asked because I thought his Italian sounded a bit
odd," said Macrea to Mr. Rumbold. "The trouble is that it

was such an unexpected answer that we weren't prepared to follow it up."

"I'll let Nap know at once," said Mr. Rumbold.

Chapter Eighteen

After breakfast on Monday morning Nap set out to visit the Rue de Gazomètre. He found that it lay in the lower part of Angers.

As he walked along the cobbled path which skirts the ramparts of the castle and slopes down to the river front, he turned over in his mind the idea which had come to him.

In the light of morning it looked, perhaps, less promising than it had done the evening before but he was convinced that somewhere in it was the hard grain of truth.

When he had called at the Bureau de Lorraine, in London, the *directeur* had given him the names and addresses of the two householders who had afforded "references" for Monsieur Sainte when the latter came over to England to open his hotel. The first of these "references" had been the brothers Marquis whose farm he had just visited. A coincidence, perhaps, that the brothers Marquis should have sold up their farm and left the district at about the same time that Monsieur Sainte had come to England? Monsieur Sainte's second "reference" had been Monsieur Gimelet of the Rue de Gazomètre. It now appeared that Monsieur Gimelet was a lawyer employed by the brothers Marquis.

"A crooked attorney," said Nap. He stopped for a moment to admire the massive chestnut trees in the avenue; their golden brown leaves were just beginning to fall. "A dime to a dollar there's some shady work going on here, and it looks as if Sainte is mixed up in it."

As he crossed the bridge he was aware that the character of the streets had deteriorated. He was penetrating the Quartier Ouvrier. The houses here were old, and thin-chested. The paint was off the wood and the ironwork was rusty.

Outside the door of Number 20 Rue de Gazomètre a chipped China plate bore the name Maître Gimelet. All the shutters were closed and the door was fast. He reflected that the corresponding street in an English town would have been alive, the open windows crowded with women, the doorways thronged with children. This street was dead.

He pulled the iron bell-pull and waited. He pulled it again. He became aware that the wicket gate had opened and a small man was peering up at him.

"Maître Gimelet?"

"Yes."

"Permit me, if I may, to enter. I have business to discuss."

The man looked undecided.

"It will take a few minutes only."

The man backed away from the door and Nap followed him into the tiled hall. No motion was made to invite him further.

"It is of Monsieur Honorifique Sainte I would inquire," said Nap. "He is now living in London—"

He was interrupted.

The door at the end of the hall opened and a huge woman in black advanced toward them. It was an unexpected but none the less an impressive performance. As she advanced she crepitated. Like a snake over sun-warmed tiles; like a razor blade across a leather hone; like the leaves of a linden tree in the faintest breeze of a summer evening. As a ship's harmony is composed of many notes, so Nap's careful ear distinguished the different instruments of Madame Gimelet's orchestra. The rustle of silk, the rumor of starched linen, the flexing of whalebone, the tweaking of elastic.

"Monsieur desires—?" inquired this female mountain coldly.

Nap repeated his request.

"My husband does not know a Monsieur Sainte."

"Indeed," said Nap. "It seems, in the circumstances, odd then that he offered his own name as a reference for Monsieur Sainte when he removed to England."

"As to that," said Madame, "it may be. One does these things and one forgets."

"Not, perhaps, quite the spirit in which one should approach an official reference."

"Perhaps not."

"Monsieur Sainte—" piped the small man.

"A business acquaintance only," said the woman. "My husband does business for many people. He cannot answer personally for all of them. What has Monsieur Sainte done?"

"Nothing," said Nap. "Nothing at all." He fixed Maître Gimelet with his eye and directed his question pointedly at him.

"As an attorney," he said, "you can tell me perhaps what was the deposit demanded by the British Government at that time before a Frenchman would be permitted to enter England and to work there."

"I think—"

"Five hundred pounds," said the woman, "it may have been a thousand. In different cases, different sums were demanded."

"Monsieur Sainte was a man of means, then—"

"Oh, yes—" began the man.

"My husband would hardly be expected to know the private circumstances of all his clients."

Maître Gimelet hastily nodded his agreement with this sentiment.

"God blast the woman," thought Nap.

He took his courage into both hands and said, directing himself again to the man, "Is it permitted to see Maître Gimelet alone?"

"No," said Madame.

Nap looked at the attorney. He seemed unaware that anything unusual had been said, but stood quite placidly, his fingers playing with a pair of pince-nez, which were hanging from a broad ribbon; his brown eyes were mild.

"In that case—" said Nap angrily. He was on the point of terminating the interview when common sense came to his aid.

"Why should I walk out on them?" he thought. "That's just exactly what the old she-mountain wants me to do." He directed himself again with laborious politeness to the lawyer.

"Do you recollect," he said, "that you acted for Pierre and André Marquis in the sale of a farm—the Ferme du Grand Puits—?"

No sooner had he spoken the words than Nap realized that he was close to something.

Maître Gimelet stopped playing with his glasses. Madame froze. There was silence in the long hallway.

"I—yes," said the man.

"One forgets," said the woman. She said it automatically.

"All right." Nap spoke with sudden savage authority. "One forgets. I ask you about Monsieur Sainte, a man for whose respectability you have vouched to the British Government. You know nothing of him. I ask whether he is a man of means. You do not know. I inquire about the brothers Marquis, two of your own clients. You have forgotten. What is all this? Is it a farce? Is it a fairy story? I speak of the Ferme du Grand Puits—"

Again it came, strong as the kick of a mine detector when it passes over hidden metal. Keep at it, thought Nap.

"What is there in this Grand Puits—"

This time it was quite unmistakable.

It was the ugly emotion of fear. He could see it in both faces; as plain as death and dissolution.

"You will go," said the woman at last. "You will go or I will send for the police."

"We shall see who will be the first to send for the police," said Nap. This seemed to be quite a good curtain line. He opened the door and let himself out into the empty sunlit street.

When he got back to his hotel he inquired at the desk for letters. There were none. As he was turning away, the manageress said: "You visitor is waiting for you."

"My visitor?"

"I put her in the writing room—that is the small room at the end of the passage past the dining room. I trust I did rightly."

"Oh, you put her in the writing room. Quite right," said Nap. "I will go along now."

In the little writing room he was not entirely surprised to find Madame Delboise.

"I trust you found your child well," said Nap. "You are tired of Paris so soon."

"He is a fine boy," said Madame Delboise. "Just seven. He is in the middle of his first love affair. However, it is not of him that I have come all the way to Angers to speak. I have come to apologize."

"For what?"

"For mistrusting you in the first place. In the second, for having you followed."

"I imagined," said Nap, "that I had managed to—er—

spare you the latter embarrassment. Evidently I was wrong."

"At Dieppe, you mean. It was charmingly done. Really, I appreciated it. That handsome suitcase—the owner came to claim it before we arrived in Paris. He was most indignant."

"He has all my sympathy. Tell me, was I very clumsy? You mean to say that someone else was following me as well as you?"

"Indeed, there was no need," said Madame Delboise. "I was aware that the only other train leaving Dieppe was for Rouen. I merely telephoned for you to be met there."

"Ah! The young man with the bicycle?"

"Philippe. Has he not a splendid body?"

"Shattering."

"So I think. One day, when things are more settled, I shall marry him. Imagine the pleasure. To awaken each morning—"

"Quite so," said Nap.

"All the same someone did come after me in Dieppe."

"No doubt they did," said Madame Delboise. "The people I am thinking of have a very good intelligence service. They would be aware that you would land at Dieppe—no doubt you would be picked up as soon as you landed."

"Look here," said Nap. "Would you very much mind explaining what all this is about?"

"Of course. First, I should explain that we have a friend in common. Monsieur Bren?"

"You know him?"

"In fact I work for him."

"My God," said Nap. "A policewoman."

"As you say it, it does not sound flattering. But it is the truth nevertheless. My assignment at the moment is to the matter of currency smuggling. It is an international organization, with its branches in all countries. Two of the strongest and best-organized branches work together on the cross-Channel service. We know a good deal about the French end—it is the English end that we are now studying in co-operation, of course, with your police."

"And the Société de Lorraine?"

"A perfectly genuine organization. I was attached there merely for cover."

"Then why should you have been interested in me?"

"Because we were not quite sure about you. And anyone we are not quite sure about interests us. You are a friend of Major McCann. He was making inquiries about Mrs. Roper —who is the friend of a man we are very interested in indeed. We felt no doubt that when you reached France things might happen. And, indeed, from what I hear, the guess was a good one. They have begun to happen already."

"You mean that unpleasant piece of work who contacted me at Rouen? How did you know about that, by the way?"

"Philippe saw him come and go."

"I see. One other thing. You said that you *were* not sure about me. Has anything happened to make you change your mind?"

"Of course. I had only to mention your name to Monsieur Bren. He gave you the best of characters."

Nap thought for a moment, and then said, "Do you like American magazines?"

"Certainly."

"So do I, for the most part. But they have one habit that I find irritating. They start a story, get you really interested in it, and then—what happens? You turn the page and find you are in the middle of quite a different one."

"I do not quite—"

"That's exactly what's happening here, don't you see?

I started out reading a murder story. It seems to have turned into a gold smuggling melodrama. What's the connection between the death of Major Thoseby last March in the Family Hotel and a large-scale gold smuggling racket?"

"Mrs. Roper."

"Yes. I know Mrs. Roper is a person who is common to both stories—but does that necessarily mean that the two stories are connected? It might have been the purest coincidence that she had the room next to Thoseby's."

"I do not believe in coincidence," said the girl. "There is a connection. It is even possible that I may be able to help you to find it. The work I am engaged on gives me certain facilities. But, meanwhile, let me warn you. Tread carefully. The state of France is not a very happy one at this moment. Sometimes, indeed, I wish that we were back in the war again. In the Resistance we were all one. Now we have gone in all directions. Some of us—the Trades Unionists chiefly—to the Communists, some of us into the administration and the police—"

"And some," said Nap, thinking of what he had read in the *Courier*, "some have gone into—into opposition."

"Yes. One sees that it was inevitable. The wilder spirits, those who had learned to live by robbing and killing Germans. Now there are no Germans. They fight society."

"I understand that," said Nap.

"Understand this, too, then. They are not easy people. Leave them to those who are organized to deal with them. Inquiries have started already. We are hopeful of that lawyer, Gimelet. We may be able to bring pressure on him."

"If you are going to do anything that will help me," said Nap, "you realize that you'll have to work fast. It's Monday afternoon. I must have all my answers by Wednesday at the latest."

"I will give you my telephone number in Angers." She

scribbled it on a piece of paper. "If you go out of the hotel, leave word where you can be found."

"Very well," said Nap.

He said it with a docility which anyone who knew him might have found suspicious.

Chapter Nineteen

"Your name is Gwendolyne Roper. You have been a resident at the Family Hotel in Pearlyman Street, Euston —for how long?"

"For more than a year."

"You were there on the night that Major Thoseby was murdered?"

"Yes."

"Will you give the court an account of your movements on that evening—from dinnertime onward."

"I finished dinner at about eight o'clock. Colonel Alwright finished his dinner at the same time and we went into the lounge together. I was there, reading and listening to the wireless, for the better part of the next two hours. I looked in at Mr. Sainte's office for a few minutes at about a quarter to ten, but, so far as I recollect, that was the only time I went out of the room."

"Did anyone else come in during this time?"

"Yes. Major Thoseby arrived at about half-past eight. He passed through the room on his way to dinner. He came out of the dining room again. At nine o'clock. The nine o'clock news, I remember, was just starting. I think he sat and read for about ten minutes—it may have been a quarter of an hour. Then he went out. I think he was going up to his room."

"What made you think that?"

"He said good night as he went."

"I see. That would have been about a quarter past nine, I take it. What happened next?"

"I went up to my room at ten o'clock. I had some letters to write. I thought I would write them upstairs."

Mr. Summers referred to the plan.

"Your room is Number 33, next to Major Thoseby's?"

"Yes."

"In the ordinary way, can you hear from your room what goes on in the next-door room?"

"You cannot hear ordinary conversation. The walls are too thick for that."

"But you can hear loud or unusual noises."

"Yes. I was able to hear—"

"I am coming to that," said Mr. Summers smoothly. "There is just one other point first. When you entered your room could you see if there was a light on in Major Thoseby's room?"

"Yes. There was."

"What about the other two rooms, on the other side of the passage? Were there people in them?"

"No. The room opposite Major Thoseby's is a bathroom. The one opposite mine is another bedroom. I don't think it was occupied that night."

"You are not sure about that."

"I think, Mr. Summers," said the judge, "that was established in Monsieur Sainte's evidence."

"With respect," said Macrea, "I don't think anything was said—"

"I could have Monsier Sainte recalled after this witness," suggested the judge.

"Your lordship is very kind," said Macrea, "but so far

as I am concerned the matter is not in dispute. Of the four rooms in the passage the only two then occupied were Major Thoseby's and Mrs. Roper's."

"I am obliged," said Mr. Summers. "Now, Mrs. Roper—what did you do next?"

"I was writing my letters and listening to the wireless."

"To the wireless?"

"Yes. I have a portable set in my room."

"I see—and then?"

"Well—I suppose it would have been about a quarter to eleven—I thought that I heard someone go past. I turned down the wireless to listen."

"Why did you do that?"

"Well, as a matter of fact, I was afraid it might be someone else going into the bathroom, which would have been annoying as I was just thinking about using it myself."

"I see. And then?"

"Then I heard a thud from the room next door and a scream—several screams."

"Would you ask the witness to be more explicit?" said Macrea.

"It seemed quite clear to me," said Mr. Summers. "She heard a thud, followed by several screams."

"No doubt," said Macrea, "but it wasn't what she said. She said she heard 'a scream—several screams.' "

"As you wish," said Mr. Summers. "Perhaps you would say again what you heard."

"I heard a thud, followed by several screams."

"Thank you. Will you go on."

"I ran out and listened. The door of Major Thoseby's room was ajar. The screaming was coming from inside. I pushed the door open and looked in. The prisoner was standing, looking down at the floor where Major Thoseby's body was lying."

"Did she say anything to you?"

"Nothing that I could understand. It was mostly screaming. I cannot exactly remember what I did next. I think I knelt to look at the body—I did not touch it. I could see that Major Thoseby was dead. Then Monsieur Sainte arrived. He told me to stay in my room until the police came."

"Thank you," said Mr. Summers.

"Mrs. Roper," said Macrea. "I am going to start by asking you a question which I put to a previous witness. Are you an accurate observer?"

"Yes, I think so. As good as most."

"You realize how necessary it is that your evidence should be absolutely accurate?"

"I should hope so."

"Very well. I will call your attention to your recent answer given to my learned friend. You stated that you heard a thud, followed by several screams."

"Yes."

"Followed, how soon?"

"Almost immediately."

"By how many screams?"

"Really—I couldn't say. Two or three."

"Not one long, continuous scream—but two or three separate screams?"

"Yes."

"Quickly, one after the other?"

"Yes, that's right."

"I see," said Macrea. "I asked, of course, because my learned friend in his opening speech—he must, I assume, have been following your evidence—spoke of *one* very loud scream, followed by further screams. Monsieur Sainte in his evidence says that he heard—" Macrea rustled back the heavy pages of his brief in a court which had fallen suddenly silent—" 'one very loud shout or scream.' You are quite certain that it was 'two or three' screams that you heard?"

"Well—yes."

"Quite certain?"

"That is my recollection."

"But you think now that you may have been mistaken?"

"I may have been."

"Very well. I would like to go on to the next point. You say that the walls between the two bedrooms were so thick that you could not hear conversation?"

"Normal conversation."

"Normal conversation, of course. And on this occasion you had your wireless set on."

"I had it turned down."

"Yes, you turned it down when the footsteps came along the corridor. But not off."

"No, not off."

"You were able to hear the footsteps in the corridor all right?"

"Yes. The corridor has no carpet."

"Quite so. But Major Thoseby's room has?"

"I—yes. I believe it has."

"And although there was this thick wall, and this carpet, and your wireless set on, you were able to hear this 'thud.' "

"Yes."

"Is that not rather remarkable?"

"I don't think so."

"I am assuming—it has not been stated—but the suggestion is that this 'thud' was Major Thoseby falling to the floor. He was not thrown down—he collapsed. On to the carpet—whilst your wireless was on—with a wall between you so thick that you could not hear the human voice through. But you heard the thud quite easily."

"Well—not easily."

"You mean you barely heard it?"

"You might say that."

"It might not have been a thud at all?"

"It was a thud."

"Then why do you say you *barely* heard it. Were you listening for it?"

"I—no—really. You're confusing me."

"The simple remedy for confusion is to tell nothing but the truth."

"I am telling the truth."

"Very well. Now going back to those footsteps in the passage. You heard them stop outside Major Thoseby's door? And you heard the door open?"

"Yes."

"How long between the opening of the door and the scream—I beg your pardon—the screams?"

"It's hard to say."

"Let me assist you." Macrea took out his watch. "The door is opening now. Tell me when the screams are due."

The silence in court was complete.

"Now," said the witness.

"Seven seconds—" Macrea shut his watch with a snap. "Rather an impetuous young woman, don't you think?"

"I don't know what you mean."

"Well, there wasn't time for much conversation, was there? She must have marched straight in and stuck a knife into Major Thoseby before he had time to say so much as good evening."

"It may have been a little longer."

"I see. It may have been a little longer. You are certain that you are not making the whole thing up."

"No, I am telling you the truth, just as it happened."

"The court will be glad to have your assurance on the

point. Let me revert to the very first question you were asked. What is your name?"

The reaction to this question was disproportionate. Mrs. Roper went first red and then white. She made no immediate attempt to answer.

"It's quite a simple question." Macrea was blandness itself. "People usually have one name at a time. Perhaps you could tell the court what your name is."

"Gwendolyne Roper."

"That is your present name?"

"Yes."

"Was it formerly Gwyneth Roper?"

"Yes."

"And before that Gwyneth Roberts?"

"Yes."

"What was your father's name?"

"I don't know." The witness gave this answer in a very low tone of voice.

"Is it correct, then, that for the first twenty years of your life you were known as Gwen Rochester—that being the name you were given in the institution where you were brought up?"

"M'lord," said Summers, "I must—"

"I presume, Mr. Macrea, that these questions are on the point of character?"

"I shall make myself quite plain, I hope," said Macrea. "I am going both to character and credibility."

"Very well, then."

"Did you, at about the age of twenty-five—your name at that time, I believe, was Gwyneth Roberts—consort with a man called Hogan? And was this man, just before the war, sent to penal servitude for robbery with violence?"

"Yes. It was nothing to do with me."

"You were not indicted with him," agreed Macrea. "Did

you, in or about 1943, under the name of Roker associate with a Polish soldier called Pakosch—and was Pakosch subsequently deported and were you joined with him in these proceedings?"

"I was acquitted."

"On a technicality, yes. But is it not true that the magistrate warned you to obtain some proper employment and were you not subsequently directed, under wartime legislation, to work in a munitions factory—a direction incidentally which you neglected to comply with?"

"I—yes."

"Are you not at the present, an associate of a man known to the police as a person who deals in illegally imported currency?"

"Certainly not."

"Then you have never met with or spoken to a Mr. Stimmy?"

"I may have done, at some time or other, I forget."

"Your memory cannot be very reliable. Were you not with him last week end?"

"It's a lie."

"And the week end before?"

"What's it to do with you?"

"Mrs. Roper. How do you earn your living?"

Mrs. Roper said something in a very low voice, which the judge asked her to repeat.

"I said, I've got money put by."

"I see. How much money? Roughly how much?"

"Hundreds of pounds."

"A thousand pounds? Is that about it?"

"Yes, about that."

"It must be very judiciously invested."

"I don't know what you're talking about."

"I will try to make myself clear. How much does the Family Hotel charge for a week's board and lodging?"

"Six guineas a week."

"And I suppose you have other expenses?"

"Certainly."

"Would it be fair then to say that you spend ten pounds a week—in all?"

"I expect that would be about it."

"In round figures that would be £500 a year—quite a good *income* from an investment of £1,000."

"My lord," said Mr. Summers. "I must object to this quite irrelevant inquiry into witness's means. Is my learned friend making any financial implication—"

"I think that the implication is quite clear," said Macrea. His voice was hard and high, the reporters' pencils scurried and squeaked. "I suggest that this witness is a criminal and the associate of criminals. That she has lived since her youth by crime. That she is supported by a man known to be a professional criminal. And that her evidence is generally about as reliable as evidence from such a source might be expected to be."

"I think you must leave this to the jury, Mr. Macrea."

"I will willingly do so. I have just one more question." He turned again to Mrs. Roper who, her dignity gone and her face white, was clinging to the rail in front of the witness box as though she derived some comfort from its physical support. "Perhaps you would tell the court—the matter appears to have been overlooked in previous examination—what exactly *did* you discuss with Monsieur Sainte when you visited him in his private room that evening at a quarter to ten—?"

"I don't think she really fainted," said Macrea callously to Mr. Rumbold as they went out of court. "She needed a good curtain and thought she might get a bit of sympathy from the jury."

"I wonder what they're making of it."

"It's difficult to say. I think they've reached a stage where they don't really believe anything."

"Well, that's a step in the right direction, anyway," said Mr. Rumbold.

He hurried off to put through a long-distance call to Angers.

Chapter Twenty

On Tuesday morning Nap visited the hotel desk on his way down to breakfast and was handed a ten-page cablegram. It was from his father and contained, in compressed form, the evidence given in court on the previous day.

He studied it whilst his coffee was percolating.

A good deal of it was old stuff but there were one or two names and facts which were new.

He concentrated on that part of the evidence which dealt with the events of September, 1943. It occurred to him that there were some people and places that might be verified.

Accordingly, after breakfast, he caught the local train, which for a pleasant hour crawled from station to tiny station eastward along the banks of the Loire and finally brought him to Saumur.

Here he made certain inquiries, arriving back at Angers for a late lunch.

The results of his morning's work were negative, and yet not unsatisfactory. He had found, for instance, that no one seemed to have any recollection at Saumur of a Monsieur Sainte, hotel proprietor. Nor was there any hotel which could be said to correspond even roughly to the description given in evidence: "On the river front at Saumur, near to the main road bridge . . . it had been completely destroyed by a bomb." Saumur had suffered from bombing, it was true, but most of the damage had been done in the station area. On the south bank by the bridge there were no hotels. On the north bank there were several hotels, but none had been bombed. There was no Rue du Pont.

Nap pondered these things as he filleted his *truite Angevine*. He found them interesting but inconclusive.

He became aware that a waiter was hovering.

"From London?"

"Yes, monsieur. The instrument is in the office. If monsieur would step this way—" Nap was pleased to detect a certain note of respect. The Hotel de La Reine was plainly not used to guests who received ten-page cablegrams with their breakfast and personal telephone calls from England with their lunch.

Over the wire his father's voice came thinly, and with intermittent clarity.

"We've only just heard," it said. "We thought you ought to know. Camino was in France for most of the war."

"Who was?"

"Camino—the Italian waiter in the hotel. He was in the Angers district, too."

"Any address?"

"No, but an Italian shouldn't be difficult to trace. How are you getting on?"

"I'm going round in circles at the moment," said Nap frankly, "but I may have something for you soon."

Over the line he thought he heard his father sigh.

After lunch he thought he would take a walk and try to straighten out his ideas.

The midafternoon quiet of a provincial town lay upon

Angers. He strolled along the main street, past the barracks and the offices of the Administration, and at the end of it he came, a little unexpectedly, upon the Jardin Planteölogique et Zoölogique. He pushed through the turnstile, made his way along the neatly kept path and sat down on a bench under a cedar tree, in front of a cageful of dispirited monkeys. He had to sort things out.

He was far from clear as to the final answer but some of the components in the puzzle were falling into place. The person round whom the whole thing revolved was little Maître Gimelet, the attorney. Maître Gimelet had lied to him almost every time he had opened his mouth; and behind him was Monsieur Sainte who had lied about his residence in Saumur, and behind him were the brothers Marquis who had stood surety for Monsieur Sainte when he came to England and who had employed Maître Gimelet to sell their farm.

What was the connecting link? What was the common factor which joined them to Major Thoseby and Lieutenant Wells—and to the grim proceedings now holding the stage at the Old Bailey?

The only possible indication which he had yet had was that it was all, somehow, connected with the currency racket. Mrs. Roper was the associate of a man called Stimmy who dealt in smuggled currency. And, if Madame Delboise was to be believed, he himself, immediately he had moved toward the Loire, had run into the people who managed the French end of the business.

There were a lot of questions to be answered, but terribly little time for the answers to be found.

He sat there until the sun disappeared and the chill of the autumn evening forced him to move.

Back in the hotel he found to his annoyance that he had been called twice on the telephone.

Not from England—a local call.

As he was talking the bell went again. It was a man's voice. He was calling, he said, on behalf of Madame Delboise. He regretted that he had missed Monsieur Rimbault on the previous occasions. He had some information for him. It was not of a nature to be freely discussed over the telephone.

"All right," said Nap. "Where are you?"

"Number 115 Rue de Piste. A wine merchant's shop."

"I'll be right along," said Nap.

When he had rung off he thought for a moment and then asked for the number that Madame Delboise had given him.

He recognized her voice at once. Shortly he repeated the conversation which he had just had.

"Very curious," said Madame Delboise. "It is true that I have some information for you, but so far as I am aware none of our people have telephoned you. I did not think that anyone but myself knew your number. Also I have never heard of the—where was it?"

Nap repeated the address.

Madame Delboise asked him to hold on. In a few minutes she was back. "The message did not come from here," she said.

"All right," said Nap. "I thought that was it."

"What are you going to do?"

"I think I'd better go along and see what it's all about. We've got to cut our corners if we're going to get to the answer in time."

"All right," said Madame Delboise. "Only wait, if you please, half an hour before you set out. If you are asked why you did not come at once say that you were delayed by a long-distance call from England."

By the time he got out into the street it was dusk—a clear autumn evening with a frosty twinkle of stars.

The Rue de Piste turned out to be a long road, which

straggled out into the countryside northward, and by the time he had reached Number 115 he was almost clear of the town. It was a moderate-sized house of pink stucco, built, he guessed, since the war. Shop below and house above. The shop windows were closely covered with white iron shutters and seemed to be in darkness.

There were lights showing in the first floor.

Nap discovered a side door and pressed the bell.

For a minute or more nothing happened and he thought that he had not been heard. Then an outside light went on over the porch and footsteps came slowly along the hall. The door was opened by a very small, very old woman, dressed in black.

"Madame Delboise?"

She peered up at him blankly.

"Madame Delboise asked me to come here."

"You are Monsieur Rimbault?"

"Yes."

"Follow please," said the old woman.

She did not go back into the house as Nap had expected. Instead she threw her shawl over her head and hobbled quickly away up the alley which separated the house from its neighbor. She did not trouble to look back.

Nap had no choice but to follow her, but he could not help reflecting that if Madame Delboise's rescue party was stationed in a car down the road it was going to have to think and move fast. The alleyway they were going up was far too narrow for any wheeled vehicle.

The old woman turned to the right, went down some steps, turned left again. They had gone three or four hundred yards and were now approaching another main road, a road which presumably ran parallel with the Rue de Piste.

She stopped and indicated the side door of a house, which

stood ajar. It was an undistinguished sort of house, but Nap
could see that there were lights in the first-floor windows.

"Monsieur will go up. He will find the door on the left."

"Thank you," said Nap.

The stairs were steep and turned twice, and being lit
only by an economical blue bulb they were not too easy
to negotiate. On the landing were two doors. Nap knocked
at the one which showed a light. A voice bade him enter.

There were three men in the room and as soon as Nap
was fairly inside one of them moved across behind him
and turned the key in the lock. It did not need this gesture
to tell Nap that he had come to the right place. As soon as
he cast eyes upon the man who seemed to be the leader of
the three he knew what he was up against.

This was a big man, thick but not heavy, strong but not
clumsy. The coat cut more tightly than was necessary
across the shoulders and the biceps. The hair black and well
brushed. The twelve hours' beard across the cheekbones.
The brown eyes expressionless. A direct descendant of
Patron-Minette. Nap had met his like on many occasions.
He had seen him put against walls and shot, blandly de-
fiant, spitting on to the floor with delicate timing a second
before the bullets went into his body. He had seen him
using a machine gun and he had seen him using a knife. He
had seen him during the great retreat, bundling up the
bodies of Germans, alive, wounded or dead, like stooks of
corn, and tossing them into the back of a blazing oil truck.

"Sit down," said the man.

"What—?" began Nap.

"And keep quiet."

At a signal the lights were turned out. The window was
opened and they all sat in the darkness and waited. A car
or two went past, but none stopped. The bell rang again.
No one moved. Nap heard the old woman's footsteps in

the hall below and the front door opening. Steps coming lightly upstairs and a knock on the door.

The window was closed and shuttered, the light turned on again, and the door unlocked. It was the unpleasant youth who had spoken to Nap in the hotel in Rouen.

"He was not followed," he announced.

"Good," said the big man. "Get out the car, if you please, and we will go. Ramon will stay behind. Coco to come with me. You will drive." He nodded to the little man who disappeared again.

It was all perfectly professional, unemphatic, almost casual, and Nap had a cold feeling that he had walked into something which it was not going to be very easy to get out of.

"Where are we going?" he said.

"I know nothing," said the big man. "I do what I am told. You are going to see those who will be able to talk to you."

"The chief of the smugglers," suggested Nap.

There was a tiny check in all their movements.

"If you talk again," said the man, "I will fill your mouth with sawdust and have your lips strapped with tape. It will not be comfortable."

Three minutes later they were in the car, an olive-green Citroen. The little man was driving, and driving well. Nap sat in the capacious back seat between the other two men.

The car skirted Angers and turned west.

They were some distance out of the town—it was difficult to judge, in the dark, and at the speed they were going —but he thought they might have gone eight or ten kilometres when the big man touched the driver on the shoulder.

"Slower," he said, "and cut out your engine."

In the silence which ensued the big man sat with his eyes closed, his chin on his shoulder.

"We are being followed," he said at last, "by a car without lights. But we are near the turning now. I think they are too far away to see us."

The driver nodded. He had switched the engine on again and they were gathering speed.

Ahead of them was a long straight stretch of white road, running slightly uphill. At the top a bend. As the car rounded the bend and started to run down the other side the driver turned out all the lights. The car barely checked, made a sharp turn to the left, and they were in a small road. The surface was poor. Then left again, the engine was cut, and the car came to a standstill.

As it did so Nap heard the noise of two cars on the main road they had just left. They were big cars and they were going fast. They went past.

"Get moving," said the big man. "They'll come back as soon as they miss us on the next straight."

The car bumped forward, forked right, and came out on to what looked like a private drive. They bucketed along for about half a mile, descending gradually. The state of the road combined with the lack of lights to reduce their speed to little more than a crawl.

Nap guessed that the river lay somewhere ahead of them.

The car swung off the road into a field and stopped. No one moved. For a long minute they listened. There was no sound at all.

"All out," said the big man.

They walked together across the grass with their prisoner a pace or two in front of them. Nap's mind was obstinately blank of ideas. He realized that the big man had lied to him. He was not being taken to see anybody. That had been said to keep him quiet. He had been taken out to be killed, and killed he would be, quietly and economically, in a very few minutes.

Suddenly he saw the river. Not ten feet ahead of him it

winked under the moon, jet and silver. It ran in a great curve through the meadow which they were crossing and Nap guessed why they had come to this precise point. The river there would be deep, with the undertow of the current on the bend.

"Stop now," said the big man. They closed up on him. Nap saw that Coco was carrying a small sack over his shoulder and from the way it swung he guessed there would be weights in it. The little man had produced a coil of insulated wire.

"Hold out your wrists," said the big man.

Nap lifted his hands as if to comply. Then, as the big man stepped forward, he jumped. He was jumping for his life and he put all his strength and agility into it. As an athlete clears a vaulting horse, with his hands ahead of him, so Nap went head-first between the two men. He saw the blue glint of a knife coming up to meet him, but he was past and going away from the blow as it landed. A hot and stinging feeling in his side, then his hands touched a tussock of grass and he doubled up and his movement became a forward roll.

Then he was falling, and stars and moon were blotted out together as he went down into the cold black waters of the Loire.

Chapter Twenty-One

"Your name is Charles Edward Younger. You are the doctor attached for police duties to Q Division of the Metropolitan Police?"

"I am."

"Were you called to a hotel in Pearlyman Street on the night of March fourteenth of this year?"

"Yes."

"What time did you reach the hotel?"

"Ten minutes after midnight."

"You were taken immediately to one of the hotel bedrooms and there shown a body that you now understand to be Major Thoseby's?"

"Yes."

"You first examined Major Thoseby's body then at about ten past twelve?"

"Yes."

"How long, in your opinion, had he then been dead?"

"Well, that is a question I always answer with some caution. Of course, in this case, I was on the scene early enough to be reasonably accurate. I should have said, not more than two hours, certainly not less than one hour. Most probably nearer ninety minutes."

Doctor Younger then gave, at some length, his technical reasons for arriving at this estimate.

"Thank you, doctor. Would you describe, now, to the court, the wound which you examined—there was no doubt, by the way, that this wound was the cause of death?"

"None at all."

"Very well, then, what sort of wound was it?"

"It was a single deep incision. The point of entry was just below the sternum, three inches to the right of the ensiform cartilage. The wound penetrated the left lobe of the liver, passing upward in the direction of the left shoulder and into the heart. Such a wound would cause death in a matter of seconds."

"Omitting all technicalities, Doctor Younger, would it

be correct to say that the weapon which caused this wound was thrust upward, under the ribs, into the heart?"

"Yes, in a left-handed direction."

"You are of the opinion that the person who used the weapon held it in their left hand?"

"It is not a question of opinion. I am certain they did."

"Very well. You have seen this knife." A black-handled, long-bladed, kitchen knife, sharpened on both edges, one of the exhibits, was handed to the witness. "Was the wound consistent with having been made with a knife such as this one?"

"Yes, I should think that was about right."

"Would it need great strength to inflict such a wound with such a weapon?"

"Not at all. A heavy, well-ground knife like this would go in fairly easily, particularly in that direction."

"Could a woman have delivered such a blow?"

"Certainly—even a strong and determined child."

"You say 'in that direction.' Do I understand that it was a skillful blow?"

"Either skillful or lucky. A little lower, it would have caused a nasty wound in the bowel, but would not have killed—or not immediately. A little higher, and the blow might have been turned by the ribs."

"I want to put to you something that was said by one of the earlier witnesses." Mr. Summers read parts of Major Ammon's evidence. "Do you agree that this was the sort of blow that Major Ammon was describing?"

"Yes. This blow was certainly struck by someone standing in front of Major Thoseby, using the knife with its point upward, with a left-handed, underarm swing. I am not an expert on French Resistance work, but that is certainly the sort of blow it was.

"Doctor Younger," said Macrea, "I would like to go back to something you said at the beginning of your evidence. You said that you were always cautious in offering an opinion as to how long a person had been dead?"

"Yes."

"Does the certainty with which you can give your opinion depend on how soon after death you see the body?"

"On that and other factors."

"Certainly, other factors must count. But is the length of time the chief factor?"

"I cannot answer a purely hypothetical question like that."

"Very well. Let me offer you a concrete case. If you saw a body within five minutes of death what would be your approximate margin of error?"

"I should know to within a minute or two."

"Right. Suppose now that you had examined Major Thoseby's body within half an hour of its discovery. It had not been disturbed. It was in the same room as that in which death took place—or so we are assuming. How accurate could you be then?"

"In those circumstances, you should be able to tell within ten minutes either way."

"Thank you. I am not going to use these figures against you, doctor, you understand. They are agreed to be approximations. Now actually you saw the body about ninety minutes after it was discovered. And your estimate of the time of death, which you have just given the court, has a margin of error of sixty minutes. 'Not more than one hour,' I think you said, 'and not less than two.' "

"Yes."

"It is true, then, that the possible margin of error grows rapidly as time is allowed to elapse between death and examination?"

"Certainly. I have never denied it. If you allowed twenty-four hours to elapse you might find it difficult to say within six hours when death took place. It is very important that a doctor should see the body as soon as possible."

"Yes," said Macrea. "Then why didn't he?"

"Really, sir—"

"Don't misunderstand me, please. I am not imputing anything in the nature of professional negligence to you, Doctor Younger. I happen to know that you were summoned, from your flat, at ten minutes to midnight and you have told us that you were examining the body at ten past—I don't think that anyone could complain of slowness there. But I would like to know the reason for the delay of more than an hour in fetching you."

"Well—I can hardly answer that. I understand there was some confusion over the matter between the hotel manager, his waiter and the inspector in charge of the case."

"I see. We can recall one of those witnesses, if it seems necessary. But no doubt the inspector will be able to enlighten us when he gives his evidence." Macrea smiled at Mr. Summers, who took the opportunity of making a bad-tempered note on his brief.

"It is true, however, doctor, that if you had been on the spot by, let us say, a quarter past eleven, you would have been able to fix the time of death very much more accurately."

"Certainly."

"And if anyone wished to conceal the exact time of death one of the ways of doing so would be to delay the arrival of the medical expert who was to inspect the body?"

"I think that follows."

"Thank you. Now, doctor, in giving your estimate of the latest time of death you said, if I have you correctly, 'certainly not less than an hour,' and then you said, 'more probably ninety minutes.' I wasn't quite clear on that. Did you mean that ninety minutes before your examination was the probable time of the murder—or the probable short limit?"

"I meant the probable short limit."

"I see. That would take us back to twenty minutes to eleven."

"Yes—I suppose that's right."

"You have heard that the prisoner is alleged to have committed this offense at about a quarter to eleven."

"Yes. I—"

"In that case, doctor, it is your professional opinion that the murder probably took place before the prisoner's arrival on the scene?"

"I don't think you can use these times quite as meticulously as that."

"I only said 'probably.' I believe that was your own word."

"With that qualification, yes."

"Thank you, doctor."

"As I understand it, doctor," said Mr. Summers, "you established two time limits for the latest possible moment of death. One of them was an hour before your examination, the other an hour and a half?"

"That is so."

"Then would it not be fair to take the average of your two times and say that the latest *probable* time of death was an hour and a quarter before your examination?"

"Yes. I think that would be reasonable."

"That is to say, five to eleven?"

"Yes."

"Ten minutes after the prisoner visited Major Thoseby?"

"Yes, that is what I meant to imply."

"I don't think he knows now what he did mean," said Macrea loudly to Mr. Rumbold.

Chapter Twenty-Two

We must return to the early afternoon of Monday.

In London, Major Ammon was beginning his evidence for the prosecution. In Angers Nap was listening to Madame Delboise's views on the state of France. Some way outside Winchester Angus McCann, in an old tweed jacket and a pair of corduroy trousers, was strolling along the Newbury road reveling in the sights and the sounds and the smells which together made up for him the feeling of a perfect autumn day.

St. Augustine's Preparatory School for Boys stands a mile or two outside Winchester. You either know the turning down to it or you don't. Gussie's would never dream of calling attention to it. The idea of some sort of painted notice board would not occur to them. It would have been an advertisement. Gussie's does not advertise.

Fortunately McCann was able to stop a farm laborer on a bicycle, who pointed out the inconspicuous entrance, and he turned to the left and made his way down the winding gravel drive: a drive which has been trodden, at one time or another, by the little feet of the sons of some of the people in England who have really mattered.

It was a long drive. But no longer than it needed to be, for it ran back more than fifty years. This was not a matter of personal knowledge. McCann had been brought up in the Scots way at a big Edinburgh day school, but he had read his *David Blaize* and his *Vice Versa*, and he knew just what he was heading for. The drive dipped and rose again. On his left he glimpsed a gaunt building of yellow brick. It looked, he thought, uncommonly like a Nazi execution shed and with this thought in his mind as he drew level with it he was startled to hear a volley ring out. On reflection he came to the conclusion that it might be the miniature rifle range.

Another turn of the road, a thicket of eminently Victorian laurels, and St. Augustine's stood before him in all its peculiar glory of red brick, curly tile, glazed slate and exterior varnished pine.

A few minutes later he was shaking hands with the headmaster, Mr. Hughenden, a youngish but impressively bearded clergyman. "Perhaps you would like to come along to my study," said the headmaster genially. "We shall not be disturbed."

He led the way down a dark and echoing corridor where a hundred maroon blazers hung on a hundred pegs, up a short spiral flight of steps and into a turret room with mullioned windows.

"My father's room," said the headmaster. "I thought it a pity to change it."

McCann could not but agree with him. It was a perfect period piece. There were dozens and dozens of photographs of Old Augustans: in scholastic dress, in athletic dress and in the uniforms of four wars. There was a superbly dreary monochrome of the Ruins of the Acropolis. There was a fire screen embroidered with the Arms of Oriel College. There was a tobacco jar embossed with the Arms of Oriel College. There was a rack of pipes. There were glass-fronted shelves of classical authors in half-calf. There was a thin and sinister-looking cupboard in the corner which McCann felt certain contained a hunting crop. There was even a marble bust of Augustus Caesar, the most arresting feature of which was a prominent and—yes, no doubt about it—a slightly rubicund nose.

"We've never quite been able to get it clean," said the headmaster, following his glance. "It was done by young

Mornington, in my grandfather's time. He painted it with a strong solution of permanganate of potash, on the last day of his last term here. He got the V.C. afterward in the second Zulu War—but I don't think he ever did anything braver than that." Mr. Hughenden gestured with his head in the direction of the outraged Caesar. "Now, Mr. McCann. How can I help you?"

McCann told him.

"That's awkward," said Mr. Hughenden. "Just the wrong year. I was away myself then—at Theological College, as a matter of fact. I came back to take over in 1939. There won't be any boys here, of course, who would remember him. The assistant staff are all new—most of them since the war. There's old Montgomery, who retired last year—he lives in North Wales. You might get hold of him. He'd remember Wells."

"Oh, dear," said McCann. "Yes. I'm quite prepared to go to North Wales—but it's the time element."

"Yes, yes. Wait a minute. How stupid of me not to have thought of it before. Tim Evans. He was here as a boy in 1937 and he's back with us now as a master—come along and let's see if we can find him."

A further journey, through a maze of corridors, up one step, down two, and they found themselves in a large, untidy annex which could have been nothing but a masters' common room. The only occupant was a thick young man, with extremely long blond hair, wearing an olive green shirt with an off-shade green collar and a large black bow tie, who scrambled out of the ruins of a wicker armchair and said, "Hullo, headmaster."

"Oh, Evans, I wonder if you could—"

"Good heavens," said McCann. "Buster!"

"Blow me down," said Mr. Evans. "Angus."

"You know each other?" said Mr. Hughenden. "Well, that's splendid. That makes everything much easier. I'll leave you to each other. You can find me in my study if you want me, Mr. McCann." He pattered away.

"Buster," said McCann sternly. "What is all this? We were never a fussy crowd in our commando. There was little of the Brigade of Guards about us. But when the hair reached the collar at the back of the neck it was usually cut. Shirts were of a decently subdued color, the collar matched the shirt and—*where did you get that tie*?"

"I know, I know," said young Mr. Evans. "Take a seat —you can put that cup of cocoa on the mantelpiece—oh, and chuck that squash racket into the corner, it won't hurt it—it's a long story."

"Never mind the story," said McCann. "Just explain what you're doing here looking like a down-at-heels student from the London School of Economics—"

"Oh, I say. Is it as bad as that? Well, the thing was, that when I came back here to teach, I thought it would be a good idea if I—if I laid it off, a bit."

"Laid what off?"

"Well—look at it this way. If I let on that I'd been in the commandos and so on—you know what I mean. It takes an awful lot of living up to. Boys are such whole-hearted creatures, you've no idea. I'd have been expected to have a cold bath every morning in the winter and— why, good heavens, if a mad bull had appeared on the playing fields it would have been 'Send for Evans.' Life wouldn't have been worth living. So I just told them I'd been a conscientious objector all the war and had been do-ing agricultural work in North Wales."

"I see," said McCann. It was an aspect of rehabilitation which had not previously occurred to him. A picture of Lieutenant Evans garrotting a German sentry with a length of telephone wire came unasked into his mind. He dismissed it and returned to the subject in hand.

"Yes, I knew Wells," said Evans. "He taught us French.

I was a precocious thirteen at the time, and he was a sort of retarded nineteen. So there wasn't all that much difference between us. Actually if the truth be told, you know, I thought he was the tiniest bit out of his depth here."

"Why do you say that?"

"Well, after all—we're Gussies! We're a survival, a genuine nineteenth-century survival. Do you know that nearly half the teaching time here is still given over to Greek? That shakes you, doesn't it? We rank the classics nearly as high as games and several points ahead of religion. Cricket in the summer and Rugby football in both winter terms. We've got our own rackets court. Boys still settle their differences behind it, with bare fists. The headmaster is called the Doctor—he's only a pale ghost of his father at the moment, but give him another ten years and he'll get into his stride. He still uses a birch. A real, genuine birch, though actually between you and me I think he could do more damage with the business end of a gym shoe."

"I see. And you think that Wells—"

"The staff in a place like this are bound to be in character, aren't they? Most of them are old Augustans, anyway. Unless you've been brought up to it from youth your system wouldn't have much chance, between the food and the sanitary arrangements. Most of them are hearty, stringy types, with big knees. Quite harmless and easy to live with and about as much sex life between them as a hot water bottle."

"But Wells—"

"Definitely other. To start with it was pretty well known that he was living with the barmaid at the Mulberry Tree."

"Pretty well known?"

"I knew it, anyway."

"Yes. You told me you were precocious. It sounds as if it might be something. It's the sort of character we're trying to build up for Wells, anyway. Do you think we could have a word with the charmer?"

"I'm afraid she's gone. She wasn't here when I came back at the end of the war. Mother Potts may know where she is. Shall we walk down?"

"We shan't be able to get in. It's out of hours."

"Don't you believe it," said young Mr. Evans. "I've known the back way into that pub since I was ten."

They walked together across the playing fields. It was very pleasant in the autumn sunshine. On one pitch thirty tiny boys were being taught the art of Rugby football by their enthusiastic seniors. An open-air gym class was being instructed by an ex-sergeant-major who appeared to Mc-Cann to be using methods which the Army had abandoned just after the Boer War. A number of boys muffled in sweaters and scarves were running round and round the perimeter of the field dripping with perspiration. Everyone in sight seemed to be busy hurting himself or somebody else.

Buster smiled genially, paused for a moment to advise two boys to "pack lower and get their heads in," and led the way through the shrubbery, out of a wicket gate, across a road and into the back yard of the Mulberry Tree.

Mrs. Potts, whom they found in her parlor, was helpful.

She remembered Ivy, Miss Ivy Pratt. A nice girl she had thought. Cheerful and a worker.

"A fast worker," suggested Buster.

"Now, now, Mr. Evans," said Mrs. Potts. "You mustn't say things like that. What's gone is gone."

"Do you know where she is now?"

"Why, Mr. Evans, you don't say you're after her?"

"That's it," agreed Buster. "She lighted a flame in my heart at the age of thirteen which has never quite died out. No, Ma. It's my friend here. He's an insurance agent. If he can find Miss Pratt she will hear something to her advantage."

"There, now," said Mrs. Potts. "Think of that. Well, she went to Winchester—the White Lion in Priestgate. But I did hear a year or two ago that she'd gone on to Salisbury. It wasn't one of the big houses and, wait a minute and I'll think of it. It was a funny name. The Dean's Frolic. That was it."

Chapter Twenty-Three

Sergeant Walter Cleeve of the Fingerprint Department at New Scotland Yard. [*An extract only from his examination-in-chief by Mr. Trouncer, Mr. Claudian Summers' learned Junior.*]

"You took this knife for expert examination?"

"Yes."

"Would you tell us what you found?"

"Fingerprints and thumbprints were visible on the handle of the knife. It is a flat wooden handle, and a very good surface for the recording of prints."

"Were these prints examined against prints taken from all the persons present in the hotel on March fourteenth?"

"Yes."

"With what results?"

"Many of the fingerprints were old and so blurred as to be unidentifiable. I was able, however, to identify one set of three prints—prints of the middle finger, ring finger and little finger apparently—with the sample taken from the prisoner. There was a clear print of the thumb, also of the left hand, corresponding with the prisoner's thumb. I found in examination of the three fingerprints, sixteen, fourteen and sixteen points of agreement. In the thumb twelve points. I have omitted a number of partial fingerprints in which four, five or six points of agreement were obtained."

"Were any of the prints identifiable with any other person in the hotel?"

"Yes. A set of right-hand finger- and thumbprints were identified as belonging to Mrs. Morrison."

"She is the cook, who comes in daily?"

"So I understand."

"Were the prints—the prisoner's and Mrs. Morrison's—clear and sharp?"

"No. It was necessary to photograph even those prints I have mentioned in oblique light to obtain a clear picture."

[*In view of Macrea's admissions in cross-examination, a good deal of technical evidence is here omitted. Sergeant Cleeve produced enlargements of all the fingerprints mentioned above and these were circulated to the jury. This part of the evidence alone occupied more than an hour.*]

"One last question, sergeant. Can you give an explanation of the consistent blurring of all the fingerprints you obtained?"

"Yes. There could be a number of explanations. Such a result might have been obtained by wiping the handle lightly with a cloth."

"Sergeant Cleeve," said Macrea. "May I take that last point first. You use the word 'lightly.' It is not, I take it, at all *difficult* to clean fingerprints from a handle?"

"No, not at all difficult."

"A moderately vigorous polishing would do it?"

"Yes."

"And once it was done, none of your oblique rays and scientific tarradiddles will bring them up again."

"Once they are gone they are gone."

"Even beyond the reach of the Forensic Science Laboratory?"

"We certainly can't produce what isn't there."

"I am not criticizing you, sergeant. I would like to say that I thought you gave your evidence very fairly. I should like to clear the air by saying that we do not deny that the three fingerprints and the thumbprint already mentioned—and no doubt many of the partial prints—were all made by the prisoner. Why should we deny it? It was a knife she used almost every day of her life. My point is this, however. You stated that *one* explanation of the blurring of the prints—the way their outlines were dragged in one direction—would be consistent with their being wiped across with a cloth."

"Yes."

"There might be other explanations?"

"Certainly."

"Can I put one to you? That after the prints were made the knife was used—vigorously used—by someone wearing a glove."

"Yes. That might produce the same effect."

"It is at least as probable as the explanation that the handle was wiped?"

"Yes."

"In fact, even more probable—since, as you yourself agreed, a person wiping the handle, if he used moderate industry, would have wiped the prints out altogether?"

"It is difficult to say that one explanation is more likely than another."

"Quite so. They are equally likely. I am quite satisfied with that. Now another point. Would you take the knife?"

The knife was handed to the witness.

"Now, sergeant. Will you assist us by imagining that you are in the kitchen. You are preparing a meal. You are cutting up meat, or chopping parsley, or doing one or other of the things people do with a knife in a kitchen. Remember that the prisoner was left-handed in all her ordinary tasks. That's right. Use the edge of the box as a chopping block and show the jury."

Macrea swung round suddenly, and said in a very loud clear voice to a solicitor's clerk who seemed to find the sight of what the witness was doing amusing, "I should have imagined, sir, that if you came to a trial, at which the prisoner stood in peril for her life, you would have the manners to remember that you were not at a performance in a playhouse." He returned as swiftly to the witness.

"Now," he said. "Would you be good enough to re-verse your grip and hold the knife in the manner already explained in evidence—with the point upward. That is correct. Would you show it to the jury, please? Now you find, do you not, that your fingers are in a very different position to what they were before."

"I am afraid—"

"There is no need, sergeant, to tell us that you are not an expert on knives. We appreciate that. This is quite a simple point that I want the jury to see and I should like your help. You can be quite a passive agent in the matter." Macrea smiled genially and turned to the jury. "I hope you were able to observe," he said, "that when the sergeant held the knife for chopping or cutting—with the point, that is, straight out and the blade downward—his thumb was the controlling factor. It was pressed very hard against the top of the right-hand side of the handle. If he had been using his right hand, it would have been the left-hand side, but the principle is the same. Once again, if you would be so good, sergeant. You see what I mean? Now when he holds the knife point upward, for stabbing, the thumb hardly touches the wood at all. The handle is gripped in the crook of the fingers. Is that not so, sergeant?"

"Well, yes. It is. The thumb might be touching the handle."

"Touching, but not pressing against it."

"That is correct."

"So that the presence of a clear thumbprint in conjunction with the three fingerprints suggests that those particular marks almost certainly *did* come there when the knife was used in the kitchen."

"I shouldn't have said that it was a certainty."

"But very probably."

"Well, as you put it, yes—probably."

"Thank you," said Macrea. "That is all—oh, no. Wait a minute. There was just one thing more."

Only Mr. Rumbold, who knew him so well, guessed that there was anything at all behind Macrea's casual manner. Mr. Rumbold had seen it too often to be deceived. The close of the main cross-examination. The witness getting ready to step out of the box, relaxing. The sudden last deadly question.

"I take it, Sergeant Cleeve, that you made a general inspection for fingerprints in the room? I mean, you didn't only examine the knife?"

"Oh, no. We looked at everything."

"There was no lack of prints, I take it?"

"There certainly wasn't," said Sergeant Cleeve with a smile. "We found prints which we identified as belonging to the deceased, the prisoner, Monsieur Sainte, Camino, the last three occupants of the room, and a man who had been in two mornings before to see to the electric light."

"And all these were people who would have had legitimate reasons for being in the room at one time or other—?"

"That is so. We didn't make anything out of them. The prints were just what would have been expected in the ordinary use of the room."

"Quite," said Macrea. "I am sure you examined the room very thoroughly. Was there a fingerprint on the bell-push?"

There was a moment of dead silence.

"No, sir," said Sergeant Cleeve, "there wasn't."

"I see," said Macrea. "Thank you."

"Sergeant Cleeve," said Mr. Summers, re-examining. "Two points that my learned friend has put to you—the absence of certain prints from the knife handle and the blurring of existing prints—they would all equally be accounted for if—I only put it to you, as a supposition—the prisoner had herself been wearing gloves at the time of the murder?"

"Yes. That is so."

"Speaking as an expert, that would account for all these —er—phenomena?"

"Yes."

"Thank you. That is all."

Macrea grinned gently. He thought that his cross-examination must have been unexpectedly effective if it had sufficed to lead so old a bird as Claudian Summers into so lightly spread a net.

Chapter Twenty-Four

Eleven o'clock on Tuesday morning. The second day of the trial. At the Old Bailey Colonel Trevor Alwright was giving his evidence-in-chief. Nap was in a train, pay-

ing a flying visit from Angers to Saumur. Angus McCann
was walking across Salisbury Market Place.

Preparations were already on foot for the next day's
market. Damp men in leggings were hammering in the
posts to which, later, the hurdles of the sheep pens would
be lashed. The weather had broken overnight and the south
wind, which reaches Salisbury fresh from the Solent, was
lashing the fine autumn rain backward and forward across
the square. It was like being underneath a giant lawn
sprinkler, thought McCann, as he turned up the collar of
his raincoat. It came at you from every direction at once.

He was looking for the Dean's Frolic and he had to ask
twice before he found it, hidden away in the egg box of
streets which have stood, little changed, since the cathedral
masons struck for a rise of pay and celebrated their victory
by naming Penny Farthing Street.

It was worth finding: real beam and wattle, not fake
Tudor, the saloon bar had one of those smooth red brick
floors which must be trodden upon for a hundred years
before they come to their prime. There was a lot of clean
brass, a cheerful fire and, at that hour of the morning, no
other customer.

The beer wasn't bad, either.

"I remember this place well during the war," said Mc-
Cann to the stout gray-haired man who drew his beer for
him into a pint glass. He looked as if he might well be the
Jas Firmin who was licensed, according to the spidery
writing over the low doorway, to sell ales, wines and spirits
by retail.

"Ah—you'd have been in camp here, I expect." He didn't
really sound interested. It was just professional talk.

"Larkhill," said McCann. "1942."

That was a safe gambit too. A million gunners passed
through Larkhill during the war.

"I thought first," said the man, "that you might have been Air Force. Then I thought, no. Not enough hair-cream."

He even managed to put this one across mechanically, as if he'd said it a thousand times before. Probably he had.

"One thing I remember about this place—you might call it a feature of the place—that very pretty barmaid you had—?"

"Had plenty of them. What was her name?"

"Wait a minute now—I'm wrong." McCann took a long pull at his beer. "It wasn't when I was here in forty-two. It was when I came back again, in forty-five. Ivy. That was her name."

"Well, now," said the man. "So you're a friend of Ivy's." McCann caught the glint of amusement in his eye, and looking past him he saw that there was a girl, standing in the hatchway which led to the next bar.

He had to take a chance on it.

"Talk of the devil," he said. "What'll it be, Ivy?"

"A gin and pep," said Ivy.

McCann saw a brown-haired, sensible-looking girl of about thirty. She was quietly dressed, had good brown eyes, bad teeth, a generous mouth and an appealing band of freckles over the bridge of the nose. McCann thought that if he had met her anywhere else he would have put her down without hesitation as a nursery governess.

She poured herself out a gin, added the peppermint and renewed McCann's beer for him.

"And how are you keeping, Miss Pratt?" he asked.

"Can't complain. How are you?"

"I can see quite well," said McCann truthfully, "that you don't really remember me at all—"

"Well—"

"I'm sure I'm not surprised, either, when I remember the crowd of admirers that used to surround you."

Ivy downed half her drink in a gratified sort of way and observed that uniform changed a man so, you could hardly credit it.

"You don't even remember my skill on the 'double-in double-out.'" McCann gestured with his head toward the dart board on the wall.

"Oh—in the private bar, you mean. We never had a board in the public during the war."

"In the private bar," added McCann hastily. "It struck me you'd shifted it."

"You couldn't have a dart board out here, not during the war," said the landlord. "They'd have killed someone —those Canadians—no more idea of darts than putting the weight."

"I've never met a Canadian who could throw a dart," agreed McCann.

All this time he was thinking about tactics. In the end it was the honesty of the girl's eyes that decided him. It didn't seem to be a situation where anything could be lost by straightforwardness. In any case, other people would be coming into the place soon. Probably only the rain had kept the bar empty so long.

The man was busy polishing glasses at the other end of the room. McCann leaned one elbow on the counter and said, in a low voice, to the girl, "As a matter of fact, I've got a bit of news for you."

"Yes," said Ivy noncommittally.

"I ran into another friend of yours a few weeks ago. A chap I used to know in the Army. Julian Wells."

For a moment McCann thought she hadn't heard. Then he saw that she had gone very white. She opened her mouth and said in the tiniest voice, as if it was coming to him through layers of folded gauze, "No, no. You can't have done that. How could you? He's dead."

Then she fainted.

The crash brought the landlord running. Together they carried her through the partition door and into the private bar. There was a sofa and McCann put her down on it whilst the landlord went for water. Before he was back she was sitting up. She still looked bad.

"What's happened, Ivy?" The landlord sounded reproachful. "You did give us a turn."

McCann had been thinking hard. He pulled the man to one side. "I'm afraid," he said, "that it's something I told her. Bad news. It was my fault. Didn't break it gently enough. I think if you'd leave us alone for a few minutes. Could we have the door shut—?"

"You could slip the bolt," said the landlord doubtfully. "But it's licensed premises, you know. It's all meant to be open to the public."

"That'll be all right," said Ivy, who seemed to be recovering some of her spirits. "Say it's being redecorated. No one'll know the difference."

The landlord looked as if he would have liked to protest, but Ivy gave him no chance. She hustled him from the room and slid the bolt. Then she turned on McCann, with a dangerous light in her eyes and said, "Perhaps you'll explain what you mean by startling the wits out of a working girl."

Then McCann did his best to explain. It took some time.

"I see. You haven't really seen—you made that up."

"Yes. I thought I'd see if I could get some reactions—"

"You got some, all right."

She was sitting on the wooden settle, in front of the tiny window, and she was watching the fat raindrops running down outside the misty glass. Her mind was far away. Ten years away, McCann guessed.

"Look here," she said at last. "I'm going to tell you something I've never told anyone before. You know about me and Julian—when he was at that school?"

McCann nodded.

"Well, that was all right. We never went too far, if you see what I mean. And when he left and joined up, and I went to Winchester, I forgot about him. And that was that. Then, suddenly—in early 1943, that would have been, because I'd just left Winchester—before I came to this place I had a job in that big café in the square. One day he blew in, all dressed up in his second lieutenant's uniform and sat down at my table. Then it started again, just as if it had never stopped. You never knew Julian, did you? If you'd known him you might have understood that part. He was a very easy sort of person to love. He wasn't big and tough and strong and rough. Girls may marry that sort, because they think they'll be a success in life and look after them—the poor saps—but when it's just love, they pick the sort they like. And it's the soft, lost type like Julian that gets them every time—or it does me."

Ivy sighed, finished her gin, and helped herself absent-mindedly to another one out of a bottle under the shelf.

"That's how it was," she said. "We started just where we left off. I was happy. He seemed happy. He was stationed at Larkhill. He was a gunner, too, you know, before he started doing that secret-service stuff. Perhaps you may have met him then."

"No," said McCann. "I was never a gunner. That bit was lies, too. Please go on."

"There isn't much else to say. I didn't know till afterward that I wasn't the only one. I don't suppose it would have made much difference if I had known, come to think of it."

"You mean there was another girl."

"Yes. The wife of one of the staff sergeants at the camp. I never met her, but I heard all about her afterward, you can bet. There's never any shortage of a girl's best friends to tell her things like that."

"I imagine not," said McCann. He felt desperately sorry for the girl. Nor could he see how any of this was going to do Mademoiselle Lamartine much good.

"That's all, really. After that he went away to do his training for that other job. Then I heard he was dead. You bringing his name out suddenly, it gave me a turn."

"You never heard from him again? Before he went over to France—or even whilst he was there?"

"Not a sausage."

Ivy finished her gin and got to her feet.

"Why don't you go and have a word with Mrs. Staff-Sergeant Bellerby," she said surprisingly. "Don't say I sent you."

"Is she still about?"

"She was last Wednesday. Her husband got a permanent job up at the camp. I sat next to them both in the cinema. I didn't introduce myself."

"Perhaps I will," said McCann.

"They've got a cottage outside Amesbury on the Tidworth road. It's just past Stonehenge Inn, on the right. You can't miss it."

"I'll do that," said McCann.

He went out to look up an Amesbury bus.

It was still raining.

Chapter Twenty-Five

"Your name is Randolph Partridge and you are a Detective-Inspector in the Criminal Investigation Department?"

"Yes."

"In March of this year, you were the Divisional Detective-Inspector in Q Division?"

"That is so."

"And Pearlyman Street is in your division?"

"Was in my division. I am now attached to the Central Office."

"I see. On the night of the fourteenth of March of this year, as the result of a message you received, did you go to the Family Hotel in Pearlyman Street?"

"Yes, I did."

"Will you tell the jury, in your own words, what happened?"

"I arrived at the Family Hotel at about ten minutes past eleven in the evening—"

Inspector Partridge was a large, sanguine man; he spoke with the point and fluency which distinguishes the habitual from the occasional giver of evidence.

"I was met by Monsieur Sainte, whom I understood to be the proprietor of the hotel. He conducted me to a bedroom at the back of the premises, where I found the body of the deceased lying on the floor. It was evident that he was dead and the absence of any weapon raised a clear assumption that he had been murdered—"

"One moment please, Inspector. Was it plain to you at that point what sort of weapon had caused the wound?"

"It was clearly a knife wound."

"Have you, in your experience, ever known a knife used as a weapon by a person taking their own life?"

"No. A razor occasionally. Not a knife."

"Then that fact also would influence you in deciding that you were dealing with a case of murder?"

"Certainly. I acted from the first on the assumption that I was investigating a case of murder."

"Thank you. I wished that to be made quite plain to the jury in view of the steps you subsequently took. Please go on."

"I understood from the account given to me by Monsieur Sainte that all the persons who had seen the body had been asked, by him, to wait in the room next door."

"The room occupied by Mrs. Roper."

"That is correct. I found there the hotel waiter Camino, Mrs. Roper and the prisoner. I asked Monsieur Sainte to join them, which he did. Before questioning them I made a quick examination of the deceased's room. I found a knife."

The exhibit was handed to the inspector and identified.

"I understood that this was a kitchen knife from the hotel. I had it placed on one side for expert examination. I did not, at that time, find anything else of significance in the room. There was a half-unpacked suitcase and some papers on a bedside table which seemed to be notes of some conference at the War Office."

"Did you then, or subsequently, get any impression of what Major Thoseby had been doing when he was interrupted by the entry of the person who killed him?"

"It seemed fairly apparent that he had been sitting at the bedside table, writing or reading. There was a chair pushed back from the table, and the table itself was drawn out away from the bed."

"It is a fair deduction, then, that Major Thoseby was sitting at the table and got up when—whoever it was—came in?"

"I think so."

"Did you draw any further deduction from this?"

"Yes. I was of the opinion that it showed a slight probability—I don't put it any higher than that—that the person who came in was a woman."

"I object to that," said Macrea. "It's the purest supposition."

"I don't think," said the judge mildly, "that the answer was an improper one. A gentleman would, I think, naturally rise to his feet if a lady came into the room—but he might remain seated if a man came in. No doubt you will be able to deal with it further in cross-examination."

"I am obliged to your lordship," said Macrea. "I certainly intend to do so."

The witness continued.

"After searching the room I questioned all four of the people who appeared to be most possibly concerned. On the face of the evidence I dismissed from my mind, for the moment, Colonel Alwright and the guests who were still out of the hotel at a quarter to eleven. Also the daily staff. Neither then, nor subsequently, did there appear to be any evidence of an intruder from outside. I took statements, therefore, immediately from Mr. Sainte, Camino, Mrs. Roper and the prisoner."

The witness read relevant portions of these statements referring, from time to time, to notes which he had made of them. These statements did not differ in any significant particular from their evidence as already given.

"When you had taken these statements, Inspector—how long did this take, by the way?"

"It was nearly one o'clock by the time I had finished. By that time I had also received the first medical report, indicating the approximate time of death and I had had a further opportunity of examining the wound and the knife."

"And as a result of all this?"

"As a result of this, at about one-fifteen, I cautioned the prisoner and told her that I was taking her into custody on a charge of murder."

"Inspector Partridge," said Macrea, "you have told us that at the time of this investigation you were the Divisional Detective-Inspector in charge of Q Division."

"That is so."

"But since that time you have been moved?"

"Yes."

"On promotion, I hope?"

"Yes."

"Not as the result of any dissatisfaction over your handling of this case?"

"I am not aware of any dissatisfaction."

"You must excuse a layman's ignorance of police procedure, Inspector, but when you were called to this crime would it not have been the normal thing for you to bring a doctor *with* you?"

"I—yes—that would have been normal."

"But you didn't do so?"

"The message mentioned that the police doctor had already been summoned."

"And you relied on this statement?"

"Yes."

"A statement which unfortunately turned out later to be untrue?"

"Yes. As soon as I realized that, I had him sent for."

"Yes," said Macrea. "Most unfortunate. Most unfortunate. Now, Inspector Partridge—you have told us you were Divisional Detective-Inspector of this division. Any serious crime would, therefore, automatically be referred to you in the first instance?"

"That is correct."

"If, at any time, you felt in need of assistance you could apply for it from the Central Office at Scotland Yard—when a chief inspector would have taken over the case—working with you, of course?"

"Yes. It was open to me to do that if I wished."

"But you never did so?"

"No."

"You did not feel in any need of assistance outside the resources of your division?"

"No."

"Despite the fact that half the evidence in this crime was to be looked for outside this country—in France?"

"I don't think that is quite correct. Only the motive was to be found in something that was alleged to have happened in France. I should not call that half the evidence."

"Even when you were investigating the murder of a man who had done most of his war service in France, by a French girl, whom he was alleged to have met in France, in a hotel kept by a Frenchman with an Italian waiter who had spent all of his war service in France?"

"No."

"A typical English crime?"

"It was an English crime. A crime committed in London."

"You persist in that?"

"You will not intimidate me, Mr. Macrea."

"Nothing," said Macrea with a crocodile smile, "was further from my mind. Now, Inspector, would it be true to say that you have always held very strong views on this case?"

"No, I don't think it would."

"You have been engaged in a number of murder cases?"

"Yes. Quite a few."

"Can you recall any other case in which you have charged the alleged murderer within ninety minutes of your arrival on the scene of the crime?"

"No, I don't think I can."

"And that in spite of the fact that there was no case here of a confession or of any very obvious guilt? There were a number of conflicting stories and from them you arrived at so definite a conclusion that you immediately charged the murderer?"

"If I was reasonably certain of her guilt, it was my duty to charge her at once."

"Why?"

"For many reasons. Among others, so that she should not have time to destroy evidence."

"I see. Yes." This answer seemed to cause Macrea some satisfaction.

"If I may revert to my former question. What was there in the evidence—I don't mean such evidence as may have come to light now, but the evidence which you gathered in the first two hours—to make you certain of the accused's guilt? Or was it just an inspired guess?"

"Certainly not. I had the evidence of the weapon. I had evidence that the prisoner had been found standing over the body, which had just that moment been heard falling to the floor."

"You had Mrs. Roper's evidence on that?"

"Yes."

"Which, at that time, you had no reason to disbelieve?"

"I'm not saying I disbelieve it now. The attacks made on her character in cross-examination—"

"I beg your pardon?"

"I said—"

"Do I understand that you were in court when Mrs. Roper gave her evidence?"

"I—no."

"Then why do you refer to 'the attacks made on her in cross-examination'?"

"I have been told about them."

"I'm afraid I don't quite follow that," said Mr. Justice Arbuthnot. "Do you mean that you were allowed to read a copy of the earlier proceedings?"

"No, sir. It was talked about in my presence. And there were reports in the papers."

"Yes. I suppose that is inevitable. You realize that it is your duty to give your own evidence, and not be influenced by what other witnesses may or may not have said."

"I shall endeavor to do so."

"Now, Inspector," said Macrea, "perhaps you will deal with my question. You have said that you had the weapon and the evidence of Mrs. Roper. Was there anything else?"

"Certainly. There was the means and opportunity. There was also the motive."

"I see. You had already considered the question of motive."

"Yes."

Mr. Macrea fixed his monocle into his eye, leaned forward slightly, and said, "*At that time*, Inspector, what evidence had you about motive?"

The witness took a minute to think this one out. Then he said, "I had the evidence of Mr. Sainte. He told me that the prisoner had been trying to get hold of Major Thoseby for some time, and that he had come to the hotel to see her."

"And, in your opinion, a desire to see someone is a motive for murdering them?"

"No. But I gathered that there was something between them."

"Will you be more explicit?"

"I gathered that the prisoner had given birth to an illegitimate child and that the father was alleged to be Major Thoseby."

"Mr. Sainte told you this?"

"Yes."

"Very considerate of him. No doubt you immediately asked the prisoner for information?"

"I put it to her, yes."

"What did she say?"

"She denied it."

"I see. Then you had two versions of it. A first-hand denial by the party concerned and a rather grubby third-hand allegation by Mr. Sainte, who never even knew the prisoner in France. What made you prefer his story to hers?"

"He had no motive for misrepresenting the truth. She had."

"I see. I take it you agree that as an officer of police it was your duty to discover the truth. Not to take sides?"

"Certainly."

"And not to act as a special prosecutor."

"I have never done so."

"Very well. May I refer to you—possibly this is part of the evidence you have *not* read in the newspapers—something that was said by Sergeant Cleeve." Macrea read the latter part of Sergeant Cleeve's evidence. "Have you any comment on that?"

"No."

"You were aware that no fingerprint had been discovered on the bell-push?"

"Yes."

"Although the bell was in working order and the room had been in frequent use. Sergeant Cleeve spoke of finding the fingerprints of the last *three* occupants in various places in the room."

"So I understand."

"Did not the absence of any print from the bell-push strike you as significant?"

"If anything I thought that it told against the prisoner. It disproved her story that Major Thoseby had rung the bell for her."

"In that case, Inspector, would you not have expected to have found *some* fingerprint on the bell? Anyone pressing a bell-push is bound to leave a fingerprint—prints last, I understand, for weeks, even months."

"Possibly the bell-push had been dusted."

"Possibly. I can't help thinking that it was a very remarkable hotel if it was so. But don't you think that the defense should have been given the facts?"

"I do not agree that there was any fact to give them."

"I see. It wouldn't be true to suggest that you were suppressing any facts that told against your case?"

"I resent that."

"Then if a fact told plainly in favor of the prisoner it would be your duty to produce it?"

"If it told plainly in her favor."

"Even though it weakened the case being put forward by the police?"

"Yes."

"I am glad to have your assurance on the point. Now might I refer once again to the extract which I have put to you from Sergeant Cleeve's evidence. Am I wrong, Inspector, in detecting a certain change of theory in the police case?"

"I'm afraid I have no idea what you mean."

"I will try to explain then. At the outset of Sergeant Cleeve's examination by my learned friend the theory which he expounded—I do not suggest that it was his own idea—I take it that it represented the Gospel according to

Scotland Yard—was that the presence of Miss Lamartine's fingerprints on the handle of the knife showed that she used the knife to commit this crime. Not to chop onions, Inspector. To murder Major Thoseby."

"Yes."

"However, when, under cross-examination by myself, it seemed that the position of the fingerprints might rule them out for this purpose, then Sergeant Cleeve reverted —or perhaps I should say moved on—to a second suggestion. That if the murderer had been wearing gloves it would account both for the absence of what I might call 'lethal' fingerprints—and the blurring over of the existing 'kitchen' fingerprints."

"That is so."

"Well, you can't have it both ways. Which is *your* theory, Inspector?"

"Taking everything into account, I think it is very possible that the murderer wore gloves."

"I see. Well, I am glad to get that settled." Macrea glanced at his notes. "Now, Inspector, in examination you indicated—correct me if I am wrong—that Monsieur Sainte, as soon as he had seen the body, had all the people concerned collected in one room?"

"In Mrs. Roper's room."

"And you interviewed them in there?"

"No. I saw them one at a time in the empty bedroom— the one on the other side of the passage."

"And it was there, after interrogating her, that you cautioned the prisoner and took her with you to the police station?"

"Yes."

"It would be part of your duty, I take it, to have the room where Major Thoseby's body was found thoroughly searched?"

"Certainly."

"And Mrs. Roper's room?"

"Yes."

"And no doubt the prisoner herself was searched when she arrived at the police station?"

"Yes."

"And the results of that search were reported to you."

"Yes."

"Then you will be able to set our minds at rest at once. Did you find the gloves?"

"I—I beg your pardon."

"I asked if you found the gloves."

"No. As a matter of fact, I didn't."

"There were no gloves?"

"No."

"None at all?"

"No."

"Neither on the prisoner, nor in any of the places she had been in after the murder?"

"Well—no."

"Never mind, Inspector. You can always revert to your first idea. Or possibly you might like to put forward a third and entirely new theory. Possibly the murder was committed by a disembodied spirit with no hands at all."

Chapter Twenty-Six

Mr. Rumbold missed a good deal of the final cross-examination.

He was thinking about a conversation which he had had that morning, before the court opened, with Macrea, in his chambers. They had sat there together for half an hour, in the sunlight under the rows and rows of King's Bench and Chancery Law Reports, in leather bindings (sometimes consulted by his pupils, never so far as anyone could remember, by Macrea).

Not much had been said. They were old friends, both of them experienced fighters at law. They knew they had reached the storm center.

"The prosecution case will be finished by lunchtime," Macrea had said. "The only important witness to come is Inspector Partridge. I'll take him as far as I can on the lines of prejudice. After that we shall have to see what we can make of it from our side."

"Have you decided what line to take?"

"Well—there are two lines. We can simply put the prisoner in the box to give her version of the story and trust her to come through the cross-examination. I think the jury'll like her. She's so patently honest. Then we'll go all out on a plea that the prosecution haven't proved their case. In short, that a number of other people could have murdered Thoseby and the prisoner is by no means the most likely."

"Only if we have to," said Mr. Rumbold.

"All right. But we've got to think about it, because that's the way nine out of ten defenses do go. It's the easiest line and the safest."

"It may be safe," said Mr. Rumbold, "but I still don't like it. What's the alternative?"

"We *do* suggest who did the murder."

"All right," said Mr. Rumbold. "Let's do that. I think I know who did it, all right," he added.

"As a matter of fact," said Macrea, "so do I. But that's a very different thing from being able to prove it. However, let's look at the four candidates."

"Four?"

"Certainly. First Mrs. Roper. She's a crook. She had plenty of opportunity. She could have stolen the knife."

"On the other hand," said Mr. Rumbold, "she had no ascertainable motive—and she doesn't look like a murderer. She's not the right caliber at all. A little crook—and an associate of little crooks. Not a killer."

"I agree," said Macrea. "Then we have Monsieur Sainte. Quite another proposition. He struck me as being a capable and quite a ruthless person. He would have had every opportunity to acquire the weapon. He may well have met Major Thoseby. It is not difficult to imagine some sort of motive. Supposing he had been an undercover Gestapo agent?"

"Well, it's possible," said Mr. Rumbold, "but it seems a little farfetched. Surely they wouldn't have waited all that long to do something about it. The war's been over a long time."

"I agree. There's a much worse snag than that, though. How did he get up to Major Thoseby's room and back again without being seen by Camino and Colonel Alwright —supposing he did the job before half-past ten? Or by Mademoiselle Lamartine herself if he did it afterward?"

"Quite so. The sealed box. What about Camino?"

"Could have had some motive connected with wartime happenings in France. Again not very likely. He's the type who might use a knife—and there's no doubt he could have got hold of this one. He worked in the kitchen."

"Also don't forget it was Camino who delayed sending for the doctor. If he did the murder at all he must have done it before half-past ten, so it would have been important to delay the medical inspection as long as possible so as to confuse the time of death."

"I'm glad you were attending to my searching cross-examination," said Macrea with a grin. "Exactly the same objections, however, apply to Camino. How did he get up there? He daren't have left the reception desk—not with Colonel Alwright calling for a whisky every five minutes, and people liable to come in at the front door at any time. The risk was too great."

"All right," said Mr. Rumbold. "You said four. Who's the fourth?"

"My fourth," said Macrea slowly, "is an unknown man operating from the street at the back. The only thing known about him is that he answers to the name of Benny."

"But—how did he do it? How did he get up there and down again? Miss Box didn't say she saw a man *climbing* up. She said she heard someone *calling* up. Who is this unknown person, anyway—"

"Dammit," said Macrea irritably, "this isn't a detective story. The murderer doesn't *have* to be one of the principal characters. It might have been any old enemy of Thoseby's, who happened to choose that moment to finish him off."

"How did he reach the bedroom?"

"I don't know. There's a lot we don't know. We want more facts. Where's that son of yours?"

"I wouldn't mind knowing that myself," said Mr. Rumbold.

Part Three

Chapter Twenty-Seven

"It is customary," said Macrea, "for the defending counsel in a capital charge to open his remarks to the court by saying that 'he has never listened to a case in which such a serious charge was supported by so little evidence.' That, I say, is the customary opening. It does not apply to this case. In this case there is a great deal of evidence. Some people might feel, rather too much evidence. The difficulty is to examine such a body of evidence critically and to see what it means.

"Upon the primary point—about the basic fact—there is no dispute. Major Thoseby was stabbed to death, in that room. It is the duty of the prosecution to marshal all the relevant evidence—*all* the relevant evidence—I shall return to that point in a minute—and then to say to you: 'On this evidence we contend that there is only one reasonable solution. The prisoner murdered Major Thoseby.'

"That is their job. Have they done it?

"Is their chain of reasoning so cogent that you *must* say to yourselves, 'There is only one reasonable explanation. We are satisfied that the prisoner struck the blow'?

"I suggest that when you come to examine the evidence critically you will find no such thing. Rather you will find that it adds up to some proposition such as this.

"The prisoner *could* have murdered Major Thoseby. It was physically possible. She could have left the reception desk, walked up that flight of stairs, along that corridor, and opened that door. Major Thoseby would, no doubt, have got to his feet when he saw her. That is in accordance with the evidence. She could have pulled out that knife

191

and thrust it, upward, in the way she had been taught, into Major Thoseby's body. She could then have hidden the knife.

"None of that is impossible.

"But—and here is where I want your full and critical attention—" Macrea swiveled round and glanced briefly at each member of the jury in turn— "this proposition is supported, in a positive way, only by a line of evidence which rests on the flimsiest reasoning. The prosecution is asking you to say that because the prisoner was the only person in the hotel who had previously known Major Thoseby, the only person who had a history of association with him, the only person, *so far as we know*, who was making actual efforts to see him again—therefore, she must be the person who killed him.

"She knew him. She could have killed him. She did kill him.

"When the proposition is put as baldly as that, I hope you begin to perceive its weakness.

"I will deal with the two parts of the proposition separately, and in some detail. I will then conclude by summing up for you what I might call the additional, or extrinsic evidence.

"The prisoner knew Major Thoseby in France. It is not denied. But look what an elaborate structure the prosecution is trying to build on that simple foundation. An attempt has been made to persuade you on evidence so flimsy that I think I can, in this case, say without exaggeration that it is no evidence at all—that the prisoner and Major Thoseby were lovers. That Major Thoseby was the father of an illegitimate child, a boy, who has since died. The only positive evidence put forward in support of this is that the prisoner and Major Thoseby once spent a night together, with fifteen other people, in a barn!

"The danger of this sort of suggestion is that it is easier to make than it is to demolish. It instills a poison which it is impossible entirely to eradicate. However, I propose to make the attempt. Our contention has always been, as you know, that the father of this child was a Lieutenant Wells, a British officer who fell into the hands of the Gestapo, and subsequently disappeared. Now the normal method of establishing this would, I suggest, have been by examination of the persons most closely concerned. One of the candidates, however, has disappeared. The other has been murdered. Different methods will, therefore, have to be employed. And, at the last moment, as the result of our investigations, a reasonably convincing method of proving this matter has presented itself."

The pressmen all looked up.

"The defense is often accused of concealing witnesses and springing them on the prosecution at the last moment. I plead not guilty to that. The evidence about which I am now speaking came to light at four o'clock yesterday afternoon. We can hardly be accused of delay in bringing it to your notice.

"I will leave that for the moment and go on to point two. The significance—the only possible significance—of the often recited fact that the prisoner *could* have committed this murder lies, I take it, in its corollary: that no one else could have done so. The prosecution have themselves used the expression 'a sealed box' in this connection.

"Now it has often been said, and I will repeat it again, that it is no part of the defense's business to suggest who, in fact, did the murder, and I will not, therefore, attempt to do so. In the face of the above allegation, however, it is open to us to show that the 'box' far from being 'sealed' had a number of cracks or loopholes in it.

"I will pass over the obvious fact that at least one other

person—Mrs. Roper—had considerably easier access to Major Thoseby than did the prisoner—and will remark on two other points. First, at almost any time in the evening, an outsider, choosing one of those moments when the waiter Camino was absent from his post, serving Colonel Alwright with a drink—quite a frequent occurrence—any outsider, I say, could have made his way into the hotel and slipped, unnoticed, up the back stairs. He could then have hidden—in the empty bedroom—come out at his leisure later and killed Major Thoseby. All right so far, you say, but how did he get down again? There is nothing obscure about that, either. When he had killed Major Thoseby he *rang the bell* and retired to his hiding place. As soon as Miss Lamartine came past and entered Major Thoseby's room the way was clear. He calmly walked downstairs and disappeared.

"Now don't start saying to yourselves—" Macrea swung round on the jury again—" 'Oh, that's just a theory.' Of course, it's just a theory. But so is the prosecution's case. There is no more and no less evidence for the one than the other. Again, the prosecution has very lightly laughed away the idea that an outsider may have made his entry by ladder from the passage at the back. No real attention was paid to the theory. It was set up just to be knocked down. I propose to treat the idea with a little more respect. I shall be producing evidence for you that there *was* some sort of secret activity in that quiet passage at the back of the hotel—"

"My God," said the *Evening Echo* to the *Banner*, "Macrea's beating his own record. *Two* surprise witnesses—"

"You will admit, I think, that if I can make good my promises on these two main points—and I assure you I shall do my best to do so—then there will be very little of the prosecution's case left. If I can show first, that the prisoner had no conceivable motive for killing Major Thoseby, and secondly, that there *is* evidence that several other people had at least as good an opportunity, then you will admit that most of the positive side of the case has gone.

"Before calling my evidence on these two points, however, I should like to sum up for you what I referred to as the minor inconsistencies of the prosecution's case. Some of them have been brought out already in cross-examination. /

"First, there was the question of fingerprints on the knife. You all saw how the police witnesses were driven to shift their ground over this. At the outset we were meant to believe that the prints on the knife handle were the prints left on it by the prisoner when she drove that knife into Major Thoseby. This was shown to be, at the least, unlikely. Whereupon, there is a remarkable change of front. Now, say the police, the prisoner did *not* make the prints at the time of the murder. She made them in the kitchen. Therefore, she must have been wearing gloves at the time of the murder. An odd fact then emerges. No gloves were found either on the prisoner or on the scene of the crime, although the prisoner had clearly no opportunity for getting rid of them unobserved.

"Secondly, there was the curious spotlessness of the bell-push. Astounding hotel, where they polish their bell-pushes!

"Thirdly, there was the knife itself. Has it occurred to anyone to wonder at what precise point in the proceedings the prisoner is meant to have got hold of the knife? Did she take it with her to the cinema? Remember that after she came back she went straight to the reception desk and stayed there. She could not have gone to the kitchen without being seen by Camino.

"Fourthly, there was this peculiar, this elusive 'thud'

which Mrs. Roper either did or did not hear. You will yourselves have formed your own opinions on Mrs. Roper's reliability as a witness. But allow for a moment that she did hear this thud. Was it not an extraordinary performance? Can you visualize a girl walking into a room, walking straight up to a man she had not seen for three or four years, and sticking a knife into him? No words, no recriminations, no arguments, no threats, no tears. The whole thing accomplished as coolly as a surgical operation. Is that your idea of the character of the prisoner? Were her screams—the most horrible, one witness said, he had ever heard—were they then faked screams?

"Is it not an extraordinary character the prosecution are asking you to believe in? A woman who can nurse a passionate hatred for three years, and yet can be so unmoved when the time comes that she will not even stay in to meet her victim. It is her night out, so she takes it—a cool customer. She walks up unobserved and stabs Major Thoseby quietly, and quickly. Then, instead of creeping away again, she clumsily hides the knife *on the spot* and breaks into screams loud enough to attract everyone in the hotel—everyone, I should say, except Colonel Trevor Alwright, sleeping a soldierly sleep, on nine whiskies. I will be excused, perhaps, if I say that the whole thing looks to me like a jigsaw puzzle which has been half done by an inexpert child. Any bit that seems to fit has been left in. Any bit that doesn't fit has been disregarded.

"Now I say again, it is no business of mine to finish this jigsaw. If, when I have done, a recognizable face should happen to appear in the puzzle it will only be by chance. But let me at least demonstrate that the picture which the prosecution is trying to fashion cannot be put together.

"It simply does not exist."

Chapter Twenty-Eight

"Your name is Victoria Lamartine?"

"Yes."

"Now, Miss Lamartine, you speak English well—we can hear that—I should just like to ask you whether you fully understand and appreciate the significance of all that you hear."

"You mean, do I understand what goes on here?"

"Yes."

"Very well, thank you. I was puzzled by the former proceedings—"

"The police court proceedings."

"Yes."

"If there is anything," said the judge courteously, "that I can explain to you, I am entirely at your service."

"You are very kind. I understand now perfectly."

"Very well. Mr. Macrea."

"I wish it to be quite plain," said Macrea, "that the prisoner understands the nature of the questions that I am putting to her. A sort of convention has grown up that they are put to a prisoner at the end of the evidence. I consider them of sufficient importance to place them at the beginning. Now, then, did you kill Major Thoseby?"

The question was rapped out like a word of command.

"I did not."

"Did you have any reason to wish Major Thoseby any harm?"

"No reason at all."

"Was he the father of your child?"

"No."

"Very well, mademoiselle. I wish the jury to hear your

answer to those questions. Now, before dealing with the night of the murder there are one or two points I should like to clear up about the earlier history of this affair. I should like you to take your mind back to the events of September twenty-sixth, 1943."

"Shall I ever forget them?"

"Would you tell the court, then, in your own words, what happened on that day."

"In the early afternoon, after lunch, I was sent out by the patron, Père Chaise, on a mission. I had to take a message—it concerned the distribution of some arms and ammunition—to another Maquis post. This post was a farm—called the Ferme du Grand Puits. It was some distance away, and stood on a hill. I took a bicycle, and part of the way I rode, and the last part I walked, through the woods. It was very hot. It was about three o'clock when I arrived. The two brothers who owned the farm, Pierre and André Marquis, were out—"

"You knew these men?"

"No. I had never met them. In fact, I never did meet them. I waited for them until nearly seven o'clock, then I started back. It was not safe, in those days, to be out after dark. As it was, I went on foot, wheeling my bicycle by a way that I knew—not along the main roads at all. It was this that led to my capture. Had I gone by the road, one or other of the Maquisards who had been posted there would have stopped me. As it was, I got back to the farm unobserved and was immediately taken by the Germans, who were waiting there hidden. One does not complain. That was how it went, in France, in those days. You turned to the left, and you lived, you turned to the right and you died. One could not foresee everything."

"Yes." Macrea took a quick look at the jury to see what they were making of this.

"Now, mademoiselle, let us turn to your stay in England. You came here in 1947?"

"That is right. In May of 1947."

"After the death of your child."

"That is so. I came here to find work. I was fortunate to find a job at Monsieur Sainte's hotel."

"You were happy there?"

"As happy as I could be anywhere."

"During that time did you make efforts to contact Major Thoseby?"

"Yes. Many efforts."

"Can you give us your reason for this?"

"Certainly. It was through Major Thoseby alone that I could hope to find Julian Wells."

"Could you be more explicit about that?"

"Major Thoseby was of your Intelligence Service. His work in Germany was concerned with tracing the victims of the Gestapo. He was my friend. It was natural that I should turn to him."

"Quite so. And did he help you?"

"He did what he could. Toward the end, I must admit, I felt that his efforts on my behalf were becoming less."

"Why do you suppose that was?"

"I think he was more and more convinced that Julian was dead."

"You mean he had found no trace of him in the Gestapo records?"

"No trace at all."

"Did you think Lieutenant Wells was dead?"

"I knew he was not."

"You *knew* he was not. Did you have any evidence?"

"No evidence at all. It is a thing one feels."

"Very well. Now what happened in March of this year? We have heard that Monsieur Sainte received a letter from Major Thoseby."

"It came on March thirteenth. I remember it well. I was very excited. I was convinced he would have news for me."

"Did Monsieur Sainte show you the letter?"

"No. He told me of it at once, though."

"Very well. What happened next?"

"After lunchtime on the next day, March fourteenth, Monsieur Sainte called me to his office. He had been speaking to Major Thoseby on the telephone. He said he would be coming to the hotel that night. Imagine my excitement."

"One minute, if you please. I wish to be quite clear about this. Did Monsieur Sainte tell you that Major Thoseby might be at the hotel early that evening?"

"No. He said, as I recollect, 'Major Thoseby will be sleeping here tonight. He will probably arrive late.'"

"What time did you imagine that meant?"

"No time exactly—about half-past ten or eleven."

"That was what Monsieur Sainte usually meant when he told you a guest would arrive late?"

"Yes. For example, there was a train which arrived at Euston from the north at half-past nine. A guest who was coming on that was always referred to by us on the staff as a 'late' guest."

"Did Monsieur Sainte indicate that Major Thoseby might be at the hotel in time for dinner?"

"Not to me."

"Thank you. Please go on."

"I got back to the hotel that evening at about half-past ten. Camino was leaving the desk as I came in. I took his place."

"Did you say anything to each other?"

"We may have said good evening or hullo. I can't remember. There was no need for any explanation, you understand. It was our usual arrangement that I took the desk after my evening out."

"Was the lounge empty?"

"So far as I could see, quite empty."

"Was anyone else about?"

"No. I could hear Camino moving in the kitchen. Otherwise, it was quite quiet."

It was quiet in the court, too. Macrea let the moment hang.

"What next, mademoiselle?"

"The bell sounded. I was a little surprised. I had not known that room was occupied. Then I noticed the key was gone so I supposed it must be occupied. I went up."

"And then, mademoiselle."

"I found Major Thoseby."

"And then——?"

"Then I believe I screamed."

Chapter Twenty-Nine

On the previous afternoon, at about the time that Dr. Younger left the witness box to make way for Detective-Sergeant Cleeve and Nap sat by himself in the Public Gardens at Angers, looking at the monkeys, McCann was getting out of a bus at the crossroads by the Stonehenge Inn.

The rain had stopped and the washed gray uplands of Salisbury Plain stretched round him, bare, unchanging and unfriendly under a monochrome sky.

The six pink-and-white bungalows looked like six little intruders.

He walked up the short gravel path, between two rows of flat, whitened stones. There were a few marigolds, a few sweet Williams, the rest was a dreary jungle of Michaelmas daisies.

For a few moments after he had rung the bell nothing happened. A spotter plane from Old Sarum buzzed slowly across the sky. It was very peaceful. McCann had spent the half-hour in the bus coming over to Amesbury persuading himself that he was on a fool's errand. He would do no good. He might easily do harm. He had no idea what he wanted to say. He felt glad, in a cowardly way, that there should be no one at home.

Then a child's voice shouted something from inside the house and there was a shuffle of slippered feet down the hall. The woman who opened the door answered one question before she spoke. The brown hair, the plain but friendly face, the kind, slightly anxious eyes, the immature tilt to the nose—even the freckles. They were all there. He had seen them all before. She was a little older than Ivy Pratt, less carefully dressed than Victoria Lamartine. But in effect she was the same. McCann knew exactly what he was looking at. He was looking at the sort of girl that had appealed to Lieutenant Julian Wells. The real likeness between the three was almost as uncanny as the real differences.

He was aware that he had been staring.

"I beg your pardon," he said. "Mrs. Bellerby?"

"Yes."

"I'm McCann. I'm quite certain the name won't mean anything to you. I'm from London. I—look here—I can't possibly explain all this on the doorstep. May I come inside?"

He observed a flicker of distrust.

"I promise I won't try to sell you a vacuum cleaner."

"I'm sure you won't." Mrs. Bellerby smiled. "Please come in. I'm afraid you caught me—I was having my afternoon nap. I won't be a minute."

She led the way down the passage, showed him into the living room and disappeared. It was a neat and cheerful room. Perhaps the nicest thing about it was the view from the big window. The garden ran away, and over the low hedge you could see an uninterrupted piece of downland. The furniture was like the furniture of all the Army families everywhere. It looked as if every stick of it had changed hands at least a dozen times but had, at last, got resigned to it.

There were some photographs on the wall. One of a young gunner wearing a side hat and a cowlick. The other a picture of the same man, rather older, kneeling beside a monstrous-looking gun with six trumpet-shaped barrels, which had apparently just exploded in his face.

Mrs. Bellerby came back. She had done the mysterious things which women do to themselves on such occasions and look ready to entertain a duchess.

"That's my husband," she said. "He's clever about everything to do with guns. They terrify me. That one with six barrels is the only one in England, and he's the only man who really understands it, so they say."

McCann thought on the whole that it wasn't an act. He thought she sounded really fond of him. It made what he had to say somehow easier.

"I'm going to tell you a story," he said, "from the beginning. It's a true story. I'm leaving out one or two names, but otherwise I'm giving you the full strength of it."

She was a good listener. She only interrupted once, when he came to the trial. Then she pointed to the evening paper and asked, "Is this the Euston murder?"

"That's it," said McCann.

"All right," she said. "I just wanted to know. Please go on."

At the end she said, "How do I come into it?"

"The young officer," said McCann, "the one who disappeared in France. It was Lieutenant Wells."

"You didn't have to tell me, really," said Mrs. Bellerby. "I guessed. He's dead, isn't he?"

"Yes," said McCann. "Yes. I really think he must be."

"Poor Julian."

She was silent for a long time. It was getting dark in the room, but there was still a little light in the sky. She seemed to be watching the clouds.

"Poor Julian. What a—what a *person* he was." It was difficult to say whether she was laughing or crying. "He used to talk to me. You know he lived here?"

McCann nodded.

"He had ideas, about himself, and the war. He wasn't content just to be a gunner. He wanted to do something real, something—dramatic. I can't explain it. He tried lots of times to get into the commandos and things like that."

"We turned away fifty a week," said McCann quietly. "There just wasn't room for them all. You had to know someone—"

"I think it made him bitter—a little. He thought they were laughing at him. Then he found out that the one thing he had never thought about was the thing that mattered—his beautiful French. He really was good. He lived in France until he was fourteen and spent all his holidays there. When they found that out they were keen enough to have him. He did a lot of special training. He wouldn't tell me much about that—because it was secret. But sometimes, he simply couldn't keep it in. I remember him sitting there, playing with a little silver pencil, and saying that he could blow us all up with it."

"Just a boy scout," said McCann. He didn't mean it unkindly. It didn't matter, because she didn't seem to be listening, anyway. After a bit she said, "Have you got a photograph—of the French girl? The ones in the papers weren't very good."

McCann took out a photograph and pushed it across the table.

"She looks kind."

"I think she is that," said McCann.

"Did she kill Major Thoseby?"

"I don't know," said McCann. "I don't think so."

"What were you hoping to find—down here, I mean?"

"We were just casting around. It seemed a hopeless chance, the time was too short. But we wanted to find people who really knew Wells. I think you did, didn't you?"

"Yes," said Mrs. Bellerby. "I knew him all right. You know that we—?"

"Yes," said McCann, "I knew about that."

"I'll do what I can. I wouldn't want to give evidence—not about us—not unless I had to."

"Of course not," said McCann. He was out of his depth. "I don't know what the law is about all this. One of the things we wanted to prove was that it was more likely that Wells would be the father of the child than Thoseby. That he was the sort of man who—"

Mrs. Bellerby said nothing.

"Another thing," went on McCann, "we thought we might get hold of someone who had heard from him when he was in France. Messages did get out."

"Not a word," said Mrs. Bellerby. "I think you were right, though. He'd have written to me if he could have written to anyone."

"Yes, I expect he would," said McCann. "I'm afraid that's all that there is to it. I'll have to have a word with our counsel."

"How old would the boy have been?"

McCann took a moment to think what she was talking about.

"Vicky's boy? If he had lived—he'd have been almost exactly five. Why?"

It was dark in the room by now and very quiet. Mrs. Bellerby turned and looked full at McCann. There was just enough light to see that she was smiling.

"Say that again," said Macrea.

The telephone clacked and buzzed.

"Can you get 'em up here by midday tomorrow? Good work. No. I don't know how we'll use it. I'll have to have a word with her before I go into court tomorrow."

The telephone said something else.

"No," said Macrea. "Highly illegal, I should think. But I'll do it gladly for the sake of seeing Claudian's face."

Chapter Thirty

"Mademoiselle Lamartine," said Mr. Claudian Summers. "Have you ever killed a man?"

"Killed—you mean in wartime?"

"Certainly. I was referring to your experiences during the war."

"Yes. I have."

"How many men?"

"Only one."

"Who was that?"

"A German soldier, of course."

"Of course. How did you kill him?"

"He would have killed me if I had not killed him."

"I asked *how* you killed him."

"With a knife."

"And in what way did you use the knife?"

"If it will save you time, I will say at once, in just the way that the knife was used on Major Thoseby."

"Thank you. Whilst we are dealing with past history perhaps I could question you on one other point. You have admitted in evidence—or if you have not actually stated it, it has been made part of your case—that you had an illicit affair with Lieutenant Wells—"

"I do not understand, I am afraid. What is that, an illicit affair?"

Mr. Summers looked a little baffled.

"You mean that he was my lover?"

"Yes."

"That is correct."

"He and who else."

"I am afraid, monsieur, that you have formed your ideas of French girls from reading romances. We do not fornicate with every man we meet."

"Very well. Now perhaps you will answer my question."

"With Lieutenant Wells alone. No one else."

"You were aware that what you were doing with Lieutenant Wells was wrong?"

"Yes—I was wrong."

"Morally wrong?"

"Certainly."

"Thank you. I am only stressing this because the defense as I understand it have endeavored to cast a certain glamour over this matter. It is even suggested that times of stress and danger excuse indiscriminate behavior."

"I am sure the jury will know better than to believe any such nonsense," said the judge.

"I am obliged," said Mr. Summers. "Now, mademoiselle.

In the interval between your release from prison and the events of last March you made, I believe, a number of attempts to communicate with Major Thoseby. Why was that?"

"I have already told you."

"Possibly it was not very clear to me. Would you mind telling me again?"

"Because through Major Thoseby I hoped to hear of Julian."

"All right. I will accept that for a moment and amend my question. Why did you wish to get hold of Lieutenant Wells?"

For the first time the prisoner hesitated.

"Of course, I wished to see him."

"Why?"

"He had been—he was the father of my child."

"A child who was—you will excuse me for reminding you—some years dead?"

"That does not abolish its significance."

"Let us be precise, mademoiselle. Did you still wish to marry Lieutenant Wells?"

The hesitation was now plain. The prisoner did not attempt to conceal it.

"I do not know," she said.

"If you did *not* still wish to marry him, why were you going to such lengths to see him. Did you hope to get money out of him?"

"Certainly not. The suggestion is infamous."

"Then if you did not mean to ask him for anything, and cannot be sure that you wanted to marry him—we are back where we started. Why did you try to see him?"

"I do not know if I would have married him."

"Not one attempt, mademoiselle, but several. You were prepared, according to your story, to urge and press a very busy officer to make inquiries on your behalf. Yet you cannot be certain that you really wished to see the object of those inquiries?"

"Must I answer this question?"

"You have already said that you do not know," said Mr. Justice Arbuthnot. "If that is your answer then I cannot see that there is any need to add to it."

"Well, then, that is my answer. I do not know whether I wished to marry him or not."

"I see. You found him attractive enough in France."

"Certainly."

"Attractive enough to live with?"

"I have said so."

"On very short acquaintance?"

"Yes. Julian had a nature very sympathetic to a woman."

"Why do you say *had*?"

"Monsieur?"

"You spoke in the past. I understand that it is your belief that he is still alive?"

"Yes. I do believe that."

"Then why did you speak of him in the past?"

"I was confused."

"It would not be true to say that you have exaggerated the incident of your brief acquaintanceship with Lieutenant Wells out of all proportion. That you have made all sorts of suggestions *knowing very well* that he is dead and cannot refute them?"

"Certainly not."

"In order to conceal your very real and very unhappy relationship with Major Thoseby?"

"That is untrue."

"Yet you admit that you do not know why you wanted to see Lieutenant Wells?"

"There was some doubt in my mind—at the last."

"I see. Very well. We will leave it at that. Now on the day of the murder, you saw Monsieur Sainte and he told you that Major Thoseby was expected at the hotel?"

"Yes."

"There seems to be some doubt as to whether or not he told you that Major Thoseby might be there in time for dinner?"

"There is no doubt in my mind."

"Very well. We will say that there are two versions of what occurred. It is not in dispute that you decided to take your evening off, as usual?"

"That is so."

"We have heard that you went to the cinema. By the way—" Mr. Summers' manner was a shade overcasual— "perhaps you would tell us what film you saw?"

"I did not go to the cinema."

"Oh, indeed. I believe Mr. Macrea stated—" Mr. Summers ruffled his papers.

"I did not say that I went to the cinema. Usually I went to the cinema. On that night, not."

Macrea said something testy to Mr. Rumbold, and scratched a note on his brief.

"Then perhaps you would tell the court what you did do."

"I had dinner first, at La Coquille. I did not hurry myself. It was after nine o'clock before I finished. Then I walked."

"Where did you walk to?"

"I do not know."

"Do you mean to tell the court that you have no idea where you went?"

"In London I never know where I go. When I have finished walking I take a bus back to somewhere I know."

"I see. Why did you have this sudden desire for exercise?"

"I beg your pardon."

"Can you tell us why you took this walk?"

"Because I wished to think."

"About what?"

"About what you have already questioned me—whether I still wished to marry Julian."

"Stalemate," said Macrea, who had been placidly watching this conversation come round in a circle. "She's a beautiful witness, isn't she? I wish she'd told me about the cinema, though."

"At what time, then, did you get back to the hotel?"

"At half-past ten."

"Who did you see when you got back?"

"Camino the waiter."

"Did you say anything to him?"

"I may have said good night."

"Nothing else?"

"I cannot remember saying anything else."

"Isn't that rather extraordinary?"

"I am afraid I do not understand you."

"Did you not ask whether Major Thoseby had arrived?"

"No. I cannot explain why, but I did not."

"Then I repeat my question. Is not that rather extraordinary?"

"Perhaps it seems so. I imagine that I thought that if he had arrived Camino would have told me."

"You imagine that you thought . . . That is a very qualified answer, mademoiselle. Can you not be more precise?"

"I am sorry."

"Would it not be true to say that you were determined at all costs *not to know* that Major Thoseby had arrived?"

"I do not understand."

"Is that not why you went out—although he was expected that evening. Why you took care to arrive back

exactly at half-past ten. Why you deliberately said nothing
to Camino?"

"You are inventing."

"I am making a suggestion."

"It is not true."

"Very well. Some ten or fifteen minutes later one of the
bedroom bells sounded. A telltale dropped in the indicator
board?"

"Yes."

"Showing that the occupant of Number 34 bedroom re-
quired your services?"

"Yes."

"You say that until that moment you had not known
that Number 34 bedroom was occupied?"

"I have said so. That is correct."

"If it had been occupied—earlier in the evening, I mean,
before you went out—you would have known about it?"

"Certainly."

"Then you knew that during your absence a guest had
arrived?"

"Yes."

"One guest only?"

"Yes."

"Did it occur to you that it might be Major Thoseby?"

"At the time, no."

"Is not that rather extraordinary?"

"I cannot explain the workings of my mind."

"You knew Major Thoseby was expected. You had
been trying to see him for years. You were eagerly looking
forward to his arrival. During the greater part of your evening you were thinking, as you admit, of matters connected
with him. When you came back, you find that a guest—
one guest—has arrived."

"Yes."

"And you wish the court to believe that it never occurred to you that it might be Major Thoseby?"

"I can only say—that is the truth."

"Hm! Very well, mademoiselle, what happened next?"

"I went upstairs."

"Yes."

"I knocked on the door. There was no answer. I knocked again and went in. I saw Major Thoseby."

"You recognized him at once?"

"Certainly. He was lying on the floor, his head was on one side. I could see his face."

"I see; and then?"

"Then I believe I screamed."

Chapter Thirty-One

It was late in the afternoon when Macrea rose to re-examine. The lights in the court had not yet been turned on, and in the lengthening shadows the observers in the gallery thought that his face looked unusually grim.

"Just two or three points arising out of my learned friend's questions. You said that you were in some doubt as to whether you still wished to marry Lieutenant Wells?"

"Yes. I said so."

"However, that is not, I take it, the same as saying that you were in doubt as to whether you wished to meet Major Thoseby?"

"Certainly not. Him I was always anxious to see."

"I mention this because the two things seem in danger of becoming confused. Your immediate wish was to see Major Thoseby?"

"Yes."

"And to have a few words with him?"

"I wished to know what he had found out. I understand that this time his information would be definite. What has happened to Julian? Whether or not he was still alive?"

"Quite so. And having got this information—if his information was that Lieutenant Wells was alive, and that you could see him—then you could make up your mind whether or not you really wished to take any further steps?"

"Yes."

The crime reporter of the *Banner* was a sharp and observant young man. It occurred to him at this point that Macrea was being unusually heavy-handed. Not only this, it occurred to him also that he seemed to be doing it on purpose. The point he was making was not a very profound one, and yet he was dragging it out as if—

Almost as if he was waiting for something. Something unconnected with the cross-examination.

With this idea in his mind he allowed his eyes to stray round the body of the court and he was thus the only person to see exactly what did happen.

A whispered confabulation at the door, the quiet entry of a woman. Nothing very remarkable about her. A plain good-tempered face, brown hair, light eyes. Not unlike the prisoner, he thought. She had a boy with her. A child of about five. At a word from the attendant, a space was made, and they sat down quietly together on the end of the front bench.

"I have one more matter to put to you." Macrea had drawn himself up and his voice had changed. It was no louder, but it had the clean edges of a word of command. He held all eyes for a moment.

"In cross-examination it has once again been suggested that Major Thoseby was the father of your child?"

"That is not so."

"The father was Lieutenant Julian Wells?"

"Yes."

"Mademoiselle. Is there anyone in court that you recognize?"

There was a moment of complete silence. By some instinct all eyes seemed to turn towards the newcomers. The boy, frightened by the sudden attention, caught hold of the arm of the woman beside him.

"Jules." It was the faintest whisper. "Jules."

The prisoner swayed for a moment. Then she seemed to be trying to leave the witness box.

A wardress laid a hand on her arm.

Then she started to scream.

Chapter Thirty-Two

"I have closed the court, Mr. Macrea," said Mr. Justice Arbuthnot, "in order that your explanations, if any, may be given to myself and the jury alone. If they are not satisfactory, I shall have to consider whether it is not my duty to empanel a new jury and take the case again."

"My lord—" began Macrea. He sounded contrite but not overwhelmed; it was in cases like the present that his long career of legal guerrilla stood him in good stead. "My Lord, I am very glad that you have decided, in view of this interruption—may I say, the *quite unforeseen* interruption—to take this part of the hearing *in camera*. It will allow me to explain very much more fully than would perhaps have been the case in open court how the recent unfortunate occurrence came about."

"Very good, Mr. Macrea."

"I trust," said Claudian Summers waspishly, "that the explanations will not prove more irregular than the circumstances that have given rise to them."

"I can assure my learned friend," said Macrea, "that anything I may say now could properly be put in evidence and will be so put if his lordship rules. My meaning was that this evidence closely concerns the private life and happiness of a third party who has no direct connection with this case. I am, therefore, glad that the opportunity should be given to discuss it, first, in closed court."

"On those grounds then—" said the judge.

"My lord. One of the greatest difficulties which the defense has labored under in this case—I have touched on it before—is that an allegation has been made which we believe to be false but which we have no normal method of disproving. The alleged motive here turns entirely on the parentage of a dead child. The prosecution says that Major Thoseby was the father. The defense says Lieutenant Julian Wells. That is the matter in a nutshell. Unfortunately one of these men is dead, the other has disappeared. The child is in a French grave. All ordinary methods, therefore, of proving or disproving this allegation fall to the ground. The prisoner, of course, gives her testimony and states that the father was Lieutenant Wells. I do not expect this to carry much weight, since, whichever way you look at it, she is bound to be a biased witness.

"What must the defense, then, do? Admit the damning suggestion? Or use every legitimate method of casting doubt on it?

"You will have noticed that in my cross-examination, I put to every witness who was likely to have knowledge of the matter, the following proposition. In your opinion was Major Thoseby a man to have immoral associations with women? You heard the answers. A clear negative in each case. On the other side of the proposition, evidence was harder to come by and was bound to be a delicate matter to produce. But I was convinced that Lieutenant Wells was the type of man who is, by nature, a pursuer of women. A lady has come forward—and it is a great credit to her that she has done so—and she is prepared, if your lordship rules her evidence to be admissible, to tell the court that she was living with Lieutenant Wells shortly before he left this country for France. I hope that her name will be withheld from the press reports and that she will be given the protection of the court. If it is thought desirable, I am ready to produce a *second* lady who will also testify to a similar course of conduct on the part of Lieutenant Wells."

"By this testimony, Mr. Macrea," said the judge, "are you hoping to establish the positive proposition that Lieutenant Wells was a man who was inherently likely to have immoral relations with any woman he met?"

"Yes, my lord. I am hoping to establish that, and something further. I am hoping to show that a certain type of woman made an especial appeal to him. A type which I should describe as a small brunette, of pleasant rather than aristocratic features. A type, may I add, to which the prisoner demonstrably belongs."

"I do not know what Mr. Summers has got to say about all this," said the judge doubtfully.

"With respect, my lord," said Mr. Summers who was clearly bursting to say a good deal, "I think the proposition is nonsensical. I do not think that the dictates of passion can be classified in any such analytical way. You cannot lay it down that certain types of men appeal to women, or that certain types of women only appeal to certain men."

"My learned friend is oversimplifying my proposition,"

said Macrea. "I do not think that the physical type of the man has anything very much to do with the matter. I do not believe, for instance, that women are necessarily attracted to a man because he is large, strong, athletic or superficially handsome. Indeed, if we may judge by some of the notorious lady-killers who have from time to time come before the criminal courts of this country, they were often small, timid-looking, sometimes rather effeminate men. Possibly such a type arouses some maternal instinct in women which later turns to passion when it is reciprocated—I do not know. What I am certain about is this. A man either is or is not a 'lady's man.' Further, if he is, then human nature being what it is, his friends will know about it. You will recollect I put precisely this point to two witnesses. And you will remember their answers. The English witness agreed with me. The Frenchman did not. I must confess that I prefer the English viewpoint. It may well be that Frenchmen are more reticent than we are in affairs of the heart. I simply do not believe that any Englishman will be a 'squire of dames' without his friends knowing all about it."

"In the United States of America," observed the judge unexpectedly, "I believe such a man is described as a 'wolf.' "

"I believe that is so," agreed Macrea, "though, as I have indicated above, the description may often prove superficially misleading."

"Very well," said the judge. "I am certain that the jury are sufficiently men and women of the world to form their own opinion." The jury all looked down their noses in a gratified way. "I shall rule that this witness may be heard— I think one witness will be sufficient, Mr. Macrea—on the grounds that her testimony may help us in the specific manner you have indicated. I must confess, however, that I am still a little at a loss to understand—"

"If I might make the matter clear," said Macrea. "I had hoped to introduce this new witness simply in the role of Lieutenant Wells's former lover. I was told that he carried a photograph of her in his pocket when he went to France. It occurred to me—such things do happen, odd though it may seem—that he may well have shown it at some time or other to the prisoner. If he had done so, and the prisoner had been able to identify the witness, her position in the matter would have been established without a number of embarrassing questions."

"I see," said the judge doubtfully. "And the boy?"

"Shortage of household help," said Macrea promptly, "was alone responsible for such an unfortunate occurrence. She came up to London at very short notice from Amesbury, where her husband is stationed, and having nowhere to leave the boy was forced to bring him with her. That the prisoner, in the darkness of the court, should have mistaken him for her own dead child is a contretemps which upset me as much as it did anyone else—"

Chapter Thirty-Three

"Your name is Irene Durvier?"

"Well—that's my professional name."

"Your—?"

"My stage name. My real name is Iris Box."

"I see—now, Miss Box, I understand you have something to tell us about the night of March fourteenth."

"That's right."

Without undue prompting, and with reasonable clarity, Miss Box then told the court what she had already told Mr. Rumbold and had later repeated for Macrea. She told how she had celebrated her birthday. How she had eaten and drunk with her friends—"not that I was paying for the party. I was far too broke. It was strictly a Dutch treat"—and had eventually set out, at about twenty-five past ten to walk, from the neighborhood of Gower Street, to her lodgings in Mornington Crescent. How she had sat down, for a few minutes of rest and reflection, on the low coping of the wall in Pearlyman Passage. How she had heard an unknown voice, from the darkened windows of a building which she now knew to be the Family Hotel, whispering the name Benny.

Mr. Summers rose to cross-examine with something like satisfaction. There were moments in the case which had shaken him considerably. He considered that Macrea's tactics had verged on the unprofessional—had indeed at more points than one passed right over the verge line. But this was the sort of witness he appreciated. There was nothing he liked more than a witness, preferably a member of the public, who came forward at the last moment with unexpected testimony in a murder trial.

"Now, Miss Box," he said briskly, "will you tell the court why you are here."

"Why—I'm afraid I don't understand, sir."

"It's a plain question, surely."

"Well—when I read about the case—"

"You read about it? Where?"

"In the newspapers."

"I see. Please go on."

"Well—I read it in the newspapers, and I said to Daisy —that's the girl I share a room with—'Why, that's just about the place where I sat down that night'—and Daisy said—"

"I am afraid, Miss Box," said the judge, "that what your

friend said to you is not strictly evidence in this case. You must confine yourself to indicating what you did."

"Oh, certainly, your lordship," said Miss Box, considerably flustered at this judicial intervention. "Well, I went back to make sure."

"You went back to Pearlyman Street?"

"That's right."

"And before that you had no real idea where it was you had sat down that night?"

"Well, no. It was very dark, of course."

"Of course. But once you had seen it by daylight you were quite certain?"

"Well, I had to look round a bit, and then I found the wall I had sat down on, and there it was—the hotel, I mean."

"Was this wall the only wall in the street?"

"It was the only one just there."

"I'm afraid I don't understand that."

"It was the only one opposite the hotel."

"Oh, I see," Mr. Summers smiled indulgently. "It was the only one opposite the hotel. Quite so. There were other walls, but they were opposite other houses?"

"Yes. But I'm sure this was the one I sat on."

"And what makes you so sure, Miss Box? Was there something particular about it?"

"Not exactly. But I know I'd come a certain way along the street, and then I came to this wall—and—that was the one I recognized when I came back to look at it."

"I see. Yes. There was, of course, a considerable interval of time, Miss Box, between your two visits to Pearlyman Street. The first visit was on the night of March fourteenth and the second one was not until after you had read the police court proceedings in the papers—August of this year, that would be?"

"Yes, I suppose that's right."

"And even after that length of time you were able to identify the particular—er—wall on which you sat?"

"Well—yes. I'm fairly certain that was the one."

"Fairly certain?"

"Yes. Pretty certain. It's difficult to be quite certain."

"I entirely agree with you," said Mr. Summers suavely. "Now on this first occasion—the night of March fourteenth. It was your birthday?"

"Yes."

"And you had been having a little party?"

"That's right."

"A certain amount of drinking—I don't suggest that anyone had drunk too much—?"

"Well, it wouldn't be a party unless you had something to drink, would it?"

"I suppose not."

"And you can't go too far on beer."

"As to that," said Mr. Summers, "being a total abstainer myself, I would not be able to give any useful opinion. No doubt some of the jury are beer drinkers and will be able to form their own opinion. It would be true to say, however, that you had taken a glass or two of beer, and that you were walking home on what you have already mentioned was a very dark night, and that you sat down for a minute or two to rest?"

"Yes."

"Now, Miss Box—" Mr. Summers leaned forward, a picture of earnest kindliness—"is it not possible—I will put it no higher than that—is it not *possible* that you were mistaken?"

"I'm afraid I don't understand. Do you mean that I am making up—"

"Please, please. Don't misunderstand me. I willingly accept that everything happened exactly as you have told us. But is it not conceivable that in all those many little streets that you had to pass through in walking between Gower Street and Mornington Crescent—is it not conceivable that you sat down to rest at some other place than the back of the Family Hotel?"

"Well—if you put it like that—yes, I suppose it is possible."

"I do not know how many streets you had to pass through—how many houses you had to pass behind—how many walls you might have rested on—dozens, certainly. Perhaps even hundreds. I am simply suggesting—it is no possible criticism of your veracity—that when you went back *five months later* you selected the wrong one."

Mr. Summers accompanied this with a broad smile in the direction of the jury, as much as to say, "See how considerately I'm treating this witness. You and I know perfectly well that she was so tight at the time that she wouldn't have known whether she was sitting on Noah's Ark or Nelson's Column, but we mustn't hurt her feelings, must we?"

"I suppose that's right," said the witness unhappily.

"Now, Miss Box—" Mr. Summers' voice took on a sterner note. "You probably know that in every criminal case—every sensational criminal case, the police invariably receive a number of communications from members of the public, who wish, from motives of notoriety, to identify themselves with the case?"

"I—"

"One minute, please. I am not suggesting that here. I am merely illustrating the point I wish to put to you. Is it not possible that the same sort of cause has produced a different effect? You read an account in the papers of this crime?"

"Yes."

"Several accounts?"

"Yes. I read it in most of the papers."

"Quite so. You were interested in it?"

"Certainly. Because I thought—"

"I am suggesting—it's no more than a suggestion—that the idea that this house you sat behind on the night of March fourteenth came into your head, in the first instance, from those accounts. Then you went back to look—and it is not surprising that you found that it was so—"

"I'm not sure that I understand."

"Counsel is suggesting," said the judge kindly, "that you read about the hotel in Pearlyman Street, that you remembered that you must have passed through or near Pearlyman Street on the night these things happened, and that you, therefore, came to the conclusion that the house you took a rest behind on that night was the Family Hotel."

"Well, I don't know, sir. I'm sure I thought it was the house I sat down behind that night. I wasn't making it up. It did happen as I said. But whether or not it really was the house, I thought I could swear to it, but now I'm not sure—or that is to say, I'm not so sure as I was when this gentleman started asking me questions."

"Your witness," said Mr. Summers, sitting down resignedly.

"Miss Box," said Macrea, "when you finally made up your mind to come forward and give evidence in this case, did you discuss the matter with your friends?"

"Oh, yes. I did. I talked it over with several of them."

"And what was their advice?"

"They said I'd be a fool to do anything of the sort."

"I see. Did they give any reason for their opinion?"

"They said I'd be asked a lot of nasty questions and

anything I said would be sure to be twisted round till it meant something else—"

"Thank you," said Macrea. "Thank you."

That night, after the court had closed Macrea and Mr. Rumbold sat late in counsel's chambers in King's Bench Walk.

Both men were tired, but they were past the stage where they felt very much desire for sleep.

Their minds still pecked at the case, in a desultory way, as an overfed chicken might peck at a plate of scraps; not wanting the food but anxious that no titbit should escape.

"I was afraid Summers would tie up Miss Box," said Macrea. "Ever since the Yarmouth case that sort of witness has been meat for counsel. He only has to mention the 'notoriety' angle and the jury automatically disbelieve every word the witness says."

"Yet you called her?" said Mr. Rumbold.

"I had to." Macrea sounded irritable. "I've got a feeling that in a case like this, in the long run, a grain of truth is going to be worth a peck of prejudice. I believe Miss Box did sit behind the Family Hotel that night. I believe it was just about the time when Major Thoseby was being killed. And I believe that somebody did call somebody else Benny. When the truth comes out that's going to be one of the tiny little pieces that will fit and clinch the matter."

"Will the truth come out?" said Mr. Rumbold.

The room was so quiet that it might have been listening for the answer. The long shelves of lawbooks were in shadow, the reflected light from the green reading lamp engraved dark lines on the tired faces of the two men. From the direction of the Embankment came up, faintly, the double hoot of a ship's siren.

"This may shock you," said Macrea. "I was going to say

that it didn't seem to me to matter. I think the truth will
come out—sometime. I'm fairly confident that Miss Lamartine won't be found guilty. You can never be quite certain
with a jury, but that's what I feel about it. I can't be certain
that they'll acquit either. A disagreement seems the most
likely. But it'll be the sort of disagreement with too much
doubt in it to make a retrial popular. The British public
don't love retrials."

"Well, I suppose that will be a sort of a happy ending,"
said Mr. Rumbold. "But, you know, it won't satisfy me a
bit. I haven't got a technical mind. I want everything to
come out. I want the knots untied and the crooked ways
made straight. I want Miss Lamartine set free and the
murderer hanged."

"And the moon," said Macrea. "Don't forget the moon."

"I want to know who killed Major Thoseby, and if it
wasn't Vicky, then the first thing I want to know is, what
motive could anyone else have had. And it's no good trying
to persuade me that there's an underground Gestapo organization working in London polishing off our Secret Service
aces—because that's not the sort of thing I find it possible
to believe in. If there is a motive it's got to be quite simple
and sordid and credible. Then, I want to know where Mrs.
Roper—a currency smuggler or associate of currency
smugglers—fits into the Family Hotel—or was her presence
a coincidence? I want to know what happened on the Loire
in September, 1943—or was it yet another coincidence that
more than half the people in this case seem to have been
there—Thoseby and Wells and Monsieur Sainte and Vicky
and Camino."

"And a million Frenchmen—and several thousand Germans."

"All right. Then I want to know how the murderer got
up to Major Thoseby's room unobserved and how he got

down again. And I want to know who said 'Benny' and who they said it to. And why."

"Anything else?"

"I wouldn't mind knowing what's happened to my son—"

"Yes," said Macrea. "Yes. Well, we shan't find out by sitting here, you know. I'm for bed."

He got up, turned out the desk light, and both men went out. The front door slammed, and their footsteps clattered away up King's Bench Walk.

In the empty room the telephone started to ring. It went on ringing for a long time and then it stopped.

Chapter Thirty-Four

Nap came to the surface very slowly. It took a long time and there did not seem to be any particular urgency about it. When he broke surface and started to breathe, then things started to hurt.

There was one pain in his lungs, which was the pain of the breath he had been holding. And there was another pain along the side and the top of his stomach, where the knife had gone into him—how deeply he did not know, and did not at the moment care to guess.

He could hear voices shouting along the north bank of the river, the bank he had just left: and he could see lights blinking. The current, however, was carrying him along more quickly than the voices and the lights could move, and this seemed so desirable that Nap set his teeth and did nothing. The merest movement of his legs was enough to keep him afloat, anyway, so long as the air was still in his clothes.

It was bitterly cold.

Up above, in the black sky, the stars looked down frostily, and by watching them swing he knew that the river was taking a wide loop, first through one quadrant, then, slowly, back through another.

He forced himself to think.

The treasure which he had to preserve was his bodily strength. The knife wound and the shock and the cold were draining it away. He must keep a reserve sufficient to get him out of the river. He would have to hoard it up, like a miser. He would have to use his head to save his body.

He thought about the ways of rivers, about rivers which curved, about the River Loire in particular. At the outer point of the arc the current would undereat the edge and the banks would be steep and difficult to climb. When the current swung away again, it ought to leave a shelf, by which a tired man might perhaps crawl out.

Nap continued to watch the stars. He had swung right round once. Now he was beginning to swing again. He counted up to ten, and then started to kick, with his legs, against the current.

The pain in his side became acute.

He turned on to his front and tried to use his arms. It was almost as bad, but the movement, slight as it was, seemed to be gaining ground. The main channel was behind him. He persevered in these tired, froglike movements, until suddenly his knees struck against something which felt like sand.

There was very little current. He crawled, on all fours, into a bank of rushes and got very slowly to his feet. He put his hands gently to his stomach and felt, across the water-sodden shirt front, a patch of something stickier than water. It was blood, but it did not seem to be coming very quickly which was encouraging.

He took a handkerchief from his coat pocket, squeezed it dry, folded it into a pad and slipped it in underneath where the front of his shirt ran into the top of his trousers. When he had tightened his belt on top of it things felt a bit firmer. It was the best he could do for the moment. He started to walk forward. It wasn't easy. First the rushes, then loose shingle, and finally a thicket of dwarf alders. The alders were particularly trying for a tiring man. Every branch had to be pushed aside by hand and the roots were alive in their venomous intricacy. He was just thinking that it could not go on forever when the ground started to fall away; the rushes reappeared and he found himself looking at the river.

He had been walking across an island.

For a moment the mere prospect of lowering his hurt and shivering body again into that cold, unfriendly blackness unnerved him. It was only the hard realization that a night in the open in his condition would kill him more surely than the gentlemen on the north bank that prodded him forward.

The swim, this time, was mercifully short. He employed the same technique as before, letting the current carry him along the circumference of its sweep and then, at the last moment, striking out against it.

A few minutes later he was on his face in a blessed piece of meadowland. More, ahead of him, about a hundred yards, but easily discernible now that his eyes had had time to get used to the night, was the bulk of a building.

He rested for a minute, then climbed to his feet and plodded forward toward it. He seemed to have got into a farm track: the one, no doubt, which ran between the building and the river down which the cattle went to drink. He followed it, and found that it circled the building, keeping outside a low wall.

When he got round to the front he saw that this was something more than the ordinary farm. It was a house of some size. It also seemed to be quite dark, deserted or sleeping.

Nap stood on the drive, turning the matter wearily over in his mind. He was well aware of the difficulty of waking a French house once it has put itself to bed. Then he saw that he was mistaken. There was a light in one of the lower windows: a gleam, through shutters.

He walked across and knocked on the door.

Nothing happened.

In a sudden fury he raised the heavy iron knocker and thundered it down on the woodwork. Very slow footsteps, a crack of light and a voice which said, "Who is that?"

It was neither hostile nor friendly.

"An English tourist," said Nap. "I have had an accident with my motor bicycle, and been thrown into the water. I fear I am hurt."

"I am not a doctor," said the voice doubtfully. "But come in."

Nap followed into the hall, then into a long room, partly kitchen but mostly dining room. There was a big fireplace with one of those everlasting wood fires, which never seem to blaze very fiercely yet never quite die. The man was throwing sticks on to the bed of white ash.

"I fear that the water—" said Nap. There was already a pool round his feet.

"They are bricks," said the man. "Water will not hurt them. I must fetch you a blanket."

He did not seem unduly surprised. Nap thought that possibly the Frenchmen in those parts had gone through so much during the war that nothing would now have power to surprise them further.

"For your wound, too," said the man. "I have a box."

By the time he came back Nap had got his shirt off. His hands seemed to be functioning clumsily. The movement had started the blood again. Now that his shirt was off he could see the damage: a long wound across the top of his stomach. The flesh, blanched by water and drawn away from the lips of the cut, made it look worse than it probably was. It did not seem very deep.

The Frenchman had come back and was looking at the wound critically. "A curious accident," he said, at last. "Here is the box."

Nap, to his surprise, saw that the man was holding out an olive green, japanned steel case. He recognized it at once. It was the excellent first-aid kit off a Sherman tank. Nap knew it well. The contents seemed untouched. He opened a packet of sulphanilamide, poured the whole contents on to a new gauze pad, and started to fasten it over the wound. It was whilst he was doing so that he found he had lost control of his hands.

"Let me," said the Frenchman. He finished the strapping of the wound deftly. Then he removed what was left of Nap's clothes and started to dry him, firmly but not unkindly with a very rough towel.

Ten minutes later Nap was feeling a lot better. He was sitting in a chair by the fire, drinking, very slowly, a tumbler of apple brandy. He was wearing a long, gray nightgown, buttoned round the neck. His drying hair was beginning to stand on end. Round his legs, kiltlike, he wore an American army blanket.

He was even beginning to review the events of the evening with a dangerous complacency, when he received the next shock.

The room, as he had noticed, was a long one. It ran the full breadth of the house and the windows at the back overlooked the river. The Frenchman had opened the shutters, said something which Nap did not catch. Then he repeated it. "Much activity."

"I beg your pardon," said Nap. "I didn't—"

"I say, possibly it is your friends who look for you. There is much activity. I can see lights. They are at the bridge over the river."

Nap thought hard. The man looked dependable. In any event he was clearly entirely in his power.

"Not my friends," he said.

"So," said the man. "Then possibly it would be better to close the shutters again." He did so and came back into the room.

"I think they are the people who—" Nap indicated the wound in his side.

"The people who caused your motorcycle accident," said the man quickly.

"Well—" said Nap. "I'm afraid—"

"There is not the least necessity for explanations. Things happen. One does what one can to help. It is preferable to know as little as possible."

"Have you got a telephone?"

"There is one in the closet. Follow me, please."

Nap gave the operator Madame Delboise's number. The bell rang once and then he heard her voice. Rapidly he explained what had happened. He described the house he was in.

"A house with a long drive and a low white wall round it, just south of the bridge—yes. You are in good hands," said Madame Delboise. "I will be with you in ten minutes."

"It's no laughing matter," said Nap.

"Your appearance," said Madame Delboise. "You look— I find it difficult to do you justice. You look like a choirboy peeping out of the top of a bell tent."

"I feel like a corpse looking out of its winding sheet,"

said Nap sourly. "Is anything else likely to happen tonight. Did you have any trouble getting here?"

"Not actual trouble. We passed on the bridge. We did not assault each other. We law-abiding members of the Resistance—the old Trades Union—rarely come to blows with our more extreme brothers, any more than your politicians of the Right actually fight with those of the Left."

"I see," said Nap. Despite Madame Delboise's assurance he felt glad of the three men who had come in with her and were now sitting sipping their host's apple brandy and talking quietly to him. They all looked capable.

Headlights flared on the road outside as a car swung round into the drive.

"I left a message," said Madame Delboise. "This may be—"

"On the other hand," said one of the men, "it may not."

The three men took up their positions quietly, one each where he could command a window and one out of the line of sight behind the door. Nap thought they probably needed no orders for this sort of thing.

A car stopped outside. Footsteps crunched on the gravel; there was a pause, followed by a very gentle knock on the door.

The owner of the house went out and they heard his footsteps clattering along the passage and the sound of the front door being opened. There was a mutter of voices and the man came back. He was followed by a thick, middle-aged man who came into the room as if he owned it.

"Monsieur Bren," said Madame and Nap simultaneously.

"It seems to me," said Monsieur Bren, "that this is a time for explanations."

The trouble was that Nap was finding it increasingly difficult to keep awake. The cold of the river and the heat of the fire, the apple brandy, the alternation of suspense and relief, and the ultimate feeling of deep security engendered by the presence of his old friend Monsieur Bren of the Paris Sûreté, all were combining to send him to sleep.

He had fought off this lassitude long enough to give a fairly coherent account of the matter which had brought him to Angers. After that things had become blurred.

He was aware that Madame Delboise was speaking. She was explaining something to Monsieur Bren. It was something that she or her colleagues had discovered. Nap had no difficulty in recognizing what it was. From out of the mists of talk, the miasma of weariness, the jumble of names and places, it stood out hard and clear. Like a spotlight in the dark, it focused on one place, picking it out in sharpest black and white, leaving its surroundings in greater gloom.

It was the Ferme du Grand Puits, as he had seen it last. Enclave, secret, set apart on its hilltop, among the woods.

He found, without surprise, that he was looking down on it from above. He could see the woods and the clearing, and the farm buildings. He could see someone moving, antlike, across the clearing. Someone who carried something in his arms. He came down closer to look. He was about to overtake him when suddenly the man turned, and he saw it was Major Thoseby who was smiling.

When he woke the sun was high in the sky. He was in a box bed, in an upstairs room. He had no recollection of coming there. His head was clear, and the wound in his side was hurting him, but in a healthy sort of way. It was stinging, not throbbing.

There was a cup of coffee on the chest beside the bed. It was cold, but he drank it and then slowly got dressed. His clothes were dry, and they had been brushed, but they felt oddly stiff after their soaking.

In the hall downstairs he found a gendarme. The gendarme intimated—it was barely a suggestion, certainly not an order—that Monsieur Bren had said that he thought it might be better if Nap did not go outside the house until Monsieur Bren returned.

Besides, the rest would do Monsieur's wound good.

"When will he be back?" asked Nap.

"This afternoon," said the gendarme. He added that Monsieur Bren was making inquiries. His friends were making inquiries, everyone was making inquiries.

All very fine, thought Nap to himself, as he sat in the sunlight, in the parlor, re-dressing the hole in his side. It was puffy, but clean. Even his inexpert eye could see that there was nothing dangerous about it. All very fine, he repeated, but here am I, sitting in an unknown house, in a district of France about which I know only that it lies somewhere to the west of Angers, on the Loire, whilst an uncertain number of people are making some vaguely comprehended inquiries. At the Old Bailey in London, the trial will be in its third day. For all the information I have succeeded in obtaining I might just as well have remained in London.

Nevertheless, although he rehearsed this argument to himself several times as the day wore on, yet he found it difficult to be dissatisfied. He had a feeling—a feeling which he shared, oddly enough, with Macrea, who was to give voice to it, that same night, to Mr. Rumbold. He felt that enough had been done to start things going. The train had been truly laid and fired and sooner or later would come the explosion and the truth would erupt from the darkness in which it had been hidden so long, into the light of day.

It was six o'clock before anyone arrived, and then it was not Monsieur Bren, but one of his assistants, a young lieutenant of police.

"Would a car ride trouble you?" he asked.

"I'm quite fit," said Nap. "Rather a fraud, really."

"Some of the going will be rough."

"To the Ferme du Grand Puits?"

The man looked surprised, then nodded his head.

Nap took leave of his host whose name he still had not discovered and they got into the police car, the lieutenant, the two gendarmes, Nap and a police driver. It was an open car, and Nap was soon glad of the leather coat which someone had lent him. They crossed the river and kept to the north bank, through Saumur and Bourgeuil, and it did not seem long before they were turning off at Pont Boutard. Nap glimpsed the corn chandler's shop in the headlights as they swung left, up on to the heath. Then a right fork, and they were bumping up the track and his time was fully occupied holding himself off the side of the car as it lurched and slid.

At the last moment, as they reached the point where the track ran out of the woods and he knew they would be coming in sight of the farm, he saw something which puzzled him. It was just over the brow of the hill, a steady glow, like the full moon coming up. As they topped the last rise, he saw that the light did not come from the farm buildings at all: it was lower down the hill. It looked like a small searchlight or an arc lamp, and it was slung on a derrick beside the superstructure of the well.

There were a lot of men there and they were doing something with ropes, which ran to a second derrick and a pulley.

The car drew up, and everyone got out. Their arrival caused a little stir among the group at the well head. The lieutenant had a word with a gray-haired man, who seemed to be directing operations, and whom Nap understood to be the prefect of the district.

"Would you care to descend?" said the lieutenant.

"Descend?" said Nap.

"It is perfectly safe."

"I'm sure it is," said Nap weakly.

The next thing he knew was that he was sitting in a sort of bosun's chair. When he looked up the night sky was a pale oval over his head: an oval with one unnaturally bright star in it. Far below him a glowworm of light came and went. The descent was jerky but controlled, and Nap, like Alice in similar circumstances, found that he had plenty of time to wonder what was going to happen next.

What did happen was that the descent ceased and a hand came out of the darkness and grabbed his boot heel. The electric torch came on again, its beams focused now on to a shallow cavity at a point where the wall of the old dry well met the floor.

The light illuminated the cavity—and what lay in it.

The little heap, the scraps of cloth, the leather belt, green with mildew, the thin, white bones.

"Allow me to present you," said the voice of Monsieur Bren in his ear, " a gentleman for whom many people have been looking. Lieutenant Julian Wells."

"Hullo Angers," said the voice, impersonally. "I have no answer from your London number."

"Curse it," said Nap. "What's the time?"

"Eleven o'clock," said Madame Delboise. "Your father must be making a night of it."

"He's more likely to be in bed and asleep," said Nap. "I'll try to get Macrea at his chambers. It's an off-chance. He might be working late."

Here he missed both Macrea and Mr. Rumbold by a few minutes. Half an hour later, in desperation, he rang his own home again. His father had just got back.

Then Nap really started talking.

Chapter Thirty-Five

The morning of Thursday, the fourth day of the trial, opened with a drenching downpour of rain. Nothing would now damp the general interest. The queue for the gallery was longer than it had been on the first day. The trial had grown, in the mysterious way that a murder trial can, and had possessed the minds of the public. "Rex *v.* Lamartine" was news.

Possibly the most worried man in the court was Macrea.

The whole case now lay in his hands. Truth had come up from the bottom of a well and he knew everything. He was now able to answer all of the questions which Mr. Rumbold had asked him the night before—and a few more. What had been dark was plain. Yet his next move was far from clear to him.

The procedure of a criminal trial was, he considered, singularly ill-adapted for the bringing out of the truth about any crime. It was shaped and constituted to one end alone: to show whether or not a particular person was guilty. This end it achieved admirably. But it could not be pushed beyond its function.

He knew, of course, now, who had done the murder: why they had done it, how they had done it and when they had done it. Whether he would be able to demonstrate this in court was another matter.

There was also the judge to consider. Mr. Justice Arbuthnot was a good judge and a likable person. But he was not a man you took liberties with. Macrea had upset him once already. Once was more than enough. None of this was betrayed by his well-trained face as he rose.

"My lord, members of the jury, I had intended to begin

the proceedings with my final address. In the interim—to be precise at ten minutes to midnight last night—information of such importance reached me that I realized I should not be doing my duty to my client—or to yourselves—if I did not make some especial effort to present this to you. My difficulty has been how to do so. Particularly since most of this information concerns what I may call the French side of this case, and the witnesses who could speak to it are either dead or not easily available.

"In the event, I have asked the co-operation of the prosecution—and I must place it on record that this co-operation has been very generously given."

He smiled at Mr. Summers who smiled back thinly. He had been roused from his bed by telephone to a conference at six o'clock in the morning and he was not feeling at his best.

"I have decided, with your lordship's permission, to recall three of the prosecution witnesses. Their attendance here has been arranged. I have further asked—as would be normal when they were giving evidence in chief—that none of them be in court when the others are giving evidence. That has also been agreed."

"I have no objection," said Mr. Justice Arbuthnot warily. "Are the matters on which you wish to question them connected with their previous testimony?"

"I shall ask them nothing, my lord, which could not properly have been put to them on the previous occasion."

"Very well."

"Call Major Ammon."

"Major Ammon, in your evidence you stated that you were responsible for the English end of Major Thoseby's operations in Occupied France?"

"I and others."

"Were you also responsible for dispatching Lieutenant Wells?"

"I certainly knew he was being sent, and assisted in some of the preliminaries. I didn't actually brief him myself."

"Now, Major Ammon. When Lieutenant Wells was parachuted into France did he—I want to be particularly careful not to lead you on this—did he take anything with him beyond the usual outfit which a man on such a mission would take?"

"Did he—oh, I see what you're getting at—yes—"

"I am afraid I must interrupt you," said Macrea with a smile which robbed the words of their sting. "I'm not 'getting at' anything. You must just answer my question."

"Very well. Yes, certainly. He took a great deal of money."

"Perhaps you could tell us why he took this money."

"Yes. We thought it important—particularly at that time, you know, when the Resistance Movement was beginning to get the support of the better class of Frenchman—we insisted that everything taken should be properly paid for."

"I quite understand."

"It was necessary to replenish funds from time to time and it so happened that Lieutenant Wells was selected as a carrier."

"In what form was money carried?"

"Sometimes in franc notes. Sometimes in gold."

"In this case?"

"To the best of my knowledge and belief, in gold."

"Can you give us any idea how much he carried?"

"Yes. The gold was cast in thin tablets each weighing exactly seven ounces. The carrier had a special belt, with slots to contain a great many of these tablets. One man could carry approximately eight thousand pounds sterling in gold without discomfort. I am speaking, of course, of gold as it was then. It would be worth more now."

"Have you any idea what happened to this gold?"

"We presumed that it had fallen into the hands of the Gestapo."

"All of it?"

"Certainly. Wells, so far as we know, had no contact with anybody, between the time he landed in France and the time he was captured, to whom he would have been authorized to hand the gold. The supposition was that it was all on him when he was taken."

"The gold was never traced?"

"Never to my knowledge."

"Thank you, Major Ammon. I do not know if my learned friend—?"

"No questions," said Mr. Summers.

"I am afraid that I do not quite follow all this," said the judge. "If this gold never reached Major Thoseby, Mr. Macrea, surely it could not constitute a motive for Major Thoseby's murder?"

"I agree with your lordship," said Macrea smoothly. "It might, however, constitute a motive for the murder of Lieutenant Wells."

"Point one slipped across," thought Mr. Rumbold.

Monsieur le Commissaire Lode was then called.

"Monsieur Lode," said Macrea, "when you were giving evidence you spoke about your work on the Tracing Staff at Arolsen. Can you tell us something more about it?"

"What exactly is it you would like to know?"

"Well, perhaps you could explain to the court, roughly, the lines on which the bureau worked."

"The work was complex. We were an international team of investigators. Our first object was to trace the victims of the war. Inquiries reached us from all parts of the world, about displaced persons, victims of the racial persecutions, prisoners of the Gestapo—"

"Let us take the latter type of case, then. Your organization would be able, in time, to determine the fate of a Gestapo prisoner?"

"It was usually able to do so."

"How did you work?"

"In many ways. We had the records of the prisoners— and even when the records of a prison had been destroyed there were often duplicate records, kept by a higher authority that we were able to consult. The German passion for order and method were very useful to us there."

"I see."

"In many cases, also, we were able to interrogate the prison staffs themselves. Unless they happened to be accused of war crimes, they had no incentive to suppress the truth. Then, their stories could be cross-checked."

"In short, Monsieur Lode, a thorough use of the investigating machinery at Arolsen would most often produce a positive result?"

"Almost always."

"And you said, I think, that Major Thoseby was pursuing his inquiries through your channels?"

"That is so."

"Let me put this to you then—as a hypothetical case. If Major Thoseby was looking for traces of some Gestapo prisoner—for the sake of argument, let us say, if he was looking for Lieutenant Wells—and if, after diligent inquiry *he failed to find any trace of him*, what conclusion would you come to?"

"You say that he had made careful inquiry—?"

"Yes. Over a number of years."

"And the prison in which Lieutenant Wells was supposed to have been confined was, of course, known?"

"Yes."

"Then I should say that it was almost certain that Lieutenant Wells never fell into the hands of the Gestapo at all."

"Thank you."

The judge said gravely, "I should like to be quite clear, Mr. Macrea, exactly what it is you are suggesting to the court."

"I am suggesting," said Macrea, "that Lieutenant Wells was murdered for the gold in his belt. I am further suggesting that Major Thoseby, slowly, cautiously—reluctantly, perhaps—had at last reached the conclusion that Wells had been murdered. I am suggesting that when you find the men who murdered Lieutenant Wells you will not have to look any further for the murderers of Major Thoseby."

"I see." Mr. Justice Arbuthnot thought this out. The silence in court was uncanny. "You wish to call one further witness, I understand?"

"If you please. I have some questions now that I should like to ask Monsieur Sainte."

An usher went out; minutes passed but the swinging doors remained closed. Then the usher reappeared and spoke to one of the policemen, who also went out. Another minute passed, and the burly figure of Inspector Partridge was seen, pushing his way through the crowd at the door.

Macrea's voice rode over the rising tide of conjecture.

"If Monsieur Sainte is not here," he said, "then perhaps his waiter, Camino, could assist us."

Nobody seemed able to do much about this, either.

A very long minute passed.

The public in the gallery were showing signs of getting out of hand, whilst the press were clearly torn between a desire to reach a telephone and an urge to see the matter through to its conclusion.

Claudian Summers was observed to be in consultation

with the clerk to the court, who got to his feet and spoke to the judge.

Mr. Justice Arbuthnot nodded briskly, and a sudden silence fell as he addressed counsel.

"It would appear, Mr. Macrea, that neither of the witnesses you have named can, at the moment, be found."

"You surprise me, my lord," said Macrea, untruthfully.

Chapter Thirty-Six

"All right," said Inspector Hazlerigg. "All right, all right. You were right and we were wrong—Inspector Partridge was wrong. But don't gloat about it."

"I'm not gloating," said Angus McCann. "I'm just glad that Miss Lamartine got off, that's all. The crowd gave her quite a reception, didn't they?"

"I'm surprised they didn't come along the Embankment and break a few windows at Scotland Yard," said Hazlerigg sourly.

"Oh, I don't think they felt like that at all," said McCann. "They were just glad that a nice girl like Miss Lamartine hadn't got to be hanged and that the villains turned out to be a couple of foreigners—that's always satisfactory, too. Where are Sainte and Camino now, by the way?"

"Somewhere in France. They slid out down one of their two-way gold-smuggling routes, I should think."

"It did occur to me to wonder why they weren't arrested when Macrea gave Inspector Partridge the news early that morning."

"You're not the only person who's wondered about that," said Hazlerigg shortly.

Silence fell again in Hazlerigg's office. It was McCann who broke it.

"You know," he said, "the whole thing was too logical. That's why people didn't see it at once. You don't expect crime to be logical. Everything that happened in England depended on what had happened five years before in France. Once you knew what really did take place near Langeais in September, 1943, you could see exactly what must have taken place in London this spring. There are a few gaps, still, of course. Do you know if Sainte and Camino really were brothers?"

"We know a certain amount about them now," said Hazlerigg. "They were both Italian citizens—we've traced them under the name of Santi—who came to France in the thirties. They took the name of Marquis and ran the Ferme du Grand Puits as brothers. They may have been brothers, or it may just have suited their book to pretend they were. When they came over here they changed roles and became hotel proprietor and waiter. Either way the deception was liable to be useful to them. They were born criminals."

"They had their nerves in the right place," said McCann. "In France, during the Occupation, they posed as moderately loyal Maquisards, but I can't help thinking that that Gestapo raid on the Père Chaise Farm was a little *too* well timed."

"You mean they had them tipped off that Wells was there?"

"Yes. I think so. The Gestapo drill, as Lode explained in evidence, was to raid at dusk. So the brothers Marquis went down with a farm cart and took Wells away at about four in the afternoon. They took him straight up to their farm—then waited to see what transpired. When the Germans shot Père Chaise and the other men in the farm and picked up Miss Lamartine *there was no single outsider left who knew where Wells was.* So they quietly cut his throat and dropped him down the well. As soon as they decently could after the war they sold the farm and decamped. They used a crooked attorney in Angers. Maître Gimelet, to do the job, and killed two birds with one stone, because he was also contact man for the French side of the gold-running crowd. They needed professional help to dispose of the gold. When they got to England they used some of the money to buy the Family Hotel, and they must have been making quite a nice thing out of it. There were only two snags. The first was that the English end of the gold-running crowd thought that they were worth watching and installed Mrs. Roper to keep an eye on them. They couldn't object to that. They were still realizing the gold, piece by piece, and it all had to be done on the black market."

"And the other snag?"

"The other snag," said McCann, "might be described as the possible conjunction of Miss Lamartine and Major Thoseby. It must have been intensely irritating to them. They were so nearly safe. If only Wells hadn't been so damnably attractive to—and attracted by—small brunettes. If only the Gestapo had finished Vicky off when they had her. If only she hadn't been devoted to the ghost of Julian Wells. If only Major Thoseby hadn't been such a painstaking investigator. There they were, miles from the scene of the crime, the body disposed of in one of the deepest dry wells in France, the gold almost all realized, many of the actors dead. Yet all the time, week by week and month by month retribution was coming up on them. Vicky Lamartine and Eric Thoseby. Of course, they had always realized that Vicky might be a nuisance. That's why they got her a job in the hotel—to keep an eye on her. What they hadn't foreseen was that Thoseby, working from another angle, was going to be equally dangerous. It only needed those two to have ten minutes' conversation—mention their suspicions to each other—and the truth would have been out."

"I suppose that's right," said Hazlerigg. "I shouldn't have thought it would have been easy for anybody to pin it on to the brothers Marquis after all that time."

"Not just anybody—no," said McCann. "I think that's the whole point. As I see it, there were three bits of information needed, and you had to have them all. The first's just guesswork. If the brothers were going to remove Wells they had to have some sort of conveyance to remove him in. Motor cars were nonexistent. They were all requisitioned or hidden away. And, anyway, it would have been too risky."

"A farm cart," suggested Hazlerigg.

"Surely, with a load of hay in the back to hide him under. But they couldn't hope to take a farm cart from up at Grand Puits all the way to Père Chaise without meeting a few people. That was fact one. They must have been seen on the road. Miss Lamartine probably saw them, herself, though they meant nothing to her at the time. Now take fact two—which was known only to the Germans at first, but had recently, by long and patient research, become known also to Major Thoseby: that Wells was no longer at the Père Chaise Farm by the time it was raided. Miss Lamartine, remember, had left him there after lunch."

"And your third fact?"

"The third fact," said McCann, "was one which was entirely harmless by itself, but which might assume a certain significance if it was considered alongside the other two. It was simply that Miss Lamartine knew that the brothers Marquis had been, rather unexpectedly, absent from their farm from before three o'clock until after seven o'clock. It had been arranged for her to meet them there, you will remember. Well, there was nothing much in any of those by themselves, but put them together and a certain pattern begins to emerge. A clear enough pattern to make it worth while instituting a little search at the Ferme du Grand Puits. And it would have been inevitable that one of the first places to be searched would have been the well. And once the body had been discovered the hunt would have been up. Photographs of the brothers Marquis in all the papers—"

"Yes," said Hazlerigg. "And they still had some of the stolen gold undisposed of. Very uncomfortable for them. So the long and short of it was, they had to take vigorous steps to prevent Miss Lamartine and Thoseby from meeting."

"Vigorous and logical. There was something almost classical about the way in which they set the two menaces to cancel each other out. Thoseby wished to come to the hotel. Very well, he should be encouraged to do so. Vicky mustn't see him at once. All right, then, tell her that Thoseby wasn't arriving till eleven o'clock. I don't know what devious and damnable alternative plans they had hatched. It all turned on when Thoseby went up to his room. He'd been allotted that room on purpose, of course. In fact, he went up before Vicky came back. That was all that mattered. At about twenty past ten—he would leave it as late as possible so that the medical evidence wouldn't conflict—Sainte walks from his office, *through* the reception desk, upstairs, knocks at Thoseby's door, goes in, says something conventional about he hopes Major Thoseby has everything and is quite comfortable. Perfectly comfortable, says Thoseby. Splendid, says Sainte, here's one thing more. Whips out the knife he's been holding in his gloved hand—a kitchen knife which he knows is already well covered with Vicky's fingerprints—and good-by Thoseby."

"And then?"

"The next bit's quite easy, too. Macrea had most of it in his summing-up. Thoseby slides gently to the floor. Mrs. Roper's wireless would drown any noise there was. Sainte pushes the knife down the back of the sofa, walks out of the bedroom and locks himself into the bathroom opposite. Then he sits—and waits."

"Yes. There was nothing wrong with his nerve, as you said. What exactly is he waiting for?"

"Why, the signal that Vicky is in the reception desk and the front hall is clear."

"And the signal is given by—?"

"Camino, of course, from the kitchen. At about twenty to eleven. That was your mysterious Benny. They were both Italians, and in a moment of stress they naturally spoke in Italian. Camino simply whispers up to his brother that the way is clear and all is well. A Frenchman would have said 'Bien.' Camino says 'Bene.' Sainte, when he gets the signal goes back into Thoseby's room—still gloved—and *simply presses the bell*. Then he comes out again quickly and walks down the passage—it's only conjecture, but it seems reasonable—as far as the empty bedroom. Vicky comes upstairs, along the passage, goes into Thoseby's room, and—somewhat naturally—screams. Sainte is well placed to pretend to be coming up the stairs attracted by her screams. We've only got Camino's word that he was ever seen on the actual staircase."

"Yes," said Hazlerigg. "I think that's it all right. I think that's how it must have worked. Mrs. Roper's statement—nerves, imagination or self-defense?"

"A bit of all three. Mostly self-defense. She saw the red light at once. If Vicky didn't do it, then she was automatically next choice. Also she had a bad record. She had only to invent the mythical thud—or so she thought—to clear herself. Only she ought to have realized that if you are going to tell a lie which is to stand up under cross-examination, you've got to think it out pretty carefully. She didn't do herself much good with that thud."

"No. After that I suppose Camino and Sainte worked together to delay the arrival of the doctor, long enough, anyway, to conceal the difference between a death at ten-twenty and a death at ten-forty."

"Yes, that's about it."

Silence fell again.

"How's Nap?" said Hazlerigg.

"Fine," said McCann, "he's fine. The wound's absolutely healed."

But he only said that absently. His real mind was still turning over the case.

"Do you think," Hazlerigg said, "that they meant her to hang?"

"I'm sure they didn't," said McCann. "The most they expected was for her to be found guilty under provocation —and either pardoned or given a nominal sentence for manslaughter. That, incidentally, was the line of legal defense that Sainte bespoke and paid for—and with all possible respect to everyone, if Vicky hadn't been so determined to change her lawyers, it's just about what would have happened."

"Yes," said Hazlerigg again. "You seem to have got everything tied up. All we've got to do now is to catch them. Then we can start all over again, trying to explain it to a jury. Not just the straight bits but the odd little difficulties, too. What's worrying you now?" he added, for McCann still seemed to be turning something over in his mind.

"It's just this," said McCann. "I'm fairly sure now that that's what did happen. It all fits together reasonably well. But there's one thing I can't understand at all. Why did

Sainte—or Marquis, I suppose I should call him—*ever allow the girl near him*? I know that I suggested that he wanted to keep an eye on her, and that may be true, but look at the risk he was running. It only needed an acquaintance from France to come into the hotel and address him as Marquis, in Vicky's presence—and the fat would have been in the fire. Perhaps the risk was small, but why run it at all?"

"Criminals," said Hazlerigg, "are people with extraordinarily acute apprehensions. They revisit the scene of the crime to see if they have overlooked some obscure clue, and a blundering policeman, who doesn't like the look of them, arrests them on suspicion. They take wild precautions to guard against imaginary dangers, and the precautions themselves lead to their undoing, long after the crime has become undetectable. In short, they make mistakes; which is as well, for if they never made mistakes we should never catch them."